THE MONASTERY MYSTERIES

HIS KINDRED SPIRIT

THE MONTCLAIRE MYSTERIES

HIS KINDRED SPIRIT

Being the further Memoirs of Colonel Sir Francis FitzMaurice, VC
Concerning Some Terrible Murders in AD 794

E. A. ALLEN

A Montclaire Mystery Novel

Published by Wildside Press LLC.

WILDSIDE PRESS

Published by Wildside Press LLC.
wildsidepress.com

Fate whispers to the Warrior, "You cannot withstand the storm."
The Warrior whispers back, "I am the storm."
                    —Ancient adage, perhaps of Samurai origin.

AN EDITOR'S NOTE

"No murders ought go unsolved, even those that have languished a thousand years."

And so begins a marginal note that Sir Francis FitzMaurice appended to his strange memoir. In it, he gives details of an extraordinary collaboration between two detectives—kinsmen whose lives were separated by a millennium. The one, his good friend Gérard de Montclaire, most renowned detective of the Belle Époque. The other, Piers de Valon—Montclaire's ancestor who acted as an inquisitor in the reign of the Emperor Charlemagne.

The story of this collaboration begins in the Christmas Season, 1918, just after the Armistice and as Sir Francis and Montclaire returned from service in the Great War. What was to be a celebration of the return of Peace on Earth became instead an exciting journey into the horrors of the remote past and into a remarkable challenge. What follows is the story of that adventure, as Sir Francis recorded it.

—E. A. Allen

PROLOGUE

Teddy's Puzzle

CHAPTER 1

Paris, 6 Rue de Longchamp
9 December 1918

Paris lay changed and lifeless in those first weeks after the Armistice. The whole atmosphere of the city remained somber, still in shock, but striving to regain its old vitality and gaiety. The staggering losses of the Great War cast a dreadful pall over the city and, despite the victory, Parisians found little to cheer.

Montclaire and I arrived home from War service at the end of November. Wounded on the Somme, and released from hospital the previous summer, it would be my last year as a soldier. Montclaire served with France's secret intelligence service—the Deuxième Bureau—until the Armistice and experienced many a secret adventure, most recently in Italy.

Even as the Christmas season approached, we found ourselves eager to remain in Paris. It was good to be home and we ventured as little as possible from the warm and familiar comforts of our *apartement* in the rue de Longchamp.

One morning in early December, while we lolled about a generous fire crackling in the library hearth, Montclaire surprised me. He announced that we would have guests for the Season. Then he ordered Petrovsky, his Russian manservant, to, "Lay on provisions and prepare the necessary rooms."

Montclaire's two sisters, Modestine and Clarisse, would arrive from Chateau d'Ecouen to stay a fortnight in Paris. Most interesting to me, we also expected Gilbert du Burney. A cousin of Montclaire's and a professor at Oxford. Teddy—as the family called him—taught Medieval History. I wondered whatever he was about.

"We are to have a considerable party for the holiday, after all, Fitz. If that's not to your liking, now's the time to high ass for London, or perhaps Rome. I hear from Madame Soyeuse that the Baroness is in Rome," he added with a playful lilt in his voice.

"No fear! I'm delighted at the prospect of such company as your charming sisters, and Teddy sounds fascinating."

"Perhaps Teddy's visit will prove more fascinating than you think. I have a note from him this morning, and he seems to promise a holiday filled with intrigue. Here. Read it and tell me what you make of it."

Gérard. My dear cousin—

I am pleased to accept your invitation for the holiday with you and your enchanting sisters. And though I have not yet met Sir Francis, I have, of course, heard much of him. All England celebrates his heroism and his Victoria Cross. I read that the President of the Republic will give him the Croix de Guerre and Legion d'Honeur in the spring. What an honor it will be for me to make his acquaintance!

I bring with me a document, which is both unique and fascinating, and which I propose to lay before you as a puzzle. I'll wager a thousand gold sovereigns that even you cannot supply a cogent solution to it. What say you?

Gil

"Of course, I have accepted his wager, and I look forward to the challenge."

"I am flattered he should know of me, but what shall I think of it, Montclaire? It says almost nothing, except that we are to read an exceptional document. Teddy is a noted professor of medieval history, so I presume it is a document of that era. He is French, so I deduce further that it likely pertains to this country, but he is at Oxford so it may be English. And clearly, the document contains a mystery of some sort that he is confident will remain a mystery, even from you. I am already intrigued."

"You have indeed milked every legitimate deduction from Teddy's note, though knowing him as I do, I can assure you that if he brings a 'puzzle' that he has not been able to solve himself, it must be a difficult one. Teddy is a brilliant man, but he is also playful in the extreme."

CHAPTER 2

Ten Days Later
19 December 1918

A rare snow blanketed Paris to greet the arrival of our Christmas guests. What began as flurries became a torrent that brought near a half-foot of snow to a city unaccustomed to it. To me, it seemed an optimistic thing, signaling the end of something and the beginning of another, a fitting conclusion to that era of dreadful War.

One morning, shortly after breakfast, our entrance foyer filled with sounds of the simultaneous arrival of all our guests. The ruckus announced the arrival of Montclaire's two handsome sisters—Modestine and Clarisse—both of them turned out in the highest fashion, had not seen their brother for a year, so the reunion was tearful. There came with them a tall, thin man of middle years, slightly balding, with a long face, a high forehead, and a neatly trimmed beard. Though his shoulder showed the beginnings of a scholarly slope, he gave every indication of remarkable vitality and energy. His peculiarly resonant voice and sparkling eyes exercised a remarkable appeal to everyone who met him, and to find Gilbert Chassin du Burney and Montclaire in the same room seemed an extraordinary assemblage of charisma.

When we assembled at 7:30 o'clock for the distribution of life-giving brandy before the dinner gong, Montclaire turned to the Professor. "Teddy, you must tell us of this puzzle you have brought for Christmas. A mystery in search of a solution, eh?" Montclaire asked, handing his cousin a snifter of brandy.

"Gérard, it's nothing less than the most remarkable document I have ever discovered, and as you know I've studied most of the archives of France and England."

"But what is this mystery?"

"For that, cousin, you and our companions must wait 'til after dinner. And, I warn you, I do not intend to spend my coin, so to speak, in one evening. I have decided upon a schedule to my revelations, which I promise, will make my gift to you last the entire Season. We will begin a journey tonight that will only end on Christmas Eve—if that is, it ends at all. That will be up to you Gérard if you are able to collect our wager."

"Ah yes, the wager. I promise only to try, and I approve heartily of your methods, Teddy. You have the gift for suspense—a rare thing."

Dinner passed in talk of the Peace, the American President Wilson, and the prospects for the coming Conference at Versailles. Afterward, we all gathered with no mention of Teddy's puzzle in the library, which Petrovsky rearranged so as to make a circle of comfortable chairs, one for each of the guests. Teddy took the head of the circle, with Montclaire directly across, and we settled into the first evening to hear Gilbert describe the strange discovery that he was to share with us.

Teddy's beginning was a tad tutorial for my taste, but he soon settled into a more congenial tone.

"I bring you a discovery, which I found among the items offered at auction last fall at Sotheby's. The bits and pieces sold belonged to an old scholar I knew slightly, and I thought to buy something as a memento, you understand. The catalogue listed something that caught my eye, 'A Latin manuscript of unknown origin, probably Carolingian,' a description I found intriguing. However, I did not have time to examine it before the bidding began, and so I raised my hand when the time came on speculation that any such document in my colleague's possession must be of some interest and would be a suitable remembrance of him. To my surprise, there was only one other bidder, who abandoned the effort upon my counter bid. The price? Ten pounds!"

"When I returned to my rooms in college, I was tired and put the document aside and went to bed. Next day was a busy one for me, so I thought little of my purchases, and soon forgot it altogether."

"You've become absentminded, Teddy. Confess it!" chided Modestine.

"Nonsense, sister! You know very well that Teddy was born absentminded. There's no 'becoming' about it," said Clarisse.

"Well, ladies, you've been onto me since we were children, so I'll not deny it. It slipped my mind entirely. Some days later I found it on my desk, which gave me the pleasure of discovering it once again. Upon closer examination, and after only one paragraph, excitement caused my hands to shake and I couldn't finish. It took an hour's respite and a bit of brandy to steady my nerves and allow me to continue."

"Mère de Dieu, Teddy! Does this document announce the end of the world?"

"To a scholar, Gérard, it might seem so. It was the discovery of a lifetime, and nothing less."

Teddy, who stood at the center of our circle, raised his arms to quiet his listeners, most of whom were demanding more.

"Ladies and Gentlemen, please. Allow me to make my presentation with the proper drama and theatricality. I promise, your patience will be rewarded."

The circle settled into silence and the professor continued. "The manuscript before me was a document of the year 821, composed by none other than Saint Theodulfe d'Orleans, who succeeded Alcuin of York as a sort of mentor to Charlemagne. I'll not tell you more, because I prefer to allow Theodulfe himself to tell his story, but the document tells of something very rare, a mission of the Missi Dominici."

"The Missi who?" I asked, in obvious confusion. "You've already lost me, old boy. My Harrow Latin is still good enough to know that Missi Dominici means 'envoy of the lord,' but what does that mean?"

"A worthy question, Sir Francis, for knowing who the Missi were, is crucial to my story."

"They were inspectors and personal representatives sent out by Charlemagne, were they not?" Montclaire asked.

"Yes, indeed. The use of traveling inspectors went back to a time before Charlemagne, who came to his throne in 768, but he used them routinely and prolifically. In order to keep himself informed of the goings-on in his vast and expanding empire, Charlemagne sent out his agents, usually to investigate a perceived problem and set things right. They exercised the authority of the King himself, and so no one, no matter how powerful. could oppose them. They were always sent out in pairs and the team almost always included a high noble and a high churchman."

"Very interesting. And you say that these fellows acted in the name of Charlemagne himself?" the Duke asked.

"Yes. They carried with them a charter from the King, called a *capitulary,* which shielded them against any danger. To molest or interfere with the *Missi* was a good as a death sentence."

"The document that Theodulfe composed is exceptional because it is literally one of a kind. There are no surviving reports of the Missions undertaken by the Missi, though we know they routinely reported to the King. Don't you see what a discovery this is? The only one of its kind!"

"Yes. Fascinating," said Clarisse, with more than a touch of ennui in her voice.

Teddy, however, did not notice it or at least was undeterred by it. He pressed on with rising enthusiasm.

"There is, however, an additional excitement attached to this document, ladies, and gentlemen, fascinating as it is in itself. You see, I soon learned that the Missi whose Mission is chronicled in this document is none other than Piers de Valon, the young Marquis de Valon et Balaincourt!"

"What!" Montclaire asked, rising from his chair in a convulsion of excitement. "Piers de Valon? Are you certain?"

"Yes!" Teddy smiled. "It could not have been more exciting for me. I felt that Fate itself had brought the document into my hands, and once more I was mystified by it. By this time the document was taking on a magical quality for me. I felt myself coming under its spell."

"But who is this Piers de Valon? You chaps obviously know him, but the rest of us are his complete strangers. At least, I know I am," I said.

Montclaire answered, though still in a state of amazement. "Fitz, Piers de Valon is the remote ancestor of four people in this room, including both Gilbert and me! And until this moment, there has been almost no documentary evidence of his life. This is indeed exciting news for the family Montclaire. Well played, Teddy! Well played!"

"Thank you, Gérard, but I can claim no credit. I was merely in the right place to benefit from good fortune."

Our company's delight erupted into applause and a chorus of hearty hurrahs. Petrovsky arrived at that moment with brandy for everyone. After a spontaneous toast, Teddy continued.

"I soon found the document was a remembrance of a strange and dangerous mission undertaken by two Missi Dominici, in the year 794. One of the Missi, our ancestor, Piers de Valon, and the other, Theodulfe d'Orleans, an abbot at the time, but eventually to be the most important churchman of Charlemagne's empire. I won't say more at this time, because I want to allow Theodulfe's document to tell his story, as only it can tell it."

"Fair enough," Montclaire responded. "It's late. I propose we convene our circle at the same hour tomorrow evening and, at that time, we will ask Theodulfe to take us into his tale."

Next evening we convened in exactly the same manner, to hear Teddy read from Theodulfe's memoir—a chronicle of each day of the investigation he and Piers de Valon had undertaken.

When Teddy began to read, we fell silent. His resonant baritone voice filled the slightly darkened library, and as the fire in our hearth crackled, I had the sensation of being conveyed back to the 8th century. I closed my eyes and then it was not Teddy, but Abbot Theodulfe who began to speak.

PART ONE

Theodulfe's Story

CHAPTER 1

The Abbey of Saint Aubin at Angers

November, Anno Domini 818

In nomini Patris et fillii et Spiritus Santi. Amen. Call me Theodulfe the Wretched, for it has pleased God that in these the last days of my life I should suffer horribly in the cold of my chamber in the Monastery of Saint Aubin d'Angers. I stand accused of taking the part of Bernard d'Italie in his rebellion against his uncle, Louis le Pieux, for the succession to the Emperor Charlemagne. Accused, I was unjustly stripped of my bishopric of Orléans and of my abbeys and exiled to this miserable place until my days are finished. My despair is now complete, for His Holiness the Pope has greeted with long silence my entreaties that he beg my release.

Foreseeing the approach of death, which I am certain is from the privation of food and warmth and from the effects of a slow poison, I have determined to write my remembrances of the most remarkable man of my acquaintance and of the strangest events of my life. If it be God's will that I may live until my testimony is complete, I will give an exact account of the horrors that transpired in the small and hapless village of Châlons, in Champagne, now more than twenty-five years past.

CHAPTER 2

A Remarkable Year

That Year of Our Lord 794 was unexceptional in my life, save for the events I am about to relate. However, all Christendom quaked at the rising danger of the Danes. In the previous year, they committed such outrages of looting and rapine at the Convent of Saint Cuthbert at Lindisfarne in Northumbria as to shock even the most hardened of hearts. It was God's will, however, that the same year also witnessed the end of the long war with the Frisians. The Great Charles led his armies into their midst and punished them for their wicked transgressions. There, too, Christianity was outraged by the murder of blessed Boniface, the butchering of priests, and the burning of Churches, as the treacherous Dukes of Unno and Eilrad led their people into apostasy—a return to pagan worship and resistance to the conscription levied by the Great Charles among the Frisians for his war against the Avars.

I had only lately been blessed by God to find even greater favor in service to the King, who placed upon my shoulders the Abbey of Fleury-sur-Loire, as well as the incomes of those of Saint-Aignan, Saint-Benoît, Saint-Mesmin, Micy, and Saint-Linfard.

In that year, also, the Great Charles summoned the Council at Frankfurt, which declared the usefulness of icons and condemned the dreadful teaching of Felix of Urgell that Our Lord Jesus Christ was merely a man adopted by God as his son at his baptism. The Council also forbade the persecution of witches and wizards as superstition and imposed the penalty of death upon those who dared burn a witch.

Then came word that the Danes had again struck the Northumbrian coast, this time plundering the Monkwearmouth-Jarrow Abbey. I recall vividly, as I and my monks at Fleury-sur-Loire prayed for the souls of our brothers lately slaughtered in Northumbria, that the King himself summoned me into association with the most remarkable man I have ever known and into the most terrifying adventure of my life.

CHAPTER 3

Early-Autumn, 974

The Monastery of Fleury-sur-Loire

It was at the Hour of Compline (6 p.m.), when suddenly there broke in upon our prayers a soldier, bearing the insignia of the King upon his cloak—a rough man who had clearly ridden hard and for a great distance. Exhausted and half-dazed, he said, "I bear a message for Father Abbot," and then fell in a heap upon the cold stones of our chapel floor.

Once revived with a cup of mulled wine, the messenger drew from his *marsupium* a small scroll of vellum. Seeing that I wore the Abbot's cross, he handed it to me.

"Father Abbot. The King summons you. Read…I beg you."

The summons, under the signature of my mentor, Alcuin of York, said that I was to come at once to the court, which the Great Charles was then holding at Rouen. The King intended to remain there through the Christmas Feast, said Alcuin, and there to hold a Great Council of his principal nobles. The message gave no indication of the reason for the summons.

Dutiful to my master, I prepared at once to travel the distance of 50 leagues to Rouen, in company with Bodo, the soldier-messenger, and two of my monks, Martin and Boethius. The change of seasons was well upon us, as autumn prepared to give way to winter, and we felt the bite of the winter cold upon the roads. Still, we urged our horses on, braving the dangers of bandits and fording treacherous rivers at great hazard. In crossing one, Brother Martin lost his seat and was washed some distance downstream and nearly to his death. Pressing ourselves, we stayed at inns only long enough to refresh and then renewed our journey. A light snow greeted us as we entered Rouen in only four days' time, on November 11, the Day of Saint Martin of Tours.

We found the King and his army encamped upon a great field to the northwest of the city, and in the city, there was a multitude of citizens and merchants—many of them Jews, who flocked to Rouen to serve the needs of the Court. Numerous leaders of the Church lately returned from the great Synod of Frankfurt, also waited upon the King. All this being the case, we thought ourselves fortunate to find rooms in a tavern of low repute. Once safely settled, I sent a message to Alcuin, to inform the Court of my arrival.

As the evening wore on, the tavern descended into near riot. The sound of cursing, gambling, and brawling mixed with the screams of whores and serving girls as they disputed prices and payments with patrons. Tavern noises troubled our sleep. Near midnight a young woman burst into our room, begging refuge from a drunken rogue at her heels. I feared for my life, but only momentarily, for Bodo awakened and put the brute to flight. The girl refused, however, to leave the foot of my bed, where she slept more soundly than I.

Next morning, after a restless night in the tavern, and as the brother monks and I broke our fast, servants of the King entered. They carried a message from the Court that ordered me and my monks to remove our accommodations to the camp. We soon found ourselves in excellent quarters, ordered by the Great Charles, who now held court at a fortress at the edge of his encampment. Another message now commanded me to attend upon the King at his dinner, which was set for the seventh hour.

CHAPTER 4

Earlier That Month
Near the City of Bourges, in the Frankish Kingdom

Scarcely a week before the messenger Bodo broke in upon my prayers, another of the King's emissaries neared the end of a more arduous and dangerous mission. I have this account of the events of that journey from the emissary himself.

Athalfe's face frightened even seasoned men of violence. He'd fought in three wars, saw a score of battles, had fallen in the field, only to rise with a wound that had left his large, heavy-featured face disfigured—a scar descending from his temple, past his eye, and carved deeply into the cheek and corner of his mouth. He had served long and well the Great Charles and had risen from humble man-at-arms when still in his youth to an officer of the Guards. He was now in his thirty-sixth year.

A sudden storm poured its cascade of rain upon the intrepid soldier. He grumbled quietly, sighed, and pressed on toward the great fortress city. He had traveled some distance in his quest, stopping in several towns and cities, but always just a little behind his "prey." Weary of his search and almost despairing, Athalfe learned from a tavern wench that Valon had told her he intended to make for the annual Fair at Bourges, where there was gambling and excitement to be had. So Athalfe made for Bourges.

Several days later on the main road he joined a river of wagons, carts, mules and people, all streaming into a city already busting with merchants and their retainers, selling their wares at the great Fair. The emissary began his search at the local taverns, where experience told him to look first for any trace of Valon. At the fifth or sixth he entered, the Innkeeper was able to give information.

"Valon, you say? A young man of about twenty-five years and a gambler. Well-spoken, eh, and handsome to a fault? Oh, yes, there was such a fellow here the night before last. He won a considerable pot at dice, in the back, but then there erupted a great brawl."

"Was Valon part of it? What of him?"

"Part! He was the **cause** of it! Indeed, he was. The rogue came to blows with the sons of Lord Halderon—one of the great nobles of our neighborhood. Those three are a terror to the same district, a bad lot, and each of them a menace in his own right."

"And you say Valon ran afoul of them?"

"Aye. They came to blows in the back," he explained, tossing his head behind him. "Their brawl spilled into the tavern, where they broke up most of my furniture, as you can well see. Then it came to swords and daggers and rolled out into the high street. The rogue you seek carved up Halderon's bastards pretty well before the Lord's men-at-arms arrived. It was the neatest piece of blackguard butchering I've ever seen, and I've witnessed many's a tavern brawl. A dozen of Halderon's soldiers finally descended upon this fellow Valon, though he wounded five or six before they subdued him—one was able to catch him a nice blow from behind."

Athalfe sighed. "Killed him, did they?"

"I doubt it. He was stunned but still fighting as they dragged him away to Halderon's Keep, not two leagues distant to the East. Valon you say? He was a fighter, he was! Never seen the likes of him, such swordplay, I mean! And quick? Quick as you please. Not surprised it took the fifteen of'em to subdue him, but I'll warrant he killed a few 'fore they got him to Halderon," the hostler said, with a hearty laugh. "If you find him, tell him I forgive the breakage. The show was worth the price!"

The emissary turned wearily to resume his search, now half believing that his mission would end in the discovery that his man had been killed by an outraged noble. Still, it was his duty to pursue his man to the very end, and then to report his findings to the King. Perhaps he would return Valon's corpse to the Great Charles. *It would be something at least*, he said and then sighed.

At noonday after next, Athalfe approached the great Keep of Lord Halderon—a black pile of stone upon a barren prominence, roughly made and hung all about with a thick mist and an air of menace. Roundabout there was little farming to support the Lord, so it appeared that Lord Halderon must be an impoverished noble, living by any means he could find, including highway robbery and any cutthroat enterprise. *A bad lot, indeed*, Athalfe mused.

At the great oaken gates of the fortress, he shouted, with an air of command, "Open in the name of the Great Charles, whose emissary stands before you."

With no word of greeting from the battlements or tower, the doors opened slowly. The rusted hinges creaked and gave into a courtyard of the meanest construction. Pigs and dogs ran about unfettered. The stink of animal and human waste poisoned the air. Despite the cold, two wenches washed in great troughs of water, while several men-at-arms—a few of them clearly drunk—lolled about the steps to the manor, chiding the naked girls.

As he approached, Athalfe remained mounted, his hand on the hilt of his sword.

"I am a messenger of the Great Charles. I seek the Lord Halderon."

The announcement caused hardly a stir among the soldiers until one answered.

"Not here. Nor his sons," he added disdainfully.

"Where then?"

"Left early to hunt wild pig. They'll be at it all morning, at least."

"Then perhaps you can tell me the whereabouts of a young man who was taken Lord Halderon's prisoner at Bourges on Monday last? His name is Valon—Piers de Valon."

The mention of the name brought the soldiers to their feet with angry looks.

"And what of it?" came the brusque reply. "What concern is it of yours?"

"It is this man, Valon, I seek. My business is with him."

"Well, your business with him is at an end, my friend, because it has pleased the Lord Halderon to hang the bastard from his battlements," said one of the soldiers, casting his gaze upward and toward the wall. Athalfe's jaw dropped as he glanced up and saw hanging from a scaffold attached to the tower a great basket of iron mesh and in it, the lifeless body of a man.

"That…that is Valon?" he asked.

"Aye," came the curt reply. "The son-of-a-whore killed three of Lord Halderon's soldiers and one son is dying as we speak. This Valon cut him in his groin…if you know what I mean."

"Castrated Halderon's heir!"

"Aye. Not the sort of thing to make him popular in the district, eh?"

"Still. Bring him down! Lower that cage at once," Athalfe demanded, summoning up all the air of command possible. "In the name of Charlemagne, I order you to lower that basket! Do it now!"

The soldiers came to greater attention but made no move to comply. One looked at the other as if in a quandary, and then one broke toward the tower to do as he was told. He reached the top and released the block mechanism and rope to lower the basket. Slowly it descended—squealing and groaning its mechanical pain—until it came to rest on the floor of the courtyard.

"Open it, at once!" Athalfe shouted, and now the soldiers obeyed immediately. It took but another minute to unwire and open the small door of the basket, but the body inside continued lifeless and apparently dead.

"Get him out!"

As the soldiers prepared to comply, a voice roared from the gate. "Who gives orders to release my prisoner? Who dares defy me?"

The challenge came from a large man mounted upon a great gray dapple horse. His hair and long beard were black as pitch and both braided. Dressed all in skins, his forearms and legs were wrapped in leather studded with brass.

"I am Halderon of Alançon and I demand to know who dares defy me!" He moved forward slowly, followed by several horsemen who bore much the same look as their leader. As they did so, dogs, geese, and pigs scattered, and the soldiers who had been idling about stood well back.

Halderon made a fearful sight, and yet Athalfe screwed up his courage, knowing that to do otherwise was certain death.

"It is the Great Charles himself who defies you, My Lord. This man is his prisoner, and I am his emissary. I charge you in the name of Charlemagne to release this man to me and give him means to travel," said Athalfe, handing over his credentials as he did so. Halderon motioned one of his sons to take the parchment scroll and read it.

The Lord Halderon paused but seemed undeterred by the name of Charlemagne. It was clear to the emissary that he intended to kill him and return Valon to the tower.

"The authorities in Bourges know I've come to your fortress, My Lord, so it will do you no good to kill me and continue with Monsieur de Valon. Behind me, there will come an army, and perhaps Charlemagne himself at its head and you will find yourself hanging from those same battlements behind you. The Great Charles is not a forgiving man to those who defy him, I promise you."

The warning, delivered with all the swagger of a soldier of the King's Guard, sobered the blustering Lord, who said nothing, but instead glanced up at the battlements. Then, after a long moment's consideration, Halderon shouted, "Release him. Release him to the Great Charles, whose prisoner he is. It is not in my power to punish the King's prisoner."

Turning to the emissary, "Tell the Great Charles that I have happily released the prisoner to him and that I, the Lord Halderon of Alançon, am his dutiful servant."

"I will indeed report to My Lord, the Great Charles, that you have done well by him this day, Lord Halderon, and no doubt, he will express his appreciation for your loyalty."

The men-at-arms now scrambled to pull Valon from the basket and as they did so, someone poured water over his head. The icy drenching revived him a little and, as he lay on the court, another bucket from the trough brought him increasingly to life. Athalfe dismounted and held a skin of wine to Valon's lips, which he drank deeply, pouring some on his head and shaking as he did so. All this revived the young man, but only for a moment.

When he tried to stand, he collapsed once more, this time into Athalfe's arms.

One of Lord Halderon's retainers appeared with Valon's horse. Together he and Athalfe hoisted the unconscious young man over its saddle, his arms dangling down the beast's side, his long, black hair dripping water and wine. Athalfe did not wish to risk a change of Lord Halderon's heart, so he quickly led Valon's horse out the fortress gates and broke into a gallop down the road toward Bourges.

By nightfall, when Athalfe decided to camp in the rough, Valon still languished across the saddle, and it seemed to his protector that he might die. Athalfe lay him on a bed of leaves surrounded by his own wool cloak and swaddled him in a think quilt of furs and wool. A blazing fire added warmth to the camp, and there the two remained until dawn, while the emissary kept his watch and Valon lingered near-death—or so it appeared.

At daybreak, as a thin mist rose from a nearby lake and meadows, a damp chill fell upon the camp, diminishing what remained of the once vigorous fire. Athalfe revived the fire and then warmed water in his iron helmet. Into it, he added crushed herbs to make a strong tea. From his small horn cup, he poured a bit of the mixture onto Valon's lips, prompting an almost immediate jolt. The young man bolted to half-consciousness, shook his head and opened wide his eyes.

"God-damn you, Evil One! What poison have you fed me?"

"Merely an herbal mixture, My Lord, which I learned in the Frisian War, from an Avar prisoner who got it from a Lombard. It is said capable of raising the dead, and I now believe it works. It has roused you, Monsieur de Valon, from something that looked very much like death."

"Who are you, Evil One?"

"I am not a Devil, nor am I Satan's acolyte. I am Athalfe—a soldier of the King's Guard. It is the Great Charles who summons you to his Court at Rouen and who dispatched me these many weeks ago to find and bring you there. I must say, Monsieur de Valon, you are not an easy man to find."

"I did not know I was being sought, and that has worked in your favor, poisoner. When I do not wish to be found, it is *not* possible to find me."

"I can believe that I swear by all the Saints! I have learned, however, that you leave behind you a path of destruction as wide as a foraging army when you do not mind being found."

"Oh! My head hurts!" Valon bellowed, then seized his head with both hands and rolled his eyes into his brow. "What is in that tea? It is a sorcerer's potion, I swear it!"

"No, hardly that, Monsieur. But it is a strong brew, I grant you. And yet, it has brought you 'round from the gate of eternity, has it not?"

"Indeed, it has, but I am unsure I would want to be brought 'round in the same way again." Still rubbing his head with one hand, Valon said wryly. "Next time, just leave me to the tender mercies of the likes of Halderon." That said, he fell back into a long sleep.

CHAPTER 5

He Revives

Athalfe stood guard over his charge all that day and through another night, tending a blazing fire and thinking that having found Valon, he must now deliver him as ordered to the Great Charles. Still, he wondered what business Charlemagne could have with such a rough and volatile young man. Athalfe himself had passed almost forty summers—most of them in the King's service. In war and peace, he had come to have a serious mind, which was mostly focused on the business of the King. *How unlike this young Valon, I am. And yet the King has need of him. How strange.*

Next morning, the pair struck out in silence upon the road to Bourges, retracing the steps that had taken them into the territory of the dreaded Halderon. As they neared the city and passed through a small village of no importance, Valon suddenly seized his head and fell from his horse, screaming in the most horrible way and chanting, "No…no, not that… No… No!" Afterward, he rolled about on the ground, screaming in fright at something he appeared to believe was attacking him.

Athalfe thought for a moment that Valon has been struck by an arrow or perhaps a stone fired from some distance, and looked about anxiously for the attacker. But they were quite alone. And yet, there was Valon, flailing about on the ground, as if terribly wounded.

Athalfe jumped from his horse, ran to Valon, and took him up in his arms, more to restrain him from harming himself than to comfort him. And still, Valon repeated over and over, "No…not that… No… No!" Again followed by shrieks of fright. Finally, the violence of his companion's seizure—for that is what he decided it was—convinced Athalfe that nothing was to be done but to sit upon Valon until the quake subsided, ensuring that he would come to no harm from himself. And so, for the next thirty minutes, the emissary straddled his charge and rode him like a wild beast, until exhaustion of body gave Valon the sleep that his mind could not find.

The hours of darkness approached and Athalfe decided to ask shelter from a nearby cottager, who showed him to a rough stable where the hay made a suitable bed. There the two passed another cold night, with only a small fire and their cloaks for warmth.

Athalfe studied the sleeping visage of his companion. What business could the Great Charles have with this man? Strange, indeed.

Athalfe sat motionless, looked into the fire, and thought of his companion. While the night passed, at about the third hour, Valon stirred and suddenly rose to his feet with a start, crouched as if prepared for combat.

"What is it?" Athalfe started, looking side-to-side. "What do you see?"

Valon relented and sat back upon his saddle, which Athalfe had arranged for him as a pillow. For the longest while, neither spoke.

"Monsieur de Valon, do you know what happened to you upon the road yesterday? Do you know that you fell from your horse and suffered a seizure? I believe you were possessed by a demon, who took command of your body."

"Not a seizure, and not possessed. But I thank you, nonetheless, for assisting me."

"It was my duty, Monsieur. The Great Charles ordered me to return you to his court—for what reason I cannot imagine—and I will do it or die in the effort. But you say that it was not a seizure or evil spirit. Then what, if you please?"

"I do not know, precisely. I call them visions, but they are not that either. They are terrible attacks upon my mind. They are thoughts that are put in my mind, maybe by the Evil One. I don't know."

"Visions and thoughts? Visions of what? And to be so violent... Visions?"

"Since I was a child, I have had premonitions from time to time. They come unbidden and at any time, but most often in that strange time of the early morning, between wakefulness and sleep, when the mind begins to stir from its slumber."

"It is a dream then...a vivid dream?"

"No. More real than any dream and more terrible than any nightmare. But there is something else..." Valon paused, unsure to continue.

Athalfe leaned forward, alert and eager to learn all that was to be known of Valon's terrifying glimpses into the future.

"What? What else, Monsieur?"

"My premonitions always come to pass."

Athalfe did not know what to make of what he'd heard. He'd never been told such a thing. And yet, somehow, he found Valon entirely credible and believed him at once.

"What manner of visions?"

"Terrible ones…almost always about death. I see people die. I seldom know who or when, but my experience has taught me that the things I foresee come to pass."

"And the one you have just had?"

"It was a vision I have seen three times in as many weeks and each time it is the same and each time it is as frightening."

Athalfe dared not ask to hear the premonition, fearing that to do so was as much as to open the Book written by Satan himself, but his face spoke clearly of his desire to know.

"Yes, I see that you fear it and yet wish to know my vision." Valon paused for a moment, collecting his thoughts. "It is a damp and bleak day and I look up to the tower of a fortress. As I do, I see a young woman in black is on the top of the tower. She is merely standing upon the tower and at first, I sense no danger for her."

"What woman is this, Monsieur? Is it a woman you know?"

"No. I do not, because I cannot see her face, but I have the sense that she is familiar to me and I care for her."

"You cannot see her face?"

"All I can say is this—she is dressed all in black and her hair is long and red."

"Red? That is something. It is not every girl, in the Frankish Kingdom who has red hair, after all."

"Yes. Well, in my premonition I watch the girl, her hair blowing in the breeze and it is a very pleasant thing. Though I cannot see her face, I know she is beautiful and I know she is pleasant to me, at least she is pleasant to watch. It is a wonderful moment."

"I cannot see what is so frightening about that, Monsieur. Watching a beautiful girl as her long hair blows in the breeze is a wonderful thing."

"Yes, but don't you see? The wonderful moment does not last. In the next moment, it turns into a horror, because of the girl… Suddenly, the girl falls from the tower. I watch—powerless to do anything—as she falls to the court below. I see her body hit the cobbles in front of me with an awful sound."

"Monsieur, you are powerless to prevent it?"

"Yes. That's exactly what is so frightening to me. I am powerless, and when I see her fall, that is always when I scream and awaken. Today is the third time I've seen this terrible event and each time it is as frightening as the last.

And yet there is one other thing, each time."

"What is that, My Lord?"

"In every instance, I have the feeling the girl's not alone on the tower when she falls…that there is another there, with her."

"Who?"

"I do not know, because I cannot see him. I only sense that he is there."

"Then it is the Evil One. He is there and caused the girl to jump, perhaps?"

"Yes. Perhaps."

Athalfe chose to say no more but sat in silence with Valon for most of an hour. Both looked into the blazing fire and found it somehow comforting. Then, with no further word, they fell to sleep.

Next morning, the two continued in silence, though Athalfe continued to wonder what strange manner of man he was charged to bring to Charlemagne's court. After only an hour on the road, Valon asked abruptly, "How long is it that you are returned from the war with the Moors?"

The question surprised the emissary, for he remembered saying nothing about the Moorish War to anyone, including Valon.

"About a year, Monsieur, but how do you know I have come from Spain?"

"It is a matter of several things, each of which contributed to my conclusion. I have noticed that you have a feeling relationship with your horse, which suggests that you have been together for some time. From the scars on his neck and rump, as well as from his breeding, he is clearly a warhorse. You also handle him in the Moorish fashion of horsemanship, though of course, I know you are not a Moor."

Athalfe said nothing but listened in amazement as his companion explained his deduction.

Valon smiled.

"Then, too, your saddle is distinctive. It is a Frankish saddle to be sure, but some of the leatherwork shows a slight Moorish influence. I would say you obtained it in the Moorish territories and it was made by a Frankish workman influenced by Moorish design."

"That is absolutely true. He was a Jew who lived in the Moorish lands for many years, and yet was keen to make saddles that satisfied the customs of the Frankish warriors."

"Then there is that slight limp of your left leg. It is not noticeable to the casual observer, but I am a noticing sort of person. The arrow you took in your thigh has left you with a weakness in your left leg, has it not?"

"Again, Monsieur, you astonish me. It is as you say, but I was certain I had entirely overcome my wound."

"Oh, you needn't worry on that score, my friend. It is noticeable only to someone practiced at noticing such things. However, there is one other thing to tell of your experiences in the south. The small clasps on your sandals are also of Moorish design and the wear upon them suggests they were purchased within the past two years. Am I not correct?"

"Indeed, you are Monsieur. They were made for me just before I left Spain. By the Lord's Mercy, you are indeed a noticing sort of man, Monsieur de Valon. I never knew anyone to know so much about me, without my telling it."

"It may comfort you to know that you are not alone in revealing much about yourself. It is the rare person whose clothing and body and manner do not tell of their experiences, and those things are there for all to see if only they will. It is a useful thing to be noticing."

"I can see that it would be, Monsieur."

The two rode on in a silence that continued even as they camped. On the third day, they approached the town of Poissy and found themselves immersed in a celebration, complete with street entertainments and a solemn procession of the town's merchants, carrying the image of their patron saint before them. The town's great market had clearly attracted sellers from a wide region.

"Our mounts are tired, Monsieur. It will be useful to rest here for a day. After, our journey to the court at Rouen should be a matter of only two days' ride."

"As you say, Athalfe. A welcome respite, and apparently a good place to find it," Valon said, clearly with an eye to the entertainment.

The two passed a delightful day among the merrymakers at the market. Soon, however, they departed toward the west, moving by Athalfe's map along a substantial road toward the city of Blois, on the Loire.

A day out of Poissy, they came to a bridge which spanned a wide tributary of the Loire, and upon that bridge stood a large man on a warhorse. He was fully armored, and beyond him, well on the other side of the stream, stood a half-dozen heavily-armed men, also mounted.

CHAPTER 6

A Neatly Severed Head

"Good day, kind Sir," Athalfe shouted, eyeing with a worried expression the man who stood upon the bridge. "May I ask if we are truly on the main road to Blois?"

"Indeed, you are, Monsieur, and you have the good fortune to find yourselves in the lands of Lord Waldgard of Blois."

As Athalfe and Valon moved to pass onto the bridge, however, the warrior moved to block their progress.

"We wish to pass Monsieur. Why do you stop us?"

"The use of this bridge and of the road to Blois requires a toll, my friend. It is Lord Waldgard's right to collect 50 silver deniers of each one who passes this toll."

"That may be so, Monsieur, but I am Athalfe of the King's Guard and this man is in my charge, and we are on the King's business. The Great Charles does not pay tolls and other fees in his own Kingdom and so we will pass and rely upon your safe conduct."

"You will pass upon payment of 100 silver deniers, to the coffers of the Lord Waldgard, my friend," said the warrior leader, and he stood a little in his saddle and his voice now menaced.

At this bravado, Valon nudged his mount forward such that he came to rest only a few feet from the leader. Athalfe remained back.

As he approached to look into the eyes of the leader, Valon's broadsword remained in its sheath, slung by a strap across his back. Suddenly, however, he stood full in his stirrups and drew the sword in one fluid motion, brought the unsheathed blade forward and severed the head of the warrior, who, for a moment, remained headless in his saddle, his hands on the horse's reins. The leader's head then bounced off the rump of his horse and fell to the ground.

Scarce believing what he had seen, Athalfe noticed the reaction of the soldiers across the stream and drew his sword as well. Looking to Valon for a notion of what to do, he heard him say, "Friend Athalfe, the road to Blois lies across the bridge."

And with that, Valon dropped his reins, drew his long knife, pointed his sword at the warriors across the stream, let out a harrowing scream, and spurred his horse onward. Still surprised at what was happening, Athalfe followed, wielding his sword in the same way and screaming in the same fashion, though not knowing precisely why.

The warriors jostled on their horses, horrified at what they had seen, and even more so to see what was coming at them—a madman who'd severed the head of their captain. Three turned their horses and spurred them up the road. The three who remained drew their swords to engage, but before the first could urge his mount Valon was upon him, passing quickly and hacking his right leg as he passed. Turning, Valon engaged the warrior directly from behind and after a brief clash of blades, ran the man through the neck with his long knife.

Meanwhile, Athalfe, busy with his own man, clashed swords several times at close quarters. Valon returned to his first adversary, who was desperately trying to stop the blood streaming from his leg. As Valon cantered toward him, the warrior hardly seemed to notice his approach but raised his sword just in time to meet Valon's assault. Quickly, however, Valon put his long knife through the man's side and he fell from his horse, screaming and flailing about on the ground.

Valon turned to see Athalfe in full combat with the remaining warrior, clearly having some success with his tiring adversary. Riding toward the two, he took from his cloak a knife and riding past, drew it across the neck of Athalfe's opponent, releasing a cascade of blood.

Not looking back, Valon continued on the road to Blois. Astonished at the quickness of Valon's attacks and their deadly effect, Athalfe spurred his mount forward to catch up and sheathed his sword as he went.

Breathless, he finally came alongside Valon. "Monsieur, I have been in battle since my sixteenth year, in Spain and in the Frisian War, but I have never seen such swordsmanship as yours. I have never seen such quickness of blade and knife. Tell me, s'il vous plaît, is it possible to learn this new and marvelous style?"

Valon smiled. "What I do is not a learned method, Athalfe, and so I do not know that is it something one could learn."

"I do not understand, Monsieur. I learned my martial skills from my father, who was a man-at-arms in service to the Duke of Etreta. I learned quickly and at fifteen I was taken by the same Lord as a man-at-arms as he answered Charlemagne's call to renew the war in Spain. In all that time, I practiced and learned from my superiors. And now, I see something that I cannot quite believe, and I am eager to learn it. Yet, you tell me that you did not learn it."

"Odd as it may seem, that is true. I, too, learned my skills with weapons and horse as a boy, from my Grandfather, the Marquis de Valon et Balaincourt. I was put in training with his own men-at-arms and his other grandsons. I learned method from his master-at-arms, but at age eighteen I was summoned to the Frisian War. It was there I learned to do whatever it is I do."

"How so?"

"My first battle was the last engagement before Boam. As the Frankish cavalry formed our lines in the morning fog, we could hear the sound of the Frisian Army, beating their axes against their shields and chanting to their gods. I sat, so frightened that I thought to vomit the little that I had eaten in breaking my fast. When the priests rode by, giving their blessings and absolution, it came to me that I was surely about to find myself in the presence of Our Lord. I prayed. My prayers were broken by the sound of the horns that signaled us to move forward at a canter. As I began to move forward, it happened, as if a gift to me from God."

"What, Monsieur? What happened?" Athalfe asked eagerly.

"I cantered forward, in line with the others, but then my mind seemed to collapse within me and I entered into a state of great peace with myself and with what I was doing. When the great horns sounded the double-quick, my mind descended even deeper within me and I sensed myself to be the instrument of another will—driven by necessity. As the horns blew the charge, I dropped my reins, drew my sword, and in my left hand took up my long knife. By this time, I had entered a trance-like state, in which my body became the instrument of the necessity to survive. Without the least thought, I gave myself over to some animal instinct, in which I am able to do as you have seen. In the Frisian War, I learned to govern my decision to behave thus, but you see I cannot tell you that it is learned because I do it in a state that can only be described as a trance."

Athalfe pondered Valon's strange story as they road.

"I am a simple soldier and have never heard such a thing," he finally said. "And yet I have seen it before my eyes. If ever you are able to convey this trance to another, I would be pleased to be your first pupil."

Valon laughed heartily but said no more.

Later, as the two approached the city of Blois on the Loire, Athalfe could see Valon was regaining his full strength from all he had suffered at the hand of wicked Lord Halderon and his sons. His wounds were healing, his muscles fully restored, and his strength was proved in his ability to once again ride long distances and for long hours. Athalfe continued to marvel at his companion's abilities in almost all things human, and in some things that did not appear to be quite human at all. In his darkest thoughts, Athalfe later confided to me, he even feared that his charge might be possessed by the Evil One.

CHAPTER 7

At the Court of Lord Waldgard

The soldiers who escaped Valon's attack on the bridge returned to report to Lord Waldgard the deaths of their fellows and the approach of the two warriors who carried a warrant from the Great Charles. As soon as Valon and Athalfe approached the city's gates, a troop of men-at-arms surrounded them and presented them the compliments of Lord Waldgard and bid them join a banquet that evening. Valon quickly accepted.

The captain of the troop—a large and well-armed man—spoke coarsely and in a tone that Athalfe took as threatening.

"The Lord Waldgard," he announced, "master of the Loir and the domain of Blois...."

"Yes. Yes," Valon interrupted. "Spare me the tedious recitation of your Lord's cursed titles and possessions. What interests me at the moment, fat one, is how long you propose to live."

The captain's mouth fell agog, his eyes grew wide, and he wheeled on his horse.

"What?" he roared.

"I mean, dense one," Valon continued, impatient, "must I kill you here, or will you allow me to pass?"

Barely restraining his fury, the captain answered, "You may pass, Monsieur, but only after I give you a message from my master."

"Well, get on with it! I am eager for my supper."

Rising to his full height in the saddle, the captain replied, "My Lord Waldgard invites you to a banquet that he has prepared this very evening, Sir."

"Good. Why didn't you say so from the outset, ugly one? Tell Waldgard that I am dubious he could prepare a banquet of sufficient quality to satisfy me, but I accept."

The captain and his troop wheeled and departed in a huff. And as they rode away, Athalfe sighed, "Monsieur de Valon, your insults leave no daylight for apology."

Later, Athalfe and Valon found the great fortress of Lord Waldgard lighted by a hundred fiercely burning torches. The Lord's Steward greeted them as if accustomed to visitors and guided them into the great hall. There, they found a numerous assembly of the Lord's friends and retainers, including a great number of his own relations who were present for a coming feast of the city's patron saint. Waldgard sat at the high table, flanked on either side by his evil-looking sons.

The warm fires in the Hall seemed to blaze forth with good cheer, as Valon and Athalfe seated themselves at a table with some of the Lord's own children and brothers. One of the Lord's children—a beautiful young woman—appeared attracted to Valon and made that clear even before the *viande* was brought to their table. Athalfe was certain that Valon would reciprocate, given the hotness of his blood, but instead of returning a welcoming smile, Valon stared at the large goblet on the table before him with a strange expression upon his face.

Athalfe whispered in Valon's ear. "What is it, My Lord? Why do you look so?"

Valon said nothing and did not avert his gaze from the cup.

Fearing that Valon was having a recurrence of his previous seizure, Athalfe repeated, "Monsieur, why do you look so? Are you unwell?"

Valon looked at him with a start. "Have you drunk, my friend? Have you?" he whispered, his voice charged with urgency.

"No, Monsieur, I have not yet."

"Then do not. Do not, by any means. Neither must you eat."

And so, the two sat, enjoyed the company, but did not take of the viande, nor of the fine wine, which flowed liberally at Lord Waldgard's table. Soon, Waldgard was himself quite drunk and shouted his glee in celebration at the head of the high table. Others of the company grew warm from drink, and at just the right moment, a traveling musician from the Moorish lands came into the Hall and began to sing of love and its gratification, much to the arousing of sinful passions in both men and women, or so I was told by Athalfe.

Still, Valon and Athalfe neither ate nor drank, and yet the two participated fully in the good cheer and enjoyed much the easy talk of everyone around them, including Lord Waldgard's lovely daughter.

Long past midnight and nearer the second hour the feast began to wane, in particular as some of the guests fell asleep at their tables and some couples wandered off to express their foul passions. Waldgard, himself, continued to make merry from the high table, where many of his fellows were to be found face down in their soups.

At times singing, or telling a merry tale of the hunting fields, the Lord eventually looked upon Valon with alarm, and asked in a loud voice, "Eh bien, Monsieur de Valon, why do you not partake of my viande and wine? Are they fouled? Do you find my vittles inferior to the provender of the Great Charles' court?"

At the question, the great hall fell to silence, except for a bit of mumbling from the outer precincts.

Valon rose, lifted his cup, and strode toward the high table where Waldgard now stood, one hand on his hip and the other on the hilt of his sword.

Standing before the Lord, Valon said in a calm voice, "This is undoubtedly the best of wine, My Lord, and so I invite you to drink it." He lifted the cup and pressed it upon Waldgard. The Lord stood speechless for a moment, and then hesitated noticeably, whereupon Valon threw the cup's contents in his great bearded face.

The hall broke into shouts and grumbling, with many curses hurled at Valon.

Wiping the dripping wine from his face and beard and restraining the hand that still gripped his hilt, Waldgard replied, "It is good for you, Monsieur de Valon, that you and your man travel under the safe conduct of the Great Charles himself. I am obliged at all hazards to give you safe passage through my domains."

"And it is good for you, Waldgard, that I do not have time to kill every fool I meet along the way to Charlemagne's court. Else I would linger a day to repay you for your effort to poison me."

Having thus scolded and affronted Waldgard, Valon turned and walked from the great hall, Athalfe following close on his heel, disbelieving what he had just seen.

When the two parted Blois on the road northwest to Rouen, Athalfe dared ask an explanation of what had happened the previous evening.

"Monsieur, by now I am practiced at understanding only half of what I see in your actions, and so I know that I may yet perceive fully what befell us last evening. May I ask…?

"Forgive me, Athalfe," he interrupted, "I should have explained last night, but I was too absorbed in my anger at the deceitful Lord Waldgard and his sons. I also feared he might make another attempt on our lives and so was preoccupied with my watchfulness in that regard."

"Another attempt, Monsieur."

"Yes, the *viande* and wine served to us was laced with a quick poison."

"But how did you know that, Monsieur?"

"Last week, before I was captured by the oaf Halderon and put in his iron cage, I stopped at a nearby inn. Having ordered my evening meal, the wine brought me was sour, so I threw it on the floor and demanded the innkeeper's best as recompense. When I sat my empty cup upon the table, I saw in my mind's eye a frightening vision."

"Another vision, Monsieur? What did you see?"

"I looked at my cup on the table and saw come from it a large rat. And then there emerged two more rats, only smaller. I jumped from the table, so startled was I, but then they disappeared, and I then knew it was yet another of the visions that I have suffered for so long."

"Last evening, at Lord Waldgard's table, when the wine was brought to our cups, I saw the same three rats emerge from my cup, and from yours. When I saw the same rats emerge from the viande that lay before us, I knew the meaning of my previous vision. I was warned that I would be poisoned, though not when or where. The three rats were Waldgard and his evil sons. It pleased Our Lord, you see, that I was warned by a vision last evening."

Hearing this, Athalfe crossed himself three times and uttered a prayer he learned as a child. "I thank God for your visions, Monsieur, for you have more than once saved me along with yourself."

CHAPTER 8

At the Court of Charlemagne

The several days that followed passed quietly, much to Athalfe's relief and surprise, for he had come to believe that violence and adventure followed Valon, as the night the day. On the third day of their journey, the two entered the city of Rouen and joined the throng of travelers, merchants, soldiers, courtiers, churchmen, and riffraff who gathered round the Christmas Court of the Great Charles.

In that same crowd, yet unknown to Valon and Athalfe, the brother monks and I rode our weary mounts out of the city of Rouen. Bodo guided us over several gentle hills and through terrain where fields were neatly divided by hedgerows, some quite tall. As we came over our final rise, we beheld before us an amazing sight. A thousand campfires of the King's enormous army wafted smoke across a broad valley, at the end of which stood a great fortress keep. Everywhere there were tents and the movement of horsemen. Carts and wagons streamed in long trains into the camp ahead of us, while others of the army's supply wagons stood motionless at the edge of the yawning encampment.

And there, in the middle of the army, I saw the most frightening creature of my long experience, for I had never thought to see it. I gasped to behold the terrible Abu-Lubahah*. His great ears extended like wings, almost in warning as we approached, and he raised his long nose as if to threaten. His legs seemed like the trunks of trees, and his color was as ominous as the gray shadows of the coming night. And withal, he stood as high as a house and was easily the size of a peasant cottage. The monster let go a horrible roar, which resounded throughout the camp, like the report of a great warhorn. The brother monks recoiled in fear, fell from their horses and began to whimper and pray that God would spare us from the creature.

"What is it, Father Abbot?" Brother Boethius pleaded from his knees.

"Do not fear, Brother. I have heard of the creature, though I never thought to see it. And now that I have, I can wish that God's grace had spared me the fright."

"But what is it?"

"It is called *The Aelephant*. It was sent as a gift to the Great Charles by the Caliph Haroun al-Rashide of Baghdad. The King is said to take it everywhere with him. I have heard he even took the creature into the Frisian War, where the sight of it spread terror amongst the foe."

Still frightened, we gave the beast a wide berth and found our way to the quarters appointed to us. There we were able to grain our horses and take our rest.

That evening, we found in the great hall of the fortress a lavish assemblage of the Court, numbering near a hundred ladies and gentlemen, and including the high churchmen and nobles of Frankish Kingdom. At a long table upon a platform raised above the rest, sat the greatest man of Christendom, Charlemagne, along with his Queen Fastrada (who was to die in that same year), several of his children, and the principal nobles of the region, including at the King's right hand, the Comte de Rouen. At the center of the encircled long tables blazed forth a great fire, which spit and crackled, its flames dancing high in the air. In that same circle, a troop of musicians entertained with the liveliest music, most of it having to do with the bravery of Frankish heroes of old—Roland and the other heroes of the Moorish War. It was the very music that Charlemagne liked best, though some thought it pagan.

Now alone and no longer attended by my brother monks, I was led to a table near the King and motioned to take my seat beside a young man who was engaged in the most animated conversation with his companions.

He was a well-made man of the noble warrior class, much taller than the ordinary Frankish man and his face long, angular and clean-shaven. His jaw was well-set and his eyes, piercing and black, moved relentlessly as he spoke. He wore no cap, and his hair he wore long and a braided topknot on the side, in a pagan style popular with those lately returned from the Frisian War.

Noticing my approach, he broke off his conversation and said, "Father Abbot, welcome. I am Piers de Valon." Standing, he held out his hand, which I took to embrace.

As we both sat to table and took meat from the ample provisions, I asked Lord Valon if he had been long at Court if he were a soldier in the King's service, and if he knew what reason had prompted Charlemagne to hold his Court at Rouen.

"I arrived at court only yesterday, Father Abbot, and am not now a soldier in Charlemagne's service, though I have been a soldier and am returned from the Frisian War. In truth, I do not know why I have been summoned to the Court. But I have already learned that the King is at Rouen to assure the nobles of the Northwest and particularly the Comte de Rouen that he will protect them against the marauding of the Danes. News of the plundering in

Northumbria has frightened almost everyone, and the King wishes to reassure, I am told."

"Well, Valon, you and I share one thing already in addition to this table. We are both summoned and we do not know why. Nonetheless, I am Theodulfe of the Abbey of Fleury-sur-Loire, and I beg you to call me by my given name." And from that time, I addressed him as Valon, and to him I was Theodulfe.

As we spoke, I noticed a strangely inquisitive gaze came into Valon's dark eyes, and I wondered what could be troubling him.

"Pardon me, Theodulfe, but I see you are a man of the old Visigoth kingdom, though you have not been there these many years. Perhaps it was your family that came of those lands."

"Yes, Monsieur, you are correct. I was born in the Visigoth Kingdom, or rather what was left of it from the Moorish conquest. My parents died there. But how do you know such things? "I have no hint of my Visigoth origins in my speech; I know that. And my dress...?"

"No, no...there is little about you that speaks of your origins, save that small clasp on your tunic, just beneath your cloak. I saw it briefly as you sat. That you use it as a clasp for your inner garment tells me that it is not decorative. And that you wear it at all tells me of your connection to the Visigoth Kingdom. Its design is distinctive, coming from the era at the end of the past century, and it is decidedly a feminine piece in the Visigoth style, which suggests that it came to you from your Visigoth mother.

"And you are also correct that your speech carries no sign of your gothic origins. You speak beautiful Latin, but you have used two words so far, the pronunciation of which tells me that you were educated in the southwestern part of the Frankish Kingdom, just north of the Pyrenees. Is that not so?"

"Yes. At the Monastery of Pau. Valon, I'm astonished at your powers of observation. Extraordinary."

"No, Theodulfe, they are not. It is all there for any man to see if he but will. Sadly, most men see, but do not take the time to know."

After this brief exchange, we lapsed into a short but welcome silence, and for the first time, I tried to take the measure of the very odd Marquis de Valon. Our conversation soon resumed and I learned that Valon's territories lay along the Loire and northwest of the ancient city of Tours. We discussed this and that, and I noted the peculiar sparkle and flash of his black eyes, the clear and incisive nature of his intellect and speech, and his wonderful command of Latin. I learned further that he spoke also the Frankish language, which was the natural dialect of the King, and also the Saxon tongue, in which he possessed a remarkable gift for reciting epic verse from memory. He spoke with authority upon subjects as varied as the monastic reforms then underway in Frankland, the culture of the Danes, and the poetry of the profane young Roman, Gaius Catullus, which he particularly admired and which led me to suspect for a time that Valon must be a disgusting sodomite. However, I was sinfully flattered that he was also familiar with my own poetry and that he pronounced it among the best produced in the Kingdom.

Why have I never before heard of this young man? Looking backward, I know now that it was because he lived reclusively for some time, distracted in self-destructive torment of a personal nature and was only just making his name in the Frankish realm, a name that would eventually achieve considerable repute, as a commander and more, much more.

Two fine ladies of the Court who sat directly across from us and two young soldiers on his left claimed much of Valon's attention, and the conversation drifted in other directions, notably toward the subject of the Danish threat. Valon's pronouncements were sober but optimistic, and it seemed to me that his mind was mature well beyond his years. I was aware, as well, that he had captured the complete attention of the two ladies.

As I listened with admiration, now upon the issue of the war against the Moors in my native land, a court messenger approached with a note from my old mentor, Alcuin of York. His message began with an apology for his absence and instructed me to appear at the fortress next morning just after Prime (about 6 a.m.), as it was then that Charlemagne would hold his first audiences. It was at that time, Alcuin said, the King himself would tell me of his reasons for summoning me.

Alcuin's reticence to explain why I had been brought to court seemed mysterious, but I resolved to return to my quarters and an early bed, so as to be prepared for my audience next morning. My sleep was fitful, however. I rolled from one shoulder to the other in my apprehension of the Charlemagne's purpose. It even occurred to me that somehow I had incurred the King's displeasure.

CHAPTER 9

Next Morning

I entered the fortress next morning, well before the appointed hour. While I waited in the King's antechamber to be called, I was surprised to meet once again the young Marquis de Valon. At first, he seemed not to recognize me, but then remembered we shared an interest in poetry and the affairs of Spain.

"Of course, I remember you, Theodulfe, but what are you doing here, and at this ungodly hour?"

"I await the King's pleasure, however long that takes him," I said, with just a bit of anxious anticipation. I am earlier than need be because I could not sleep for wondering why I have been summoned."

"What a strange thing. I, too, am called for the same unknown purpose. Do you suppose you and I are summoned for the same purpose?"

"That would be odd indeed, young Valon—two strangers? What possible connection could we have?"

As our speculations began, Alcuin appeared through the large doors of the Audience Chamber and, without a word, motioned the two of us to come forward.

"That answers my question," said Valon, as we scurried forward.

We entered a large and barren room, appointed only with a single tapestry that hung from the far wall, behind the throne. Charlemagne's throne, a plain stone chair raised the length of a man's arm above the floor and approached by three steps, dominated the room. On it sat the most powerful man in Christendom.

"Come forward good Theodulfe," he commanded in his thunderous voice. "And you, Valon. Come!"

We approached together and at the foot of the throne, knelt on one knee until told to rise. Then we stood, eager to hear finally the reason for our summons. It was not long in coming.

"I have commanded you hither because I have a mission for you and it is my will that you should carry it out together. You see, I am appointing you as my Missi Dominici in a matter of grave importance and in a role that I believe you…both of you…are uniquely capable of fulfilling."

"Indeed, Sire?" Valon asked, clearly eager to hear the nature of the mission that the King meant to assign.

"Alcuin has drawn up the special *capitulary,* which will guide you and give you authority to act absolutely in my name. He has also assembled the necessary documents that will tell you of the problem I wish you to resolve."

"You said, Sire, that it is a grave problem…" I ventured.

"Yes. You will travel some distance to the east, to the village of Châlons upon the River Marne. There, you will investigate and do justice concerning a number of horrible murders that have driven the neighborhood into hysteria and even into reprisals against the Lord of the region. In fact, I'm told the entire district of Châlons has been tormented these many months by a beastly murderer who preys upon innocent girls in the most savage way. Alcuin's documents will provide you a full history of the problem, as the facts of it are known to the local Bishop—Ambrose of Rimes. It is he, you see, who begs me to intervene. The decision is made, then. And, you, Theodulfe of Fleury sur Loire, and you, Piers de Valon, are my Missi Dominici."

The Great Charles stood and spoke these last words with his voice ascending and the palms of both hands raised toward us.

I clasped my Abbot's cross. Valon drew his sword and held it high. We both knelt and in unison repeated he obligatory oath-taking—*"Capio meum sacramentum."*

CHAPTER 10

The Strange Testimony of Ambrose, Bishop of Reims

When it pleased God that our audience with the Great Charles ended, Valon and I retreated to a quiet precinct of the fortress, where we read the letter Alcuin gave us. Bishop Ambrose's account of recent events in Châlons was both frightening and remarkable. Addressed to Alcuin of York, it read as follows:

Brother Alcuin,
*   In the name of the Father, the Son...*
*   I send this to you in the hope that you will find it in your heart to bring it to the attention of the Great Charles, and at that time beseech him on our account to act upon our desperate plight. I urge you further that there is no time to wait, for the Evil that has come upon this poor district seems to multiply its horrors each week.*
*   That Evil first appeared in our midst, in the village of Châlons-sur-Marne, in the early autumn. Then, on an evening after Michaelmas, a peasant girl of the village, on her way to visit a neighbor, was attacked in a street just off the main road and there was beaten and cruelly violated. Her attacker then strangled her, while at the same time leaving the most horrible marks of biting and tearing of flesh on her innocent body.*
*   The outrage of this crime seized the entire village and as the townsfolk began to contemplate the event, it seemed to all that it must be one among them who was guilty.*
*   Then, not one week later a girl of about the same age was similarly murdered, while on her way home one night from cleaning the village church with other women. She was dragged into a stable, where she was beaten and raped. Then her throat was cut, but once again the poor girl's body was covered with bites. This seemed tell-tale evidence that the same creature must have done the second murder. I say, "creature," for what man would behave thus, and because by this time, the simple village folk had begun to speak that a diabolical animal of a sort—perhaps a loup-garou (werewolf)—was loosed by Satan among them.*
*   Once more the villagers were shocked at the horrors before them. Grieving soon gave way to anger and the mood of the village became even more outraged and guarded. This time, however, one of the women*

who had been in the group who cleaned the church reported that she had seen a figure in the vicinity of the stable. Although this woman, a simple and elderly person, was unsure who she had seen, she later told Father Draco—the serving priest of the village—that the figure seemed familiar. Pressed to say who she thought it was or might be, she confessed privately to him that it appeared to be Ethelred, the Lord of the Manor of Châlons and Passy. The Lord is a tall and large man, who might well be recognizable even in the dark. Father Draco decided to hold in closest confidence what the old woman told him because he was loath to believe it and credited it to poor eyesight and a simple mind.

Two days later, the murderer stuck again. This time he invaded a cottage on the outskirts of the village, where he found two young girls who had been left to themselves, while their parents and brother traveled to a nearby town. When the family returned, they found a horror in this cottage. The walls and floor were covered with blood. Both girls were found to have been bound and tortured before they were killed. And again, both had been horribly violated.

The revulsion and anger that swept the village at the news of this latest horror ignited a white-hot determination among the townsmen to find and punish the murderer. It was then that Farther Draco told me the tale the old woman confided to him and he had discounted as certainly in error.

We had no time to decide, for the old woman broke her silence and began to tell what she had seen, making the most vocal and extreme vows. Now she professed herself certain that she had seen the Seigneur de Châlons that night near the stable, and this aroused the villagers as nothing before. A mob marched one night to the house of Dagbert, the Lord's Steward and Seigneurial Judge, demanding that the Lord of the Manor account for himself.

The respect that was customarily due the Lord and which had previously been given without reservation melted away in the villagers' outrage at the terrible crimes. It was in this atmosphere that the worst happened. One evening, as the Lord Ethelred de Châlons returned to his manor he was viciously attacked. A crowd of masked men began to pelt the Lord with rocks and even knocked him from his horse to the ground. At that moment, several of the Lord's men-at-arms came down the same road—clearly intending to meet and escort him to the manor. They rushed upon the rogues and drove them away and thereby managed to rescue their Lord.

An attack upon the Lord of the Manor is a most serious crime. The injured Lord Ethelred was put to his bed treated by the apothecary of our nearby Abbey of Saint Benoît du Lac. Meanwhile, the Lord's sons—Godfrey, Humphrey, and Guillaume—led a band of men in a reprisal against the village. One night—not three days later—marauders attacked the village, burning several houses and the smithy and killing several men. The father of one of the murdered girls, who was said to be a leader of those who had attacked Lord Ethelred, was dragged from his cottage and hanged from a tree near the Abbey gates. While the attackers were not apprehended and no one could bear witness to the identity of any of them, the villagers believe that the attack had been ordered by Lord Ethelred or his sons, the latter of whom has an evil reputation among the local folk. Guillaume is especially despised by the villagers and peasants, for he is known often to molest the local girls. In fact, there are some in the village who believe that it is he who is guilty of the murders.

Lord Ethelred, meanwhile, has recovered from his injuries and has told me that he is troubled that his villagers should hold him guilty of such crimes and he cannot forgive them for it. For their part, the villagers are both sullen and terrorized.

Then, last week, there came yet another murder. Monica, the daughter of Osbern the Miller, was attacked and murdered in the same way as the others. Her battered body was found next morning to the side of the path where she had walked. Though there were no witnesses and no evidence of the Monster who had done it, the villagers have been quick to assign guilt. They are now more enraged than before.

This atmosphere of blind anger and desire for retribution amongst the local folk has prompted me to dare put my fears before the King himself. It has seemed to me that only he can bring justice in this situation and perhaps prevent even greater violence. At the very least, I dare to hope, and the Brothers of the Abbey pray daily, that the King will take pity upon us and intervene to bring his peace and justice.

I am your Brother in Jesus Christ

Ambrose

Valon was moved to deep emotion as I read this letter and afterward lapsed into a long silence, from which I decided it would be inappropriate to rouse him. It was an instance, as I came to know later, of his extraordinary passion of justice, which I now suppose was the reason King Charles had chosen him for our mission.

CHAPTER 11

Valon the Rogue

I did not see Valon next day and could not find him in his chambers. I sent the messenger, Bodo, in search of him, and he found Athalfe, also in search of Valon. In that entire morning, the two soldiers became fast friends, united by their common interest, as they searched the precincts and environs of Rouen for a young man who Athalfe testified could at times be difficult to find. During their search, Bodo learned of Athalfe's recent experiences with Valon and his opinions about the Marquis, and Bodo prevailed upon him to convey those same experiences and opinions to me. It was from Athalfe in the next two days that I learned much of what I know of Valon's past and his strange talents. Of course, in the next month, I had myself ample opportunity to observe the same things, but I was grateful to Athalfe for his warnings.

As the two scoured the taverns and brothels they learned that a man of Valon's description had set himself to gambling in one of the town's roughest houses, but then ran afoul of the owners of the game, then initiated a brawl that spilled into the street, and had been arrested by the soldiers of the Count of Rouen.

Once Athalfe and Bodo found the prison, they were able to release Valon, on the dubious assertion that he was even then acting under a commission from the Great Charles himself. And yet, Valon's injuries from the brawl were serious, causing Athalfe to suppose that a considerable troop of the Count's soldiers must have descended upon him at once.

Bodo and Athalfe returned Valon, half-conscious, to the great fortress, and there tended his wounds. When Alcuin heard that Valon had been found he summoned me to his study.

"Brother Theodulfe, welcome. I have heard of the difficulties that beset the Marquis de Valon in Rouen." He hesitated but then continued. "I think it is only fair that I tell you more of the man you are about to join as Missi Dominici."

"There is need of that?"

"Yes, I believe so, because Monsieur de Valon is in many ways a difficult person. His connection with our King goes to the Frisian War, where he distinguished himself many times in battle. He quickly gained the King's admiration and that is significant. The Great Charles, as you know, does not easily bestow his admiration."

"Yes, I am aware of it."

"Then, too, there is Valon's disposition, which is troubling. It even troubles Charlemagne. Since returning from the War, Valon has been despondent. He has vented his despair in debauchery, violence, gambling, and drunkenness, and appears intent upon destroying himself. You yourself have heard of his misbehavior and because you are about to embark upon a difficult and even dangerous mission with him, you have the right and a need to know as much as I know of him."

"And what is that, Brother Alcuin?"

"The King and I believe that Valon behaves as he does because of events that occurred while he was away at the War. Before he left, Valon fell deeply in love with the daughter of a neighbor. Her name was Véronique, and the two planned to marry. While Valon was at the War, Véronique was brutally violated and murdered. The villain was never apprehended, and so it was thought to be a crime beyond solution. However, just after Valon returned, his elder brother, whom he idolized, committed suicide, from guilt. This brother left behind a confession, telling the story of his rejection by Véronique, his evil crime, and his unbearable guilt. He asked Valon's forgiveness. Well, as you can imagine, Valon was devastated, doubly so, because the two people he loved most in the world were dead. And that is the source of his despair, and what will be the end of it?"

"Brother Alcuin, you are certainly right to tell me. Such a thing is significant, surely. But tell me this, dear friend. How is it that the Great Charles would entrust such an important mission to so unstable a young man? And, how can the King expect me to proceed with a person whose behaviour is so disturbed? Surely, that is too much?"

"You may ask that, Theodulfe, and the answer I may give you is not entirely satisfactory, I'll warrant. And yet it is all I can offer. The Great Charles believes strongly in the talents and character of Monsieur de Valon, and he wishes to challenge him to be the man that he may yet become. The King you see has a paternal regard for the young Valon and wishes to redeem him, or rather to give him a challenge, which will cause him to redeem himself. I put it to the King that it is unfair to Valon and to you to launch such a mission, but his faith in Valon, which is born of their soldiering experiences, is unshakable and he is determined. He did assure me of this much, however. He wishes me to apprise you of everything that should be known and he assures you that should you refuse the commission with Valon, he will understand and will think no less of you. He is your friend."

"Well, that is something," I said, I am sure with a tone of dismay in my voice. "The soldier Athalfe, who brought Valon to Rouen, has told me a great deal more about him—things that would give anyone pause. To put it bluntly, Athalfe paints Valon as an incorrigible rogue and bounder. But, in all that I have also heard, I have marked him down as an exceptional person and, if Athalfe's evidence is to be believed, this Valon is capable of feats of mind and body that lie well beyond the merely human. Such testimony makes it almost irresistible to me to learn for myself what is the truth of the man."

"Do you then wish time to consider, or reconsider?"

I thought for only a moment on all that I had heard and though I cannot now say why I told Alcuin outright. "I will do as the King wishes, and I will join him in hoping that Valon may redeem himself."

Alcuin smiled his approval and took my hand in both of his, assuring me that my decision would have the happiest effect on the King, and in his view, on Valon also.

"Let us hope, Brother, let us hope," I said, as much to myself as to Alcuin.

CHAPTER 12

Our Progress toward Châlons-sur-Marne

The special *capitulary* under which we departed early next morning ordered Valon to direct our investigation and named me as his recorder and advisor. Due to the changeable nature of Monsieur de Valon, I was gratified that in all important matters the Missi Dominici must act together or not at all. Although the order gave Valon the option to take whatever force of the King's soldiers he considered necessary, he decided nonetheless to go virtually alone. He relented only so far as to permit me to take my two monks and to bring the soldiers Athalfe and Bodo, who had proved so valuable in my travels to Rouen, and in Valon's rescue from the torments of Lord Halderon of Alançon.

Mounting our horses and taking to the main road, I decided to commence our journey with prayers for the success of our mission and then several hymns that seemed appropriate for the beginnings of travel. To end, we sang the *Agnus Dei.*

In three days of travel upon good roads, we reached the environs of the ancient city of Paris and stopped in view of the great Cathedral of Saint-Denis. We found lodgings among the pilgrims at the Abbey of Saint-Denis and joined the Brothers of the Monastery at Vespers. The Father Abbot, Michael, accommodated us well, as befitting the Missi Dominici. Though Valon was eager to press on to our destination, I prevailed upon him to allow my monks and our horses rest for a day at Paris and in the precincts of the beautiful Abbey.

I soon learned that Valon was remarkably well versed in a multitude of subjects, but he particularly interested himself in the strange subject of **murder**. He allowed that his interest had clearly come to the King's attention, and he supposed that was the reason he was named to this special mission.

"What is it that interests you so in this subject, master Valon," I asked, not knowing what would come in reply.

"Justice, Theodulfe! Only that." His black eyes assumed a strange intensity as he said that word, *Justice.* "It is the function of civil government to do justice. It comes to us from the Romans, at the very least, and from earlier for certain. No society is worthy of the name that does not do justice, and it is most important to do justice in cases where the innocent have been made to pay the greatest price, the forfeiture of their lives."

Our dialogue on this issue led me to know better of Piers de Valon and in particular that he seemed a man driven by justice, and in a very conscious way. He was a philosopher upon the subject, as much as he was a hunter after those who had violated justice. In the very words of Our Lord himself, Valon hungered and thirsted after it, and I came to trust that in the case before us he would surely find it.

At the outset of our mission, I was gratified to see no hint of Valon's inclination to riotous behaviour, even at Saint-Denis and the environs of Paris, where there was ample temptation to gamble and whore. Throughout, Valon remained a steady and serious-minded man, and from his talk, he seemed to be increasingly focused on the problem before us. I gained some confidence that he could control his impulses and that, in this instance, he had decided to put them aside.

We broke our rest at Saint Denies in two days' time and struck out on the main road to the east, which took us directly toward the Marne. We passed through country laid down to crude farming of grains and foodstuffs, vines devoted to the making of a wine that was notable for its stout body, and to a modest fruit culture. There also were great forested lands, and as our road brought us into the thickness of those forests, we became more conscious of the danger of wolves and of bandits.

About the afternoon of the third day out of Saint-Denis, we passed through a densely forested region that had no substantial towns. We came upon a hamlet of cottagers, tenants of a great lord of the area, who were ploughing a long field at the road's side. As we passed close by the workmen, the rough harness of the oxen broke suddenly, and the beasts ran down the furrow and into the wastes. At the sight of the escaping oxen, the Lord's overseer—a big man of the roughest sort—approached on horseback and began to flail the hapless peasant whose bad luck it was to see his oxen escape.

As we passed, I crossed myself and offered my blessing to the peasant abused by his overseer, and then thought to pass on. Valon, however, did not pass. Instead, he diverted his horse into the field and approached the beating, which continued as he came. Halting within a few feet of the two, the overseer stopped to look at Valon. Saying no word to either and smiling his greeting to the overseer, Valon dropped his reins, placed both hands on the flattened pommel of his saddle, and the raised himself such that he was standing on his hands, while still in his saddle. It was withal a strange and amazing feat of agility, and yet it was what happened next that left me agog.

After only a few seconds of standing in this manner, Valon lowered his feet to within a foot of the overseer's face and kicked him full force, so that he flew from his horse. In the next instance, Valon vaulted over the riderless horse and onto the overseer, where he kicked the brute's face with such force that blood and teeth flew from his mouth. Saying no word to the peasants, who stood gaping at what they had witnessed, Valon jumped upon his mount, took up the reins and continued upon the road. The brother monks, soldiers, and I rode after him, only a little less amazed than the peasants at what we had seen.

On the fourth day out of Paris, we rested ourselves and our beasts at the town of Epernay, a possession of the Archbishop of Reims, but in the territory of the Count of Champagne. Surrounded by great forests, Epernay, we were warned, was notable for the excesses committed by bandits, some of them quite organized, who set upon innocent travelers and pilgrims bound for the great Cathedral city of Reims.

We approached the substantial village through what seemed to me a thickening forest, which I knew stretched far to the east and north from this point.

Valon noted it too, and observed, "This is what the Romans called the 'Silva' and it has changed little from their day. And by that, I mean it undoubtedly holds as much danger for honest men today as it did then."

There was a cool darkness to the increasingly dense forest and a wintry odor of must and rotting leaves that seemed to cast a pall over our progress. As we ventured deeper into the forest, our road narrowed and was made all the more menacing by the heavier vegetation on either side.

We emerged from our narrow forest path and came into the environs of the town, where we now passed through a substantial patchwork of fields and meadows. Here and there stood small cottages, but we soon came onto the high street of Epernay.

At the stabled of the inn where we decided to put up the ostler told of recent attacks by bandits that had left travelers, merchants and even religious, beaten and dead.

"We have begged protection from the Count and from the Archbishop, but neither has taken pity upon us," the stable owner complained in his slow-witted way. "There's no rest for the weary," he quoted Scripture, "and no protection from our lords. This life is but a Vale of Tears."

Valon said nothing, but his look told me that such stories and complaints aroused his sympathy.

"There is an air of lawlessness in this region," I lamented, as we made our way from the stable to the Inn. "The local authorities seem to take little interest in the villains who prey upon ordinary people."

"Indeed, Theodulfe, and that leads me to consider that some of the lawlessness may be the work of those very authorities. Who can say in such places as this? We have fallen among thieves, I think."

"Perhaps instead of keeping ourselves in the Inn, we should make ourselves known as Missi Dominici to the local bishop's agents and prevail upon them to accommodate us in greater comfort?"

Valon looked at me in disbelief. "Not at all, Good Theodulfe. It is in our interests to alert no one in Châlons of our approach. In this mission, we will hunt best by stealth."

When we entered the Inn, I noticed six or seven men lolling about the great hearth, most of them with cups in their hands and all of them with a look of rascality about them. There did not seem to be an honest farmer or herdsman in the lot.

The open-faced hostler greeted us warmly at the door, and his wife, a large and smiling woman of middle years, asked for our cloaks. Immediately, the innkeeper showed us to a comfortable table by the fire, which scattered the ruffians like cockroaches, who now took refuge in a distant corner of the room. There, they talked in undertones among themselves, occasionally casting a sidelong glance at us. I did not like the look of them, and their demeanor toward us caused me even greater alarm. Still, Valon seemed to take no notice of them, so I trusted his instincts that all was well.

We warmed by the fire, my monks rubbing their hands and placing their feet near the hearth. Valon opened his mind to me, just a little.

"Those no-goods in the corner," he whispered without looking at them, "are very likely bandits."

"How so, Master Valon?" I asked eagerly.

Bodo listened intently as well, sniffing his disdain for the fellows.

"Notice that one wears beneath his chemise an undersuiting of chainmail, which is protruding slightly from his rope belt. The small part I could see is slightly rusting, which tells me he's not a soldier but has probably been one in the past."

I might have marveled at Valon's perceptiveness, except that I was already coming to understand how extraordinary were his powers of observation.

"Another—the big one with the bushy beard—wears bull-leather leggings studded with brass. No one who does not expect some combat requires those and certainly not a workman. He's been a man-at-arms in the employ of some lord or other, I'll wager. And then there are the two horses we saw in the stable."

Chagrined to admit I had not noticed the other horses in the stable, I nonetheless uttered, "You mean…?"

"Yes, the mare and the aged roan gelding. Both bore several scars on the head and shoulders. They were war-horses at one time and now are likely retired with their masters to the equally dangerous business of highway robbery. Yes, those are men to avoid and we must be on our guard about them."

"Praise God, Monsieur de Valon, that you are a noticing sort of man," Bodo whispered. "I had not gleaned near so much from what I saw."

"Well then, Valon, since those toughs are up to no good, perhaps we should seek an escort of trusted men from the local lord on the last leg of our journey to Châlons?"

"No, Theodulfe. It will be to our great advantage to appear suddenly in Châlons. The approach of a troop of men would reach the village long before we arrive. News travels by strange and rapid means in lonely neighborhoods such as this."

While we spoke, the rogues grew louder as they consumed more of the hostler's cheapest wine. I noted that they tended to come and go, signally and in twos, to climb the narrow stairs to the Inn's loft where they had rented a room, and then to return. A little later, we began to hear noises coming from above, muffled noises at first and then protests and screams. They were clearly the screams of a woman, at which Valon's face darkened and his jaw set.

Just then, the landlord approached with our meat and more wine and seeing our alarm at the screams he said in a low voice, "They have with them a slave girl, Monsieur. They've been enjoying her all day. A terrible thing, but what's to be done? She's their chattel. They may do with her as they wish."

Almost as soon as the landlord finished, the noises from above ceased, perhaps because the poor girl had lapsed into unconsciousness, or more likely, had passed out from wine given to assure her greater compliance with the vile wishes of her owners. Afterward, and for some time that evening, I considered the evil of slavery, which though growing less prominent in the Frankish Kingdom, was yet permitted and defended in law. I am sure I would have encouraged Valon and the two soldiers to intervene, except to interfere in the relations between master and slave was a strictly punished crime in the Kingdom. Then, too, we did not wish to draw attention to ourselves, so close to Châlons.

Still, I could see that Valon remained disturbed by what he'd heard, and I wondered what he might do to ease his own mind about it.

Next morning at dawn, as the monks and I broke our fast, it pleased me that the tavern seemed a much happier place, without the company of the six roughens. *They've doubtless gone to prey upon unsuspecting travelers such as ourselves. May God help those who fall within their path!* I prayed.

Strange, I thought, that Valon should come to break his fast dressed as he was. He wore beneath his tunic a shirt of chainmail, and upon his legs, he wore a covering of bull-leather studded with brass beads. And, most interesting of all, he carried at his side, a brass helmet with its visor and a pair of gauntlets that were, like his leggings, studded with brass.

"Valon, you are suited for combat. May I ask why?"

"It appears, Theodulfe, that it is best for Bodo, Athalfe, and me to take precautions for the final leg of our journey. We pass through dense forest until we reach Châlons-sur-Marne. Such places are nests of banditry, as might be expected from those men we encountered last evening. But there is another reason."

It appeared that Valon did not wish to confide his additional motive for such precautions, but I pressed my interest, on the thought that I was his full associate as Missi Dominici and therefore entitled to his thinking. My annoyance prompted him to say, "But of course. I should not hold back from you. It occurs to me there may be those in Châlons who would fear our approach and would take precautions to ensure we do not arrive."

"But surely, Master Valon. We go to survey the work of a madman. The killings, as we have heard them from Bishop Ambrose, are most certainly a reflection of insanity, or perhaps the work of a..." I caught myself, lest I say too much. But my hesitation caused Valon to narrow his eyes, and ask, "...of a what, Theodulfe?"

"The work of a diabolical presence, Master Valon," I said defiantly. "I have been thinking much in our journey from Rouen and particularly since we departed St. Denis. This thing smacks of the Evil One, himself, and I have decided we cannot discount his direct presence in these events."

Valon's cold eyes betrayed not a jot of what he was thinking, but I suspected he dissented from my opinion.

"I will leave the diabolical safely in your hand," he said, just a little of the sardonic in his voice. "I'll prepare for battle of a more earthly kind. In any case, from this time in our mission, we will find ourselves in combat with a great Evil. If my presentment is correct, it may be a desperate combat."

Our morning's journey southeast, through the dense forests of the Marne, was pleasant enough, though I could not quite escape the grim forebodings that Valon's warnings left in my mind. The forest, at times, seemed to close in upon us, and the brother monks responded to the air of creeping danger by making the *Angus Dei* into a litany of sorts. In it, they invoked the saints to intercede with Our Lord for our protection from all the menacing forest could hold for us. They began with the saint on whose day we traveled, and we each of us joined in the response.

Angus Die, qui tolis peccata mundi, (Lamb of God, who takes away the sins of the world,), the brother monks sang, and we answered,

Dona nobis pacem. (Give us peace.).

Saint Nicolas de Myra, they sang, as we responded,

Miserere nobis. (Have mercy on us.)

And so, we rode in this way the entire morning, through a forest that seemed to grow denser and more menacing as we went.

When afternoon's dapple shadows fell upon our path, we neared the small village of Matougues, near our objective, Châlons. I began to feel a sense of relief that our long journey was nearing its end, when ahead of us, at a distance of perhaps twenty yards, I detected something cross the path. At first, I concluded that it was likely a deer, several of which we had seen in the corner of our eyes throughout our ride. Then, yet another shadow flitted across the path, and I began to think of wolves, whose howls we'd heard the previous night.

Then, as if from nowhere, there stepped into our path, only a short distance ahead, a man I had never seen. He wore the distinctive clothing of a warrior, but was well outfitted and, as he spoke, I was relieved that his speech was that of a gentleman. He spoke a very credible Latin.

"Good-day to you, good sirs," he hailed in a jovial tone, which disarmed my anxiety.

"Greetings to you, Monsieur," I replied in the same amiable tone, noting however that our companion's left hand rested upon the hilt of his broadsword, and that he wore a metal helmet which carried the dent of a previous altercation.

"Father Abbot, I have noticed your progress through our forest and have felt obliged to come myself to warn you."

"What warning is that, kind Sir?"

"A warning of extreme danger, Father. These forests teem with rascals of the worst sort. Cutthroats whose sinful ways make them stop at nothing to rob the poor and particularly the rich, such as yourselves—you and your retainers."

"I am obliged to you, Monsieur, for your notice of such danger. It will be all the better for us to continue our journey to Châlons, so as to arrive there before dark," I said, hoping that the visitor would step from the path and allow us to pass.

But as we started, he raised his hand in a motion to halt us and continued.

"Father Abbot, I cannot in good conscience allow you to continue into such danger without my help and protection."

"Your protection?" I repeated.

"Indeed. I and my friends, who remain in the underbrush on both sides of the path, are prepared to guarantee your safe-conduct as far as Châlons. And the cost for ensuring your life, and those of your monks, is a pittance."

"A pittance? What cost do you demand, kind Monsieur?" I asked, now fully aware that we were being robbed and the gentleman in our path was, in fact, a gentleman bandit.

"Yes, well the matter is easily resolved. The fee for our services is your purse and all its contents, good Father. And we will require as well, the *sacullus* of your monks and those of your men-at-arms as well. And I caution that withholding is a gesture that I and my companions will regard as ungenerous and uncooperative."

At that, Valon jostled forward and alongside me on his great horse, though not in a threatening way, and my brother monks remained well back.

"Your price, mon cher Monsieur, is far too high. We are but poor men and the contents of our purses are dear to us. You would leave us destitute in a strange and forbidding land," Valon pleaded.

"I will answer you, Sir, by two ways. First, I ask who are you to negotiate in the stead of the Father Abbot, to whom I spoke? And, also, I say that I cannot be responsible for the condition of your purse, for my men and I have needs as well. They are but poor men of mean upbringing and rely upon me as a river of prosperity, you see."

I glanced farther up the road, and there could see the same roughs we had encountered in the tavern. And seated upon a donkey—her hands shackled, her clothing torn and dirty, her face bruised and scratched—the young slave girl whom we had heard but not seen the night before. She was a pitiful sight and seeing her suffering made my heart grow sad.

A mirthful quality entered Valon's voice as he answered the bandit leader. "I shall answer your last first, Monsieur. I must ask that you accept a gold piece for each of your men as the price of our protection, and consider that the only prosperity you and your companions may know from this venture. And, second? Well, I am not as you suppose the Father Abbot's retainer, but rather his traveling companion. My name is Piers, Marquis de Valon et Balaincourt, and I tell you this because I have always believed that one should know the name of the man who kills him."

The bandit leader's jaw dropped. Valon's unexpected bravado caused me to swallow hard, and the result was much as I expected. The leader of the brigands drew his sword, and from both sides, we were set upon by rascals wielding cudgels and knives.

Bodo rushed forward to join Valon, who had drawn both his broadsword and his long knife. With reins in his teeth, he maneuvered against attackers on either side, eager to get at the leader, who Bodo had engaged. Athalfe busied himself with fending off the other bandits.

As I moved back in the path, I saw Valon's sword come down upon the head of one assailant, splitting his skull like a melon and emptying the contents upon the shrubbery to one side. His long knife then penetrated the chest of another, causing blood to spout as the knife withdrew. The attacker on the left withdrew to the side, both hands now on his chest to stop the blood that poured from him. Valon pushed him back with one foot, and the brigand behind him fell back as well. He tried to recover his balance but found Valon's long knife in his neck. He died as he stood.

Even as I averted my eyes from the dying thief, I saw Bodo suffer a terrible blow to his helmet from the broadsword of the leader—a blow that knocked him backward on his mount and almost to the ground. Then, another of the attackers delivered a terrible blow with his cudgel at poor Bodo's arm. He managed to recover and run the bandit through with his sword.

Valon came quickly upon the same attacker, who did not raise his club again before finding Valon's long knife in his ribs.

Athalfe engaged the largest of the bandits. He scored several blows against the well-armored thief, none of which managed to wound. Still, Athalfe was clearly the superior warrior, so the bandit's defenses finally collapsed, and Athalfe hacked him across the head with a blow that caused his helmet to fly. Athalfe turned and swung again, this time he landed a deathblow to the bandit's neck.

To my delight, Bodo was able to recover his balance, and with his good right arm engaged the two remaining thieves. Valon, now dismounted, confronted the leader, both men in the center of the path. It was the highwayman who spoke, as Valon raised the visor on his brass helmet.

"So pleased these others are safely out of the way, my friend so that you can make good your boast."

Valon said nothing, but merely put aside his long knife, and now with his sword in both hands, he pointed it directly at the leader, clearly taking his measure.

"Remember. Piers de Valon," he repeated slowly, distinctly. When you arrive at the River Styx and Charon asks who sends you, tell him simply, 'It is Piers de Valon.' He will know immediately, you see, for I have sent many such as you to the frontier of Hell."

Not allowing time for a response, Valon lunged so quickly that I scarce saw him move. I marveled at his swiftness as he swung from one side of the path to the other, but each time he missed his target and the broadswords met in mid-air with a terrible clang.

So busy was the highwayman with Valon's maneuvering at his front, he appeared not to notice when Bodo finished off the remaining ruffian. I saw that each man was the equal of the other in combat. When Valon attacked, the highwayman was able to parry the assault, and when the brigand went on the offensive, Valon was able to defend. The clash continued for what seemed a half hour, with neither of the combatants tiring of it. Keeping to the middle of the path, they circled, swinging and lunging, but with no apparent advantage.

Then, a dramatic gesture by the bandit. Instead of swinging at Valon's torso, he moved his head in one direction but then swung his broadsword in the other, only this time low, in a clear effort to hack at Valon's legs.

Valon, however, was undeceived by his adversary's feint and jumped what looked like a yard above the ground to avoid the sword's low swing. The agility of both men seemed almost beyond the human, but it was Valon's grace and swiftness that made the combat reminiscent of a dance in the Hall of some great Lord. It was poise itself.

The combat now stretched into the hour and for the merest moment, I saw the highwayman drop his arm as if tiring. I doubted what I had seen, however, such was my admiration for the brigand's stamina. *Still, is he wearying of the pace?* I wondered also if Valon had noticed what I had seen, but that thought flew immediately from my mind as my eyes witnessed something that, to this day, I do not quite believe.

In the blink of my disbelieving eyes, Valon circled his opponent, then leaped a great distance into the air, knowing it would prompt the highwayman to raise his sword in an effort to defend. But instead of making his strike, Valon plummeted to the ground, and as he fell, plunged his tip into the brigand's belly.

The scream that exhaled from the highwayman sounded like nothing so much as the opening of the Gates of Hell. Valon leaped to his feet, and with his sword now buried even deeper into his opponent, who was stunned to find himself impaled upon its tip, he withdrew the blade. I gasped to think what Valon would do next, but had no time to speculate, for after he withdrew his blade, he spun upon one leg and separated the bandit from his head.

The brother monks dismounted and rushed to Valon who collapsed in the center of the path. He lay exhausted while Brother Boethius gave him wine from a skin, and Brother Martin removed his helmet and poured water over his head. Such ministrations seemed to revive Valon. In a short while, he stood and drank by his own hand. He stripped off his chainmail and leggings to allow the coolness of the approaching night air to dry his undersuiting and cool him further.

When he could speak, it was to comment upon our assailants.

"Did you notice, Theodulfe, that those are the toughs we saw in the tavern at Epernay? Their leader was not with them last evening, but they clearly chose us as their prey for today."

"It was almost our misfortune. But Praise God, it was theirs. They chose poorly," I said with some heartfelt satisfaction at the suffering of our assailants, may Our Lord forgive me.

Valon ordered Bodo and the brother monks to search the assailants and remove their belongings and valuables, so we could give half as alms to the poor of the village of Matougues. He ordered Athalfe to search for a key to the slave girl's shackles, which the soldier soon found in the bandit's *sacullus*.

Valon walked toward the girl, who sat calmly upon her donkey. Her gaze remained fixed on the ground, as it was during the combat, and she made no gesture at Valon as he approached. While he unlocked her shackles, she continued to stare silently at the ground.

"What is your name, girl?" Valon insisted, holding the reins of the donkey.

She made no answer but continued to look at the ground.

Valon gave me a puzzled glance and then repeated, with greater authority. "What is your name?"

Still no response. And, still staring at the ground.

Valon moved to interrupt her stare, lifted her chin with his hand so that she looked at him. "What are you called? Do you speak Frankish?" He repeated the question in Latin. Then in the language of the Danes. Then in the Saxon tongue. Frisian. And to all these, there was no answer from the girl. She remained silent and her stare told me she was in a daze.

"I fear, Valon, that the girl has been so brutalized by these no-goods that she is dazed. I've seen the condition before, and it is a profound one. You will not wake her."

"Well, I doubt we can safely leave her to her own resources in this condition and in this forest. Her masters are dead, and so I am liberating her in the name of the Great Charles, under my authority as Missi Dominici, and you are my witnesses. But I allow that we must take her with us and see to it that she comes to no harm until she can fend for herself."

I did not like to agree, for our mission did not profit from the distraction of caring for a helpless girl, but Valon was right. To leave her in the forest was as much as to condemn her to an early death, either by beasts or by the same sort she had recently belonged to.

Valon mounted and guided the girl's donkey behind him.

"We must hold half of the belongings confiscated from the bandits for the girl. When she is able to care for herself, she must have some resources, and I believe it is no more than her due, considering the suffering those louts inflicted upon her."

Athalfe handed Valon a substantial purse of silver and gold coins, which he found upon the bandit leader. "The others had very little. Only their weapons and clothing. Of course, there are their mounts."

"All those we will give to the poor of Matougues. The coins will go to the girl," said Valon.

As we made our way along the road, I noticed something that had been only vaguely apparent to me at the scene of our recent combat. The girl stanketh, such that I sometimes gagged. Her stink was noticeable to all, for I could see the expressions made by my monks. In less than an hour, we came to a shallow crossing of a narrow stream that was doubtless a branch of the Marne. Seeing the opportunity before him, Valon dismounted, took soap from his *sacullus,* and lifted the girl from her donkey. He tore off the few pitiful rags and dragged her naked into the stream where he proceeded to scrub the stink away.

The girl remained in a daze and made no resistance to the washing. It was a matter of only a few minutes before Valon had washed every inch of her stink, including her matted hair. When she was fully soaped, he submerged her several times in the running stream, which washed away the soap and left her clean. And gasping.

Once out of the stream, he dried the girl with a wool blanket belonging to one of the dead bandits. Taking his own brush, he combed out the dreadful tangles in her hair. During all of this, the girl said nothing, did not resist and continued docile.

I thought it best to avert my gaze from the naked girl, as did the brother monks. I advised the soldiers Bodo and Athalfe to do the same, explaining that it was an occasion of the sin of lust to look upon her nakedness. All the more so as it became clear she was a beautiful girl, fair of both face and form. Still, I am not certain that the soldiers obeyed my priestly command.

"Bodo, give me the chemise, pants, stockings, and boots of the smallest bandit." Valon ordered. He clearly intended to dress the girl in confiscated and cleaner clothing. When she was thus dressed, we once again shifted our gaze, and I could see that the dead bandit's clothing made a reasonable fit.

Valon put the girl back upon her donkey, and we proceeded across the stream and toward Matougues.

"We must stay the night in Matougues," Valon observed, with some impatience, "for this delay means we can no longer reach Châlons by nightfall. And there, Father Abbot, you and your monks will be able to offer mass as thanks to God for our salvation from the brigands. It is His doing, you know, that we may continue our mission."

"Indeed," I added, "*Deo gratias.*"

CHAPTER 13

December 20, 1918
Montclaire Responds

The hour grew late, and Teddy paused in reading Theodulfe's narrative. "It is," he said, "a good place to stop for now."

Montclaire, however, seemed excited with greater energy from the story as we had just heard it. It had stirred his imagination.

"What a treasure you've brought us for Christmas, Teddy! To be reunited, so to speak, with our ancestor and to learn things about him that until now we've only wondered. Speculated about."

"Yes," Teddy replied, "until this document came my way, we had only read the name Piers de Valon and knew almost nothing of his life. But there is something even more singular. To my knowledge, this document is the only account of the actual investigations of the Missi Dominici. We historians, of course, have long known of their existence, and we have had a few decrees from Charlemagne and others under which they carried out their missions, but we have never before read the actual story of one such mission."

"All well and good for the scholars," I intervened, "but it's the story that interests. It's a murder investigation, for Heaven's sake! And to think, Montclaire, that your ancestor showed such passion for crime-solving. And for Justice. Must be in the blood, as they say. You come by it honestly, after all," I joked, much to everyone's enjoyment.

"Yes, and that's what makes it so delightful," Montclaire observed. "Thanks to Teddy, we find ourselves in the middle of crimes."

Mademoiselle Modestine, Montclaire's elder sister, asked, "But, was not Valon exceptionally young for such an office? Theodulfe seemed to say as much."

"Yes, he was," Teddy replied. "We do not know how young he was, but our family's best records have it that he was born sometime around AD 770 and so he was about 25, eh? His title also indicates that he had not yet come to his inheritance, for we know that he was later Count of Anjou."

"Yes, a title that our family later lost to the English," said Clarisse, Montclaire's other sister, as she hissed a little at me.

"Remember the Alliance, dear sister. Les Anglaise are now our friends and so we must forgive the past misbehaviour," chided Modestine.

She continued, "Valon was also a bit of a buck, eh? How could so wild a youth be seen as competent for such a mission?"

Teddy intervened. "The fact that Valon was so young and wild and was yet named as a Missi Dominici shows that he nonetheless held Charlemagne's respect. And that speaks volumes about his qualities, which we and Theodulfe have only begun to glimpse. Charlemagne was a keen judge of men."

"Yes, but what can we know of this pairing?" Montclaire asked. "Valon and Theodulfe? Makes me wonder about the King's reasons for bringing the two together. I wonder what Charlemagne had in mind."

"Wise counsel, perhaps?" I ventured. "Theodulfe was an older, wiser man. Clearly, Valon could profit from that, if only to constrain his own rashness. Perhaps Charlemagne believed Theodulfe could somehow redeem Valon, or more likely, help him redeem himself?"

Montclaire did not seem to agree, but gave only a Gallic shrug and offered no alternative.

"But, what of the murders?" Clarisse asked. "They are the issue here. They interest me far more than the characters of the Missi at least at this point."

"You are exactly right," said Montclaire. "Shakespeare said it. 'The play's the thing,' and my old teacher, Dupin, agreed with you. He said, constantly, '*La crime, la crime. C'est toujours la crime. Remarquez la crime,*' he would lecture me. Indeed, it is the crimes that are at the center of this thing. It is they that are the most interesting feature of this story."

"I disagree, old friend," I intervened, with an authority that unnerved me just a little. "These crimes are so obviously the work of a madman as the Father Abbot remarked. There seems little detecting to be done, except to smoke out the blighter and hang him from the nearest gallows. Er, or did you French guillotine chaps even then? Well, no matter. Valon and Theodulfe are riding into the work of a maniac of some sort."

"You are correct, in the first instance, Sir Francis," Teddy replied. "We French were content to hang the deserving criminal at that time. We owe Madame Guillotine's popularity to the Revolution."

Montclaire added, "Your suspicions may prove accurate, Fitz, but it's far too early to assume that the crimes are what they seem. Let us reserve that conclusion and see what Valon discovers. I am certain that he is reserving judgment."

"But is there anything at this point to make you suspect otherwise?" Modestine asked.

Montclaire smiled and slapped his knee. "Excellent, Sister, simply excellent! And the answer is, 'Oui,' there is one thing that makes me suspect the obvious, but I am not prepared to name it just now. Later, please. Allow me to say it later."

Montclaire's coyness on the issue gave pause to everyone. In the lull, as we thought, the Clarisse said, "Well, I intend to consider the issue in my sleep." And that seemed a good idea to the rest of us.

With a bow to Teddy, Montclaire resolved the issue. "We will reconvene our Christmas Season Crime Circle at the same time next evening."

I suppose that the adjourning of our Circle was the formal end of the evening, but it certainly was not the last of it for Montclaire or for me. During the reading of Theodulfe's narrative, I often looked at Montclaire—at his facial expressions and especially at his eyes. Often, they showed no feelings at all, but at other times they flashed emotions that ran the spectrum from extreme delight to profound sadness. Interested as I have always been in my friend's thoughts, I watched closely his reactions and wondered much about them after the fact.

The strange parallels to Montclaire's own life tragedy could not be lost upon anyone who knew him, and particularly myself, who had been so intimately engaged in his efforts to overcome them. The death of Montclaire's elder brother in a fall from a horse was I knew the greatest blow of his young life, and it affected him in much the same way as Valon's loss of his own elder brother, though not nearly so dramatic. And then there was the rape and murder of Véronique—so distressingly similar to the rape and suicide of Montclaire's beloved wife, Jeanne.

She had jumped from the roof of Chateau d'Ecouen with her infant son in her arms. She committed suicide because that baby was conceived as a result of rape, by a gang of toughs who were never caught. The deaths had driven Montclaire to alcoholism and intermittent insanity. He was suicidal himself when I determined to save him, mainly by drawing him once more into the life of criminal investigation—that tangled affair of the tragic Marie Collot.

How could life provide such a strange parallel, I wondered, between two kinsmen, separated by more than a thousand years? A remarkable thing, to be sure, and I wondered how it would resonate with Montclaire. How would he filter it through his imagination and what sense would he make of the connection between his own tragedies and those of his distant kinsman? I worried just a little that reliving such tragedies through Valon might trigger something unwanted in Montclaire, that they could carry him back into a morass. I worried even that his empathy with Valon might unleash something in him that would drive him back to whiskey, to debauchery, and even to insanity. And so, our Christmas puzzle with Teddy came to hold almost from the beginning a frightening possibility for me, and for Montclaire.

I observed that Montclaire did not go to his chamber, but instead took up a chair at the darkened end of the library, where he lighted his pipe, asked a brandy from Petrovsky, and lingered long into the night. I did not need to wonder what thoughts preoccupied him in that long silence.

Next evening, we renewed our circle, and again Teddy stood before us, reading from Theodulfe's strange memoir.

PART TWO

Hildegard's Witness

CHAPTER 1

Theodulfe Continues His Narrative

We passed a restful night in Montague and next morning, after the mass Valon ordered, we continued our progress toward Châlons. So confident were we of reaching Châlons by nightfall we stopped at mid-morning at a peasant's cottage to water our horses and allow them to graze the grass at the roadside.

I sat under a small tree and sipped a bit of wine from my skin. I noted that the mute girl dismounted and tethered her donkey and then sat only a foot or two from Valon, who did not seem to notice her at all. She looked neither right nor left, but kept her gaze on the ground in front of her. She kept her silence so completely that I would have thought her mute from birth, except that we had heard the horrendous screams she made that night in the tavern.

She looked to be no more than eighteen years and slight of build. Her hair was a light color, as was common among the northern tribes. Her cheekbones were high, her eyes large and green, her lips full, and her movements graceful. *Were it not for the bruises and scratches about her face one might even consider her beautiful, or at least comely, in the way a young girl sometimes is.* I wondered whatever Valon would do with her.

In a short while, he turned to her as if decided upon that very issue. He smeared mud upon her chin and cheeks, then took from its sheath his knife and cut off her hair, well above the shoulders.

"During our journey and time in Châlons, girl, you are officially a *boy*. Do you understand me? As far as anyone is to know, you are a boy and you'll dress and act as such. It will be too much trouble traveling with you as a girl. From this moment forward you are an apostolate of the good Abbot's Monastery who has not yet taken the tonsure. As such, you are a servant to all of us.

"What is your name, girl?" Valon demanded.

The girl made no reply but moved her eyes from side to side as Valon chopped her hair and gave his instructions. It was clear that she understood.

"Well, No matter. Your name is now Pepin, and that's the name you'll respond to."

While I did not like Valon's pretense about the girl, I knew the girl could not pretend to be Valon's daughter or mine. It would simplify our work if we did not have to provide all that was required to travel with a female. Meanwhile, as Valon thus turned the girl into Pepin, I decided I would insist with him that she must eventually go into a convent.

While we lounged upon the winter dry grass and watched our horses, a commotion erupted upon the road. It was the father of the peasant family, returning from his early morning's delivery of grain to a nearby convent.

The excitement caused Valon to ask, "Whatever is the distress, good man? Calm yourself and tell me at once."

Breathless from his hurry, the old peasant took some time to recover his wits, but then unburdened himself of a terrible tale.

"At the convent, Monsieur. There's a murder! A horrible murder, God save us from Satan's doings! In a convent, Monsieur…in a convent."

"You say, 'murder.' Who was murdered?"

"A young nun…found this morning, near sunrise, Sir. Found dead on the path that leads from the convent down to the road that travels to Châlons. I saw the poor little thing as they carried her body back to the convent. It was terrible… There was blood!" he exclaimed.

Valon gave me a knowing look. Not wishing to ask more of the poor fellow than he probably knew, Valon asked, "Where is this convent?"

"A distance of a quarter-league, no more, Monsieur. You'll see it on a rise above the road, to the north. The Convent of Saint Agnes."

"May God preserve it," the cottager's wife added, a tear in her voice.

We now rode at a canter toward Châlons, and I knew why we hurried. Valon and I both suspected there had been yet another of the murders we were charged to investigate, but oddly, one to greet our arrival. We soon came in sight of a large square structure of gray stone with a single bell tower, standing upon a gentle rise above the road. A gently winding lane led us to a large oaken door with iron hinges and studs. We rang the bell and demanded entrance, but when the Sister Warder answered—through a peephole—and saw our party was composed only of men, she asked in a worried voice what prompted us to ask admittance.

"I am Piers de Valon and this is my companion, Abbot Theodulfe of Fleury-sur-Loire. We are Missi Dominici in service to the King and we ask entry. We have heard that a murder has occurred here this morning, and we wish to know of it."

The elderly nun closed the peephole and disappeared. After a few minutes, she opened the great gate, and there a woman of remarkable presence and authority greeted us.

"I am Sister Felicitas, Mother Prioress of this Convent. Welcome, Missi Dominici. Greetings from our poor community."

We entered the courtyard, which led on one side to the cloisters and on the other to the main block of the building. "Please," the Prioress urged. "Come with me."

Followed by the elderly Sister Warder, and now joined by other nuns, we scurried toward the entrance and then down a wide corridor, past a large room that looked to be the convent's refectory. The corridor beyond opened to a sizable chapel, with rows of pews along each wall, and at the end stood a small altar, one side of which held a crucifix and the other a statue of the Saint Patron—the beloved Saint Agnes.

We lingered only a moment in the precincts of the chapel, then continued down a narrower corridor lined with the cells of the resident Sisters, and at the end a slightly more substantial chamber. A hearth blazed in one corner of the Prioress' room. Beyond there was a small chapel and just off, a bedchamber.

Having arranged at the refectory to care for the needs of the brother monks and the soldiers, only Valon and I accompanied Sister Felicitas to her rooms.

Once there, she bade us sit by the hearth. "What is it, Monsieur de Valon and Abbot Father, that you wish to know of the unfortunate death this morning?"

"We understand that it was not merely a death, Prioress, but a murder. Is that not so?" Valon asked, taking in the room as he spoke.

"Yes. I've seen Sister Helena's body when she was brought up. She had been killed. Strangled. There were bruises about her neck, you see."

"Then she was murdered outside the convent?"

"Yes, on a path to one side of the convent opposite the main gate. It's a path that goes down to the main road, as it winds around the hill on which we sit. Sister Helena's body was found near the junction of that path and the road. There's a bench there, for resting, and I suppose that's where she was attacked," Sister replied, her voice full of distress.

"I know this must be a terrible thing for you, Mother Prioress, but we must ask," Valon soothed.

"These questions go to the heart of why we are here in the first place, you understand," I reassured her.

"Thank you, Father Abbot. I quite understand, and will help however I can."

"Well, then," Valon continued, "can you think why Sister Helena would be there, at that bench, at that time of the morning? It must have been close to dawn. Am I correct?"

"Yes, it must have been. And no, I cannot think why she would be there. Sister's duties were entirely in the refectory and chapel. That's where she would have been today. Sister was at Matins. We follow the Rule of Saint Benedict and so it must have happened sometime after that."

Valon seemed to puzzle a little about this latest information, a slight furrow across his brow as he gazed down. Then he asked, "Prioress, did Sister Helena have any special friends in the convent? Someone in whom she might have confided more than others?"

"Oh, yes, Monsieur. She was especially close to Sister Céleste, whose cell is next to hers. They were good friends, and both worked in the refractory. Sister Céleste assists cook and also cleans the communal areas of the first level. The two were about the same age and so the friendship was a natural one."

"I know, Sister Prioress, that your nuns are cloistered and seldom leave the convent, but did Sister Helena have access to the outside world? Did she leave the convent, ever, I mean?"

A good question. Valon is probing to find if anyone from outside might have had access to Sister Helena. Was the one who killed her from the convent, or from outside?

"Well, Monsieur, she once visited her family, but that was over a year ago. You see they are at quite some distance and so she visited them only the once, and they have not come to see her. The only other times she left the convent were to travel as escort to Céleste—to stay briefly with Céleste's family."

"Oh? You said they were friends, but how came she to visit Céleste's home?"

"Eh bien, Monsieur, it is our Rule. The Rule of Saint Benedict, that a nun who leaves the cloister and goes into the world must have an escort. So our nuns may go out, but only if they are accompanied. On those occasions that Sister Céleste found it necessary to return to her home, she was accompanied by Sister Helena, at her own request. As I said, they were friends."

"I see. And how often did this occur?"

"I am not quite certain. Perhaps four or five times in the past two years. One was at the tragic death of Sister Céleste's mother, I remember."

"And did the two travel alone? After all, it is but a short distance to Châlons."

"No. Each time, one of Sister Céleste's brothers came for her. Lord Humphrey came last, to accompany them the short distance to Châlons. Sister Céleste will be very upset to hear of the tragedy."

"You say, 'will be.' She's not here?" Valon asked. "Then where is she?"

"Sister Céleste was summoned home to her family, two days ago. She is in Châlons. She is a daughter of Lord Ethelred of Châlons."

Valon and I exchanged glances.

"Then on this occasion, Sister Helena did not accompany her. Do you know why?"

"No, I do not, Monsieur. I only know that Sister Céleste took with her Sister

Imelda—another of her friends."

"And one of Sister Céleste's brothers came for her?"

"Yes. Lord Humphrey."

Valon said nothing in response to this information, but I could see from the look in his eye that he found it most interesting. He looked at me as if to underscore his reaction.

"Mother Prioress, we are most eager to make Châlons by nightfall, and yet it is important that we investigate this murder before we leave. I wish to go to the precise spot where the body was found, and then, with your permission, to examine Sister Helena's corpse itself."

The Prioress showed obvious reluctance at this last, but agreed to Valon's request, very likely because she could not refuse a Missi Dominici.

"Sister Martha, who greeted you at the gate, will guide you to the place. It was she who took some of our local farmers and carried Sister Helena up this morning. And then, you may see Sister Helena. Her body is in the apothecary rooms, where she will be prepared for burial."

"One last question, Sister Prioress, if you please."

"Yes, Monsieur."

"Was...eh...was there any indication from the condition of her body that Sister Helena had been...er...?"

"No, Monsieur. None," she cut him short.

Valon clearly wished to move rapidly, so made no long good-byes to Sister Prioress, but rose to depart.

"Before we find our way to the gate, Sister, could you direct us to Sister Helena's cell? It might be useful to look in there first."

It turned out that Sister Helena's chamber was only a short distance from the Prioress' own rooms. There was no need for a key, for the room was open. It was small—no more than ten feet by ten, with a window to the outside wall, and under it a cot with a straw mattress of rough muslin. At another wall stood a rough table and chair, and upon the table lay a wooden bowl, the stub of a candle in its pot, and a rough wooden cross. Everything was visible, so it hardly seemed necessary to enter. But something caught Valon's eye. It was a minor thing, but he went right to it.

CHAPTER 2

The Dead Nun

His eyes fixed for some reason upon a rustic copper bowl, which sat in the middle of the table.

"Look you here, Theodulfe. In the bowl."

"What is it?"

"It's not food. Appears to be the ashes of something burned. A piece of vellum, maybe parchment. If so, it would seem the Sister burned something on which a message might have been written. Perhaps the message that drew her to the hillside and to her death."

"But surely we cannot know that," I objected.

"Aye, unfortunately, we cannot," Valon agreed, with just a touch of condescension in his voice.

As he picked up the bowl to examine it more closely, something of infinitely greater interest appeared from under it. "And what is this?" he asked as he took it in hand.

"Bless me, it's a ring. A gold ring!"

"Aye, and hardly the sort of thing to find in a young nun's chamber. An otherwise appropriately austere cell."

Valon turned to Sister Prioress, who stood in the door, her face betraying her puzzlement.

"Was Sister Helena given to such fancies? Did she come of a family to provide such finery?"

"I can say no to both, Monsieur. She was a modest girl, and her family is of modest means."

"Odd," I observed and probably should have kept my silence, "Odd to find such a thing in a nun's cell. It is a ring as would be worn by a bride rather than a nun."

Valon shot a glance at me on hearing that, then looked to the inside for an inscription. Without a word, he showed it to me. There was indeed an inscription, and an interesting one at that—*E. Meus Uxor*.

"But what can it mean? An initial 'E,' followed by the phrase, 'My Wife?' It is a marriage ring, but to what purpose? The initial is all wrong to refer to Sister Helena."

Neither Valon nor Sister Prioress replied, but I could tell both were thinking the same thing.

"I don't suppose Sister Helena's name before the convent began with an 'E?'"

"No. Her name was Beatrice, Monsieur."

"Perhaps it was her mother's, or belonged to another who was close to her?"

"Her mother was Helena, Monsieur. I know that because that was why Sister chose the name. To honor her mother."

"Then it must be a mystery, for now," Valon concluded, a note of irritation in his reply.

With brief good-byes, we left Mother Prioress to close the cell. I noticed Valon kept the ring. We made our way down to the great gate, where Sister Martha stood her post. She guided us through the cloisters to a small oaken door in the wall, which opened onto a narrow path that meandered down the hill toward the main road, which was always visible. There were few trees on this side of the convent, and so the path itself was not secluded from view of the buildings. However, as we soon learned, the area of the bench where the body had been found, and where Sister was killed, was shielded from view of both the convent and the road by high shrubs and some trees. *The murder must have occurred in relative seclusion*, I mused.

"There." Sister Martha pointed. "There's where Sister lay. You can yet see the stain of blood that was at her head." She stifled a sob and pointed to a dark spot on the stones of the walk.

"Thank you, Sister. I know this is difficult for you, as it is for everyone at the convent," Valon consoled, his hand on the elderly nun's shoulder.

Then, much to my surprise, he fell to the ground and began to examine with minute precision the area where the body had lain. At first, I wondered what he was doing, but then it became clear he was viewing everything to be seen upon the ground. Rising slightly, I noticed that he took up a rock, no larger than a man's fist, looked at it and then put it in his *sacullus*. I wondered whatever he did that for.

As he jumped to his feet, he exclaimed only, "Interesting! Very interesting, indeed." Which, of course, left me to wonder further what on earth was interesting, for I could see nothing at all, save the blood, which was infinitely more disgusting than it was interesting.

"And now, Sister Martha, if you would be so kind as to guide us to the Apothecary's rooms, where Sister's body is kept."

We made our way up the path toward the convent, and then down a long stairway to the subterranean level where the Apothecary worked. As we went, I continued to wonder what it was that Valon had found so interesting.

CHAPTER 3

Valon Startles Me

The Apothecary's workroom was filled with jars, bowls, and baskets, and above all with the smells of herbs, roots, and flowers. The walls were hung with bunches of drying herbs and there on the stone table where the Sister Apothecary customarily did her work lay a covered corpse.

The linen wrapped around the body was an unnatural luster of white, except at the young nun's head, where there was a large blotch of red blood.

Valon moved swiftly to the table. As he unwrapped the body, I grew uneasy about our work. Soon, though, the linen was gone, and there lay the naked corpse of a slender young woman of about eighteen years, eyes closed in death, hands folded across her stomach, and her complexion drained of all color.

My companion commenced at once to examine the body, at first taking in the entire tragedy before us.

"Notice, Theodulfe, that except for the ugly gash at the right temple and bruising about the neck there is no sign of damage to the body—no scrapes, no cuts, no bleeding anywhere."

"And no bites," I said. Valon shot me a quick glance.

"Yes. That is entirely interesting." Then, taking from his *sacullus* the smooth rock he collected at the place of the murder, he held it to the gash in Sister Helena's head. It fit.

"I thought so. Although the stone had no residual blood upon it, perhaps because it was wiped by the murderer, it fits nicely. It is the weapon that killed this poor girl. And, that, too, is interesting."

"Er…ah…yes, of course," I muttered, still mulling in my own mind why I had not seen as well that the rock was interesting.

"Notice here, as well, Sister's fingers. The nails are clean and show no hint of blood or damage."

That fact prompted me to finally ask, "Valon, could you explain to me just so that I may concur with you in my own perceptions, mind you what it is that you find interesting in each of those instances you have mentioned?"

"Certainly. That a stone was used as a murder weapon tells us this was a crime of passion, rather than premeditation. There was likely an argument, at the end of which things became so heated that the murderer seized the first thing at hand and bashed the poor girl with it, perhaps so much in anger that he or she did not mean to kill. The blow was delivered either by a left-handed person from behind or a right-handed person from in front. As you well know, no mother would tolerate a child to become left-handed in adulthood, for it is the most malevolent of signs, and thus there are very few left-handed people among us. I will assume, therefore, that it was a right-handed person, who faced the victim. That would indicate they knew each other, and that suggests to me that Sister Helena was at that spot at such an unusual hour to keep a prearranged meeting with someone she knew."

"By all that's Holy, Valon, I believe you are right."

"There's much more, of course. But, to confirm that, I must examine further."

"What do you mean?"

Instead of answering, Valon proceeded to remove the girl's hands from her stomach and to spread her legs.

"What on earth are you doing, Valon!" I exclaimed, alarmed at the intrusiveness of his examination, though I had all along fretted at examining the naked body of a young nun.

"I intend to confirm that the girl was not raped, Father Abbot," he explained, even as he examined the girl's genitalia.

"You must not, Valon!" I objected strongly. "It is a violation! It is surely sacrilege!"

"No, Theodulfe," he protested as he continued to probe, "it's our duty, from the King."

Then looking up, he said it again. "Very interesting."

At first, I was so annoyed by his nonchalance in fending off my objections I forgot to ask, but then it struck me. "What is interesting, pray, Monsieur?" I asked coldly.

"Two things. This girl was clearly not raped, as were the other girls reported to us. That in itself sets this murder apart, for although Sister Helena is like the others a young girl, she was not brutalized, either before or after death."

"You said two things," I huffed, still annoyed.

"Yes, and the second is in some ways more interesting than the first. Sister Helena was not a virgin."

CHAPTER 4

Valon Attempts a Sacrilege

I am sure my face fell agog at this last, though I quickly recovered to protest. "Sin knows no special person or age, Valon. Girls are sometimes brutalized much younger than poor Sister, and so is it not unusual? What you have discovered signifies nothing."

"We cannot know, good Theodulfe, and I would not dare to speculate how many women in this convent are virgins. I merely place that fact in evidence with all else we have learned. We will assemble our facts later, perhaps, in finding a solution to this terrible crime."

"Yes, and now let us cover the poor girl and return to Sister Prioress," I said, hoping to hurry Valon away from Sister's body.

Valon made no move as I expected but instead continued to look at the corpse. Then, to my astonishment, he took from its scabbard his sharp knife and gestured toward the girl.

"Good Heavens! What are you doing?" I protested and seized the arm that held the knife.

Looking me boldface in the eyes, he said, "I am going to cut open the girl's stomach."

"No! You cannot do it! Think Valon. It is truly a sacrilege to do as you plan. It is a desecration of the sacred temple that God Himself created and that once was the vessel in which this poor girl's soul was held. You cannot do it! Why in God's name would you do it?"

"'Tis quite simple, Theodulfe," he said in a very matter-of-fact way, without emotion. "I wish to know if this girl is pregnant."

Still seized of his hand and holding it fast from his evil intention, I asked, now pleading, "But, why would you wish to do that? What reason do you suspect even?"

"Notice the unusual rise in her lower abdomen. That, and the fact that she is not a virgin pose the question for me. Is she with child?" His black eyes flashed.

"That rise is merely a bit of fat. Not unusual in a young girl, even one that is otherwise slender. No, Valon. You must not!" I insisted, still holding fast his hand and more determined than ever to prevent yet another crime, even if I had to struggle with him for the knife. "You are a sinful man, Valon. Repent your intention to do such a thing!"

Valon continued to look in my eyes, now with a coldness that the deep blackness of his eyes could assume, but I knew he could also see my resolve. "I am the Missi Dominici, Father Abbot, and I will do as I think best."

The assertion hit me a strong blow, somewhere between my lower chest and upper abdomen. Now for the first time in our association, emotions of astonishment and bewilderment gave way to anger.

"No, Monsieur, you are not *the* Missi Dominici. Though it is often used otherwise, you know very well that 'Missi Dominici' is a plural Latin form. *We* are the Missi Dominici. And the King's capitulary insists that we always act from a common purpose, *or not at all*!"

My retort clearly struck Valon a blow. His eyes closed and the muscles of his arm relaxed. "Aye, of course. It is as you say, Father Abbot. I forgot my plurals," he said apologetically. And then came his winning smile.

We took our leave of Sister Helena and the convent within the hour, though Valon was a little late to our departure. As we road in silence toward Châlons, I began to reproach myself that I had hindered Valon's investigation while contributing nothing of my own. In my mind, I fought the battle between the moral and the necessary and struggled mightily to find the balance. I knew Valon could see my anxiety and I half knew also he could read my very thoughts, for he said as we neared our destination, "Rest easy, good Theodulfe. All things are sorted out in the balance." And then he smiled such a smile as to set my mind immediately at rest.

CHAPTER 5

The Bishop Tells More

It pleased Our Lord that we came in sight of Châlons on the Day of Saint Budo (8 December) in His Year 794. As we progressed, Valon continued to say little but observed the hustle and bustle on the road around us. He finally said, "We seem to arrive amidst the market day, Father Abbot. Châlons is a town well on its way to becoming a city, it seems."

And, indeed, it was larger and had more people and activity than I anticipated. The high street led through a row of shops, houses, and the smithy, into the square where the morning's market was already underway. To one side of the large square and up a slight rise, stood the church and walled confines of the great gray blocks of the Abbey de Saint Benoît du Lac. A kind of gatehouse guarded its approach, and beyond that stood a large wooden gate fitted with giant pieces of iron. It seemed more a fortress than an Abbey.

To the right, beyond a Commons on which several cows grazed, and on a steeper rise, another large structure sat. Its massive gray walls seemed to grow naturally out of the rocks upon which it perched. In the mist of the lifting morning fog, it gave off an almost ethereal quality, as if perhaps those who lived there were not quite of this earth, or at least not quite the same earth as those who now flooded the market square. It was the fortress manor of Lord Ethelred.

When we'd passed into the square, a small man in monk's robes approached. "Are you Monsieur le Marquis de Valon?" he asked, with a warm smile.

"I am he, Brother. And what is your business with me?"

"I am Brother Otto, servant of the Lord Bishop of Reims, who is in residence at the Abbey de Saint Benoît du Lac. He instructs me to wait upon you and to bid you come to the abbey where he might speak with you, as soon as you should arrive."

Valon regarded me with a quizzical look in his eye. "By all means, Brother. Tell the Lord Bishop that we will wait upon him as soon as we have stabled our horses."

"The Lord Bishop has ordered me to see to your horses, Monsieur. There are provisions for them at the Abbey."

"In that case, Brother Otto, lead on, if you please."

The jovial little monk struck out across the square, winding his way through the maze of vendors on the market day. We dismounted and led our mounts by the same twisting path until we reached the gates of the monastery. After a few words from Brother Otto to those inside, the giant gate's hinges creaked their welcoming song. As the door moved slowly forward, I had the impression that another world entirely was opening before us.

In contrast to the noisy market square, the great court of the monastery was eerily quiet. Once in its precincts, Brother Otto assumed a hushed tone. In deference, I concluded, to the silence observed by the monks during most of their day. A monk took our horses to be stabled, and Brother Otto motioned us up the short stairs to the monastery's main block—a forbidding facade of gray granite—and through its heavy oaken doors.

Leaving the monks and soldiers with the horses, Valon and I followed Brother Otto into the great hall of the building, which opened to several corridors, going in every direction. Otto led us to a second storey, which also opened on several passages. As we walked briskly down one, I noticed on each side the doors to what were certainly the monk's cells. At the end of the long hallway, where there was a small window, Otto stopped to knock on the last door.

"Enter," came a kindly voice from inside. When Otto opened the door not ten feet away stood an exceedingly small man, no more than five feet tall and very thin. I reckoned him to be at least fourscore years.

"Gentlemen," Otto announced. "My Lord Bishop of Reims."

"Welcome, Welcome, Welcome!" the old Bishop hailed, as Otto made his exit. "Won't you have a seat here on my bench, by the fire? I find that days are growing very chill, and my aging bones are quick to feel the sting. Not nearly as much meat on them as in the past, so I feel the chill more readily than in my youth," he smiled, his voice and movements suggesting a still-vital man.

We took our seats upon the bench, which was nicely cushioned of pillows made of wool, and I thanked the Bishop for his welcome.

Valon came straight to the point of our interview, in his own reassuring way. "We are delighted to find you here, My Lord, and to find you in good health. We had not expected to meet you so soon, though you must know we have come largely at your summons."

"Yes, my letter to dear Alcuin and the King. I have expected you these many days, for Alcuin sent me notice by rapid messenger when you left. It was he who suggested it might assist your investigation if I were to present myself at Châlons. Dear Alcuin sensed, you see, that I did not say all I knew or suspected in my letter."

"Yes, that occurred to me, as well, My Lord," Valon ventured, "but I did not think it wise to take the time to divert to Reims. That is why I am so pleased to find you here. And, I am especially grateful to you, because I know that traveling has worked a hardship upon you."

"Well, I am not so quick to travel as I once was, young Valon, and I daresay I have few such travels left in me. But here I am eager to assist as I can."

With this last, the old Bishop smiled. "I knew your grandfather, Valon, you know, and it pleases and amuses me that you resemble him so fairly. He was a bit of a buck, you know, clearly not intended for the Church, as I was. Still, we were great friends. and I have missed him these long years. Does he yet live?"

"No, My Lord, I regret to say that he died last year before I returned from the War. But I count it one of the great boons of my life that Our Lord granted me the privilege to know him and to grow to manhood in the light of his example."

"Well said, and from what I've heard of you and from no less a personage than the King himself, your grandfather would be well pleased.

"But, enough of these greetings. I know you have work hereabouts and wish to get to it. So, I will come to the point."

"Thank you, My Lord."

"There are three things that have come to my attention that you must know as you begin your work. I considered them very carefully during my journey from Reims, and I am more convinced than ever that they may be important to this matter—this horrible affair."

"Three?" I asked.

"Yes," the old man confirmed, his deep blue eyes glistening with an intense gaze. "The first concerns the Abbey here, while the other two concern the Lord of Châlons et Passey and his family. There are things to be said, which I dared not put in my letter."

"Which pertain to the events of late, I take it?"

"Yes. First, you must know of the bad blood between the Abbot Hugo and Lord Ethelred. They have disputed the possession of lands these many years, and they are even now at law over their dispute. I am not myself certain of all the facts, but it seems that Ethelred's father—his name was Ergard—gave certain lands to the Monastery to ensure that prayers were offered regularly for the repose of his soul. There is, you see, a Chantry within the Abbey, and so it was a natural and saintly thing for the old Lord to do."

"Ethelred has disputed the bequest since coming into his inheritance and refuses to accept the documents the Abbey offers on their side. Against the documents, Ethelred offers the testimony of the old Lord's Steward, Dagbert, that no such bequest took place.

"Abbot Hugo and Lord Ethelred have had words in the past, but now seldom speak. Bad blood, as I say, and it seems to me to be entirely from Ethelred's side. The Abbot is a congenial man and does not begrudge the Lord his point of view. I'm told that Ethelred has even talked of burning the Abbey—an evil man!"

"That is useful to know," Valon said, though, with a dubious tone in his voice, I thought.

"Yes, and now for what I know of Ethelred and his family. Monsieur de Valon, the Lord of Châlons is a profane and godless man. No question of it. His reputation is perhaps the worst of the nobility in this entire region. Since youth, he has engaged in every depravity imaginable, and in this regard has set a low standard for his sons, some of whom are following in his path."

"But, Lord Bishop, there are many such profane men in the Kingdom. The point is, do you suggest that Lord Ethelred is capable of the crimes committed?"

The old man paused a moment to consider. "Let me answer by this. The Lord of Châlons has been married three times, and in each case, his wife died. In our times it is not unusual for a woman—even a young woman—to die in the childbed, but in this case, none of Lord Ethelred's wives died in that way. Nor did they die by illness."

Valon's jaw stiffened.

"They died by terrible accidents, and the last apparently by her own hand. And now, it is a scandal that he is attempting to take to wife a young kinswoman of his own who is but thirteen years!"

"That, too, is not unknown, My Lord," said Valon. "I will join your suspicions that so many deaths have been mere accidents or even suicide, but, do you have more to offer than your suspicions? My investigation must go more to facts, you see—useful as suspicions may be. Tell me of his last wife—the suicide."

"The Lady Editha—daughter of a distant noble house of Provence. She was in her youth a beautiful woman but had grown older than her years as Ethelred's wife. She was the mother of Mordune and Céleste, who are fraternal twins. The others of Ethelred's children were born of previous wives, including his heir, Godfrey."

"And how, precisely, did the Lady Editha die?"

"A terrible thing, Monsieur. Now, more than a year ago, in the midst of heavy snow—as we are sometimes wont to have in these parts—she threw herself from the tower of the Manor. Evidence in the matter was taken by the judge of the Comte de Meaux, to whom Ethelred is a vassal, and it was determined that the tragedy was suicide. The evidence taken, and it was damning of Lord Ethelred, was that there were strong words between the Lord and his wife, overheard by a large number of servants and men-at-arms and that the Lady Editha ran to the tower and jumped to her death."

"Strong words?" I asked. "Any testimony what about?"

The Bishop paused and looked at his hands. "Yes. It was said that Ethelred proposed to put the Lady Editha away, in a distant convent, so as to enable him to marry again. It is not uncommon for the Frankish nobles to do such a thing."

"May Our Lord preserve her," I lamented, as we three crossed ourselves.

"It has circulated for years among the townsmen and peasants that Lord Ethelred was responsible for all those deaths, and it is even said that he murdered some. Ethelred is generally unpopular amongst his people, for he deals harshly with them. In fact, he has been generally disliked since his youth. And so, this reputation has encouraged suspicions that he is also responsible for the recent murders."

"Yes, I quite understand," said Valon, "but can you be more specific of evidence, My Lord?"

"The murders that have so upset the village of Châlons are blamed on Lord Ethelred, as I conveyed in my letter. That was as much as I dared say in writing, but now I can tell you more." Valon's eyes grew wide.

The old man heaved a sigh, hesitated, and for a moment gazed out the window of his chamber as if collecting his thoughts, or perhaps his courage. I noticed that a gentle snow was falling.

"I am privy to some information—in part, from Father Draco, who serves in the local parish—that certain things have happened of late that have driven the town even deeper into the gloom. Feelings against Lord Ethelred have so intensified among his own people that they seethe with hatred, Draco says. Last week, as Ethelred rode through the town, he was struck by an arrow, fired from atop one of the buildings. The arrow struck his thigh and hardly penetrated the leather leggings he wore, but still, what an offense against order! It was not certain who fired the arrow or even from whence it came, precisely, so, of course, Lord Ethelred blames and suspects everyone. Shortly after—two nights to be exact—ten or twelve horsemen attacked the town at night and burned a merchant's storehouse and the baker's shop. You can imagine the difficulty the loss of both has caused the local people, and they know that the attack was a reprisal, undertaken by the Lord Ethelred's sons. They are mostly hotheads of the worst sort, and as I said, every bit as profane as their father. The difference is that most of the time they are somewhat restrained in their behavior by him. This time, perhaps not."

"Yes, I noticed as we entered the town that several buildings had recently burned. Is there any evidence that the attack was a reprisal? Any direct evidence?"

"None, according to Draco. But that does not stop the townsmen from being certain that it was yet another assault by their Lord, though this time no young girl was ravaged."

"How are the townsmen so certain that Ethelred murdered the girls? It is one thing to be debauched, another to be an insane murderer of innocent girls."

"Yes, and that takes me to my second revelation—one I dared not put in the letter to Alcuin."

The Lord Bishop paused once more and again looked out at the gently falling snow. "Valon, Theodulfe, what I am about to tell you I half disbelieve myself, so it is difficult to convey. And yet, I trust Father Draco's testimony. Nonetheless, I charge you to speak with him yourself. Learn what you can from him, as I am sure you will question those who inform him. He is a good man, but a simple one and perhaps too credulous."

"I shall speak to him, My Lord," Valon agreed, with a note of uncertainty in his voice.

"Yes, well. I can tell you this. According to Draco, there was a witness to the last murder, a nighttime strangulation, and rape of a girl in the street near the smithy."

"A witness?" Valon's eyes opened wide.

"Yes, a witness hiding in the shadows who saw the murderer at close hand and who identifies that murderer as Lord Ethelred. She is unswerving in her testimony that it was Ethelred and no other who did it, for she says she saw the dead girl being raped!"

"Mother of God! Protect us!" I could not help responding, and again crossed myself.

"Father Draco believes the woman. He puts absolute confidence in her witness! And there it is. Lord Ethelred, seen in the act."

"And so, can this witness come forward?" I asked.

"That's the rub, Father Abbot. She cannot be brought forward. While Father Draco may believe her, I fear no one else would."

"And why is that?" Valon pressed.

"Because she is a witch!"

CHAPTER 6

A Witch?

The word caused an odd sensation among the hairs at the back of my neck. Valon's face darkened.

"A Witch?" I repeated.

"Yes, and a brazen and notorious one at that. Hildegard—an old hag who is well-known in this district to be a true daughter of the Evil One. And worse, she's known to be in league with the Jews, who kidnap Christian children. There's no question of it! It's well known that the Jews must have the blood of Christian children in order to prepare their sacred foods. And, because old Hildegard is the Devil's own foe of Christianity, she has conspired with the Jews for years."

Valon said nothing but waited for the old man to continue.

"Well, don't you see? What sort of witness could Hildegard be? More likely, a court would decide to gibbet her, rather than anyone she gave testimony against! She would need be tortured to determine if what she said were lies."

"An unreliable witness, at best, I suppose," Valon concluded. "But how is it then that Father Draco has such confidence in her testimony?"

"A good question, young Valon, and one that I challenge you to put to Draco yourself. He will be at your service. I have advised Draco to keep a distance from Hildegard, lest he fall into her evil. There is always a great rejoicing in Hell when a priest succumbs to Satan. But first, I wish to give you the last of my advice, which I did not include in my letter."

"Yes, of course."

"It concerns Lord Ethelred's family—well, mainly his sons."

"He has four sons, I understand."

"Yes, and none of them of much account in my opinion. Godfrey is the eldest and in line to succeed. He is a morose and vengeful man, who has a reputation as clever but malevolent. The common folk call him Godfrey Malfait, in part because of that and in part because he was born a hunchback. He is a dreadfully misshapen man. You will do well to examine him carefully."

"The second son is Humphrey. He is the only one of the litter who seems the least redeemable. It is said that he wishes to enter the Monastery, but his father won't allow it."

"The third son is Guillaume the One-eyed—in many ways, the worst of the lot. He has all of his father's debauched ways, and yet is a warrior of considerable skill. I believe you were in the Frisian War, were you not, young Valon?"

"Yes, Lord Bishop, I was."

"Well, I don't suppose you encountered Guillaume, though he was also in that conflict, and by all accounts acquitted himself well in the slaughter. He is known to be fond of killing, you see."

"There are such men, and I have known one or two. But most who know war, detest it and crave peace."

"Yes, well Guillaume does not. He practices his martial skills constantly, as does his younger half-brother, Mordune. They are alike as two wicks in the same candle, and the younger looks constantly to the example of Guillaume—such as it is.

"Still, I know of nothing against Mordune. He is a twin of his sister, Céleste, and the two are devoted to each other from childhood. Mordune is also said to be fond of poetry, which as you know can be a gateway to sins of lust.

"Well, there you have it. A despicable family, at least in the male line. Ethelred's daughters are not nearly so bad, and Céleste, of course, has escaped the dreadful company of her father and brothers to become a cloistered nun."

"Yes, we have learned of her by stopping at the Convent of Saint Agnes on our way from Montague. It was there that we investigated briefly the murder of one of the nuns, Sister Helena—who was a good friend of Sister Céleste."

"A murder!" the old man exclaimed. "Yet another murder! At Saint Agnes?"

"Certainly a murder, My Lord, but not a murder like the ones in Châlons. Sister Helena was bludgeoned over the head by someone she met on the path leading down from the Convent. Still, it is an odd thing to happen, and it may well prove to have something to do with the sad events in Châlons, though at the moment I cannot see what."

The old Bishop sat for a long moment, stunned by word that a woman of the church had been killed in such a dreadful way. It seemed that the compounding evil of recent days was becoming too much for him to shoulder. When he revived, his eyes tearing, he reached out to Valon, took his hand, and said, "My son, I beg you to drive out the evil that has come amongst my people, I beg you! Until you have done so, I will remain here in the Monastery, praying to Our Lord for your success."

Valon seemed moved by the old man's emotion. "Yes, pray, My Lord, for one thing, is clear. A great evil has come amongst us." And with those words, we knelt for the Lord Bishop's blessing, which he gave and bid us good-bye.

Our leave-taking of the Lord Bishop put Valon in a determined state, but I sensed also that he was puzzled about much we had heard. Grist for his mill, I thought, as we walked down the dark and narrow corridor toward the great hall.

"What is it that makes you look so, Valon?" I asked.

"Something I had only suspected 'til now, in this problem, Theodulfe, there are plots within plots. Schemes within schemes."

CHAPTER 7

The Abbot Says His Part

At the end to the corridor we found Brother Otto, Bodo, and the brother monks, and with them, a tall, slender man with long features, large dark eyes, and a hairless domed head. It was Abbot Hugo.

We embraced and exchanged blessings as one Abbot to another. But even in the warmth of Father Abbot's fraternal embrace, I felt a coolness about his regard for Valon and me, which made me wonder if there was something about Hugo that we had yet to discover. I could tell in the glances exchanged that Valon felt the same sensation, but I dared not yet tell him of my apprehension, because I feared his suspicion of all things concerning the Church.

"Forgive me, Father Abbot, that we did not pay our respects to you first, upon our entrance into the Abbey. The Lord Bishop summoned us to wait upon him immediately."

"Think nothing of it, Monsieur de Valon. A Bishop may decide as he pleases, and I have not the least concern about it."

Valon begged an opportunity to speak with Hugo about the events that brought us to Châlons, and so we repaired to his rooms, which were just off the great hall. Once there and seated before the crackling fire in the small study, Valon begged any information that Abbot Hugo could offer.

"I know what the Lord Bishop has told you, Monsieur de Valon, for we discussed his testimony before you arrived. There is little I can add, except to say that I concur with his views. Father Draco will tell what he knows and believes. I will not speak for him. I will say, however, that I believe Draco is a simple man and as such he is far too trusting of old Hildegard's testimony. She is an evil woman—a true daughter of Satan—and dare not be trusted in any manner, except that she may be expected to deal in evil in all things. Unlike poor Draco, I believe that one may reliably believe the opposite of what she says, and doubly so if she takes her diabolical oaths!"

"Then you doubt that Lord Ethelred is guilty of the crimes?"

"Not at all. Ethelred is an evil person and may even be as deeply en-snared by Satan as old Hildegard, though I have no evidence of it. I do not doubt that God's judgment will strike him a fierce blow. But I do not know his guilt, especially from what the witch says. So, I can prove nothing," the Abbot said with a shrug. "I can only say that I do not put such things past him. That is all, Monsieur," he concluded, crossing his arms and raising his chin.

"Then, Brother, you must suspect Lord Ethelred of insanity—murderous insanity—for these crimes must be the work of such a person?" I pressed the Abbot. Valon said nothing. Instead, he watched for Hugo's reaction.

"You must judge Ethelred's mind and soul for yourself, Brother Theodulfe, that is your duty as Missi Dominici. I am merely a monk and it is not my place to make such judgments," he said, evasively I thought. And yet he said it in such a way that I knew he did indeed deem Ethelred capable of such madness. Valon could see it too.

"And what of the Lord's family?" Valon followed. "The Lord Bishop told us but little of his sons."

The Abbot's face seemed to darken even further. "If it is possible, Monsieur, in God's great scheme for this sad world in which we live, that there could be worse even than Ethelred himself, then that is surely the spawn he has given to the future. With the exception of Mordune, they are surely worse than he."

"That is a terrible judgment, Father Abbot. On what do you base it?"

"For one, some of Ethelred's own children believe he murdered the Lady Editha, his wife."

"Which children?" Valon asked.

"I am not sure, but I have been told by one who knows that some certainly do. There are things, Monsieur, which even the Lord Bishop does not know, or does not know entirely."

"That is far too vague an answer, Father Abbot." Valon pressed.

Abbot Hugo considered for a moment. "I will tell you this. It has seemed to me that since the death of the Lady Editha, relations between Lord Ethelred and Mordune have suffered most. But then, one cannot know why such things happen. And Sister Céleste…well, she seems as close to her father as ever."

"And Guillaume?"

"As like his father's twin. Since Guillaume returned from the Frisian War, he seems each week to exceed himself in evil-doing, Monsieur. He is a drunken lout, who spends much of his time abusing the peasants. Sometimes he and his friends rob travelers upon the main road. And, of course, they routinely ravage the daughters of the local cottagers and they do it as they like. There is no restraint upon him. Ethelred does not care, and no other human has the least influence with him. He and his roughs are a terror in the countryside, Monsieur de Valon, and we are defenseless against them. That is my testimony."

"You say 'with the exception of Mordune'?"

"Not a bad lot, but still…"

Hugo huffed and then sighed a little as he excused himself to his monastery duties, but in leaving he commended us to seek out Draco and discover what he might tell. As we walked through the great court of the Abbey to find Father Draco, however, we heard a loud commotion in the square just beyond. A roar of shouts and screams rose even above the considerable din of the busy market. Valon ordered the Brother Warder to open the gate quickly and as the massive structure moved before us, we could see a crowd moving toward the far side of the square, where the source commotion was apparently to be found.

CHAPTER 8

Valon Stops a Flogging

"What is it?" I asked the first townsman we met. The small think man wore a drab tunic, and by his hat and beard, I could tell he was a Jew. Clearly, his dress indicated a man of property.

He outstretched his hand. "I am Mathias of Tours, Father Abbot, a merchant in grains. I make my headquarters here in Châlons."

"Do you know what is happening here?"

"They say it is the One-eyed, Father Abbot. Violence, I do not doubt. The One-eyed is a master of violence. It is his trade, you might say."

Valon and I pushed forward behind the throng of market-goers who surged toward what I remembered as the location of the smithy. Athalfe preceded us, and Bodo and the brother monks pressed close behind. When we came to the far side, those in front of us halted, and we found ourselves at the back of whatever was happening. We heard shouts from the crowd of, "No!" "No!" "Stop, we beg you!"

Valon snatched Bodo to his front and used him to plough his way through the crowd. Poor Bodo tried to save himself by shouts of, "Stand Aside! Stand aside for the Marquis de Valon!" It hardly made a difference in the noise and tumult of the moment, but we slowly pushed our way to the front.

Soon we broke into the open, and I saw before me what was exciting the calls to stop. Just in front of the smithy, a giant of a man stood with whip in hand, flogging a poor fellow who they'd pulled over an anvil by several soldiers. The half-naked victim of the beating was apparently the blacksmith, dragged from his shop to be punished for some offense. Meanwhile, armed men pushed back against the crowd and kept them at a distance of ten feet or more from the flogging."

The giant stood in full leathers, studded with brass buttons. He wore a cloak, tied at each side by metal clasps. On his wrists and forearms, the size of a big man's legs, he wore leather wraps, also studded with brass buttons, and upon his chest, a shirt of polished chainmail that glistened in the sunlight with each flail of the whip.

As he whipped the hapless blacksmith, the giant roared and laughed with a booming, guttural sound that seems not quite human, but to me rather what must have greeted Odysseus in his encounter with the Cyclopes. His head was large, in perfect proportion to the rest of him, which must have been at least half again as tall as me. He was shaved, except from the very top of his head sprang a braided shock of bright red hair, which hung down the giant's back almost to his waist. His brow lay broad and flat, and upon it ran a deep scar toward his left eye, which was clearly dead and useless. As he laughed, he snorted and breathed from a large flat nose.

The poor smith's back was a bloody mess and as we stood, helpless to save him, I wondered what had been his offense. I considered too if the punishment resulted from some trial at law. Almost as soon as these thoughts came into my mind, Valon rushed forward and with a sword drawn so quickly it seemed to materialize in his hands, he sliced the whip as it moved to deliver another blow. The tail of the whip fell to the ground. The crowd gasped and then grew silent.

Startled by the affront, the giant glared at Valon, half in disbelief, half in building rage, but clearly uncertain what had destroyed his whip.

Valon explained. "Your whip is useless, my slow friend. And now you must take care I do not ruin that fine *chemise* of chainmail you are wearing. Would be a pity to get holes in it."

Valon's chiding came as an added insult to the giant, who only snorted his anger. Finally, there came a response. "For a small man, you have a large mouth. I am going to enjoy closing it forever, Monsieur. But first, I must know who it is that comes before me with a wish to die."

"Only too pleased to oblige, my fat friend. *I am Piers de Valon.* Do I have the doubtful honor to address Guillaume, son of Ethelred, who is called the One-eyed? And who is known to the entire Kingdom to be a witless oaf."

"None other, Valon. I have heard of you. You were in the Frisian War, and your reputation has followed you into the peace, Monsieur. 'Tis a pity that I must kill one with whom I served in Charlemagne's army, but that is as it is." He shrugged.

With these last words, the giant drew his massive sword, which seemed as long as Valon was high, and the two warriors began immediately to circle, their swords taking the measure of the other. As they did so, the circle of the crowd expanded. The giant quickly delivered his first blow, a savage effort that Valon caught with his blade and easily fended-off. Almost in the same motion, Valon fell to the ground and delivered a blow of his own, catching the giant on the top of his left foot.

The pain of the cut caused the One-eyed to let out a howl as big as his body and

immediately blood spurted from the top of his leather boot. The crowd began to shout in disbelief.

The Giant responded with a wild swing of his blade, which just missed Valon's head. The momentum of his arms pulled him round, so that Valon was able to answer with a blow from the broadside of his sword at the Giant's back.

Staggering back in some surprise at Valon's apparent ability to touch him with his sword, Guillaume backed up slightly and again took the measure of his adversary. Clearly, now he was not so confident of punishing the smaller man.

Guillaume set his heels and raised his sword to make another blow when a loud voice came from the back of the crowd.

"Stop!"

All eyes now averted to the direction of the shout. The crowd grew silent. A large, heavily armored man, with a bold red beard and long red braided hair, advanced towards us. His eyes blazed fiercely, and he held himself erect. I knew, somehow, that it was Lord Ethelred.

CHAPTER 9

Lord Ethelred

The horseman's advance cowed the giant, and the men-at-arms with him, stood rigid.

"What is this!" the rider roared, as he prepared to dismount. "Guillaume, you dog, account for yourself! Release that man, and see to him!" he ordered, nodding toward the blacksmith.

Two of the men-at-arms untied the smith from the anvil and supported him as he stumbled into his forge and the arms of his wife. I ordered Brother Martin, who had some skill as an apothecary, to tend to the man.

Meanwhile, the giant merely hung his head and made no response to his father's demand.

"And who are you?" Lord Ethelred asked Valon, turning his glance upon me and Brother Boethius.

Valon responded immediately. "I am Piers de Valon, My Lord Ethelred." He pulled from my *sacullus* the *capitulary* and handed it to Lord Ethelred. "I am here with my companion, Abbot Theodulfe of Fleury-sur-Loire," he said in a loud voice, directed as much at the crowd of townsmen as at Lord Ethelred. Handing the Lord his commission, he continued. "We are sent by the Great Charles as his Missi Dominici. I instruct you to read his capitulary before the people of Châlons." There was a loud murmuring in the crowd.

The announcement, delivered as it was in a voice of such authority that it resounded throughout the square, threw Lord Ethelred back momentarily upon his heels. I noticed that Guillaume retreated several feet toward the crowd as if seeking refuge from his former adversary.

Lord Ethelred took from Valon the commission, looked at it briefly, and read:

> I, Charles, King of the Franks, do declare these my servants, Piers, Marquis de Valon et Balaincourt and Theodulfe, Abbé de Fleury-sur-Loire and other abbeys, as my Missi Dominici and instruct them to investigate the murders that have been perpetrated in the region of Châlons, in Champagne, and all other circumstances that may seem to them useful to investigate and to determine the nature and manner of the crimes, to do justice

in my name, and to report to me the consequences of their investigation. Know ye all, my subject, from the very highest to lowliest, that these men act in my name and with my authority. Woe to him who resists them,

Charles

This last rang throughout the square as it rolled from Ethelred's tongue, and upon reading, he turned to the both of us and bowed as if before the Great Charles himself.

"I and the people of my domains are at your service, Missi Dominici. You have but to command and it shall be done."

Valon looked at Lord Ethelred in the piercing way his eyes could sometimes assume, and then walked through the parting crowd toward the Abbey. Surprised at this sudden departure, I and the others of our entourage followed, now wondering, I confess, what Valon had in mind.

Half-way to the Abbey's gates, which seemed to swing open in anticipation of Valon's arrival, I understood perfectly his gesture. His silent departure was likely to reassure the people of Châlons while disconcerting all those associated with Lord Ethelred. Not for the first or last time in our association, I stood in awe at the presence of my companion, and I feel the sensation of it to this moment, more than twenty-five years past. It felt as if Charlemagne himself was among us.

CHAPTER 10

Mathias of Tours

As the Abbey gates closed behind us, Valon turned to Brother Boethius. "Did you observe, Brother, the small man in monk's garb who cowered near the smithy?"

Boethius nodded.

"Quick. Go find him, and bring him to me. I'll wager that was Father Draco, and I wish to see him as soon as possible."

Boethius departed, still without a word, while Valon and I entered the great hall of the Abbey.

There we found Abbot Hugo, a distracted look about him. "Father Abbot, if you please," Valon hailed. As Hugo drew near, Valon asked, "Do you know why Guillaume the One-eyed should wish to flog the blacksmith, and in such a public way? What was his crime?"

"Crime, Monsieur? There was no crime, and the flogging was not a punishment for any crime. Cathar, the blacksmith, is a freeman and a village leader. He has spoken out about the murders. One of the murdered girls was his sister's child, you see. He has dared to demand that Lord Ethelred should find the villain. In recent days, he has even joined those who say that Ethelred himself is the Monster. That was his 'crime,' Monsieur de Valon… to say aloud what the entire town is thinking."

"It would appear, however, that the flogging was Guillaume's notion and that Lord Ethelred did not know of it in advance."

"That is possible. The One-eyed is a brute, as you've seen. I observed the fracas from the bell tower of the Abbey, you see. He might have acted on his own, he is a dull-witted lout after all and his kind is the authors of many poor ideas."

Just then Brother Boethius returned with a priest by the hand. Valon excused us from the Father Abbot, and as Boethius advanced, he handed Valon a small scrap of parchment, which he said a man in the square had given him. He read it quickly and then passed it to me, without comment.

Please to come to my house in the Street of the Grain Merchants at your convenience, My Lord. I have much to tell that may be of use to you.

Mathias of Tours.

Valon did not pause to consider the invitation, but took the priest to one side and asked, "You are Father Draco, who serves in the parish of Châlons?"

"Yes, My Lord," the humble priest said, head bowed and eyes down.

"You needn't call me, 'My Lord," Father Draco. Monsieur de Valon will do nicely."

"Yes, Monsieur. How may I assist you?" Draco said, bowing slightly as he did so.

"I wish to know about the witch."

CHAPTER 11

Father Draco is Surprised

The directness of Valon's demand surprised the timid priest, and at first, Draco seemed not to know how to respond. His eyes shot from side to side as if seeking an escape. Valon snatched him up by the sleeve as if anticipating his attempt to flee.

"I wish to meet the witch, Draco," he said in a confidential undertone.

"You must mean Hildegard, Monsieur. She is the only known witch in my parish, though I have no doubt there are more of the vile creatures about. The night is full of them, and I can tell you they spread their evil at will in the hours of darkness. You have only to witness the murders," he said, almost in a whisper. "The dreadful spirits that abound in the night are tied up in that business, I know it!" he insisted.

"Yes, well that's useful testimony, Father. We will, of course, take that sort of intervention into account, but I wish to speak with the witch Hildegard because I understand from Father Abbot that she has specific evidence of the murders and that you have been privy to her testimony."

"Indeed, she does, and I've heard what she says. She tells of seeing the murder last month of Monica, the young daughter of Osbern, the village miller. A terrible thing…shocked everyone in the town. Her father's been insane with grief since that night. But, can one believe a witch? What part of what she says is true and which part a lie? How can one know! Oh, they are so treacherous and deceptive!"

"Do you know where we will find this Hildegard, where and when?"

"Yes. Yes, I do. I certainly do, Monsieur. But I warn that it's a dangerous thing to go looking for Hildegard because one must do it in the night, and at the hour when the powers of the witch are at their fullest."

"What?" I intervened. "We must find her at night! Why is that?"

Draco looked at me as if he could not believe I had so little knowledge of the ways of witches that I should ask such a question.

"But of course, Father Abbot. 'Twas always thus with the witch. They cannot be found in the light of day, for God's own sunshine is a terrible thing to the witch, something to be avoided. Hildegard is no different. She seeks the darkness, where rules her Master, and where roam the creatures—demons, trolls, wizards, weasels—much like herself. A word of caution on this point, if I may Monsieur," Draco's voice fell as his eyes grew wider. He leaned closer, almost as if to whisper in Valon's ear.

"Of course. What is it?"

"The folk here 'bouts say the witch is guarded by a horror, Monsieur, a monster that protects her from any force she views as hostile. The horror keeps constant watch over her, particularly in the night." Draco's eyes grew dark. "Some say the horror is her own son, who is a *loup-garou,* consecrated to Satan as his instrument. Oh yes! One who goes in search of Hildegard runs a certain risk, no doubt of it," said Draco, his voice trembling.

Draco's warning that a werewolf protected Hildegard had no effect on Valon. "Well, Father, my companions and I are prepared to do so. If you will guide us, we will go in search of Hildegard and if she is only able to be found at night, we will search her out tonight."

"May God protect us as we go, Monsieur," Draco whispered and crossed himself.

CHAPTER 12

Deus meum est scutum.
God be my shield in the face of Horror.

Valon sent word to Father Abbot that we would remain at the Monastery that night. We passed the remainder of the afternoon in making our preparations, in the hostel used to accommodate pilgrims. Draco disappeared to his parish duties but agreed to return at nightfall and then to lead us to Hildegard's cave. All who traveled with Valon gathered for the evening meal and then prayed the office at Compline. I invoked God's grace in what we were about to undertake and asked his protection against the gathering forces of evil. I shuddered with fear that King Charles had called me into such an evil world.

Just after Compline, we found ourselves following Father Draco down a dark street and then into the heavily wooded hills to the north. Passing through a wooden gate of the village Commons, we came immediately upon rough terrain, where there was no hint of a path, not even the worn trek of cows. In the cloudless, moon-bright sky, we came to a stream, surely a branch of the River Marne.

Draco turned and instructed, "Take care, brothers, as we cross. The water is icy and undercurrents are treacherous, but this is the only ford available to us at night. Lift high your *sacullus*. The stream is chest deep in the middle."

Once we made the ford, Draco took a flint and the stub of a candle from his *sacullus*, lighted it, and gave the fire to Bodo and the brother monks, each of whom also carried a good candle. They then formed a phalanx of light to the front and guided us steadily up a steep hill and into a far denser forest not yet entirely denuded of its leaves. As we went, I looked for any sign that Father Draco was unsure of his way or that he had lost the path. There was none. He did not hesitate but moved steadily forward and up the hill. I did not bother to question him as to his destination, for it seemed a distraction. As we went, I confess I harbored many fears. *How is it, for example, that Draco knows a witch? Has he become a servant of the witch and of the Evil One? Are we following a servant of Evil to our deaths?* Such thoughts troubled my every step.

It surprised me a little when we soon found ourselves on a well-worn trek, which turned and followed a more level course to the west. Then it occurred to me. *Whose trek is this? Who, or What has made it?"*

The smells of the forest—the musty scent of decaying oak leaves, coupled with the dampness of advancing fall—wafted through the chill night air and gave me increasingly a sense that we were moving well beyond the safe and familiar world of the village and into something else altogether. And then, the night air gave a new odor—something of the stink of an animal.

As we advanced, I looked constantly beyond the candle bearers in front of us. Then, out of the corner of my eye and not reliably within my vision, I thought I saw something flit across our path, at a distance of perhaps a half-furlong. *Was it an animal? If so, it was large, else I would not have seen it.* The sensation that we were stalked by someone, or perhaps something, grew steadily sharper in my imagination, and that brought on the frightening recollection of Draco's warning that the witch was guarded by a horror.

"Deus meum est scutum," I repeated just above a whisper. "Did you see that, Valon? Whatever it was ahead of us?"

"Yes, but I made no more of it than you," he said, drawing his long knife as he spoke. Bodo and Athalfe did the same, while Martin, Boethius, and I held fast our pilgrim's staffs, against the chance that we might need them to fend off an attacker.

A noise soon answered our quandary about what we had seen ahead. First, there came a sudden and shrill yip, followed by a prolonged howl.

"It's a wolf," I whispered to Valon, my voice trembling.

"Yes," he said, "and by the sound of it a large one."

At that moment we heard the howl answered by a more distant howl, even more, prolonged and plaintive. We felt our way along the path, anxious and looked to either side for any noise or rustling in the scrub that might signal an attack. Out front, Father Draco continued to hold high his candle and to maintain his measured pace to who knew where.

Then, without apparent reason, he stopped and looked intently to the east of the path—a direction up a slight hill. My heart froze as we now followed him off the path and into the thicket, but still, he seemed sure of his way.

Not one hundred feet into the underbrush we came to an outcropping in the hill, and there, to the left, the mouth of a cave. I saw no sign around the opening that it was inhabited, but Draco assured us it was. We stood a moment in silence, listening for any rustling in the brush. Then, Draco spoke, not to us, but to someone we could not see.

"Hildegard. Come out!" he demanded, in a voice more commanding than I gave him credit for having. No response.

Draco insisted again, with even greater authority. "Hildegard, I charge you to show yourself!"

Then, out of the chill silence of the night, there came a mournful sound that I took for the faint cry of a child.

CHAPTER 13

Hildegard

Soon, there emerged from the cave a shrunken hag of about four feet, whose most distinctive feature was the terrible stink that announced her arrival in the most distressing way. Her matted white hair stood out in blotches upon a mostly bald scalp. She wore a common linen shift with a rope about the waist, and on her feet, she had wrapped wool cloth. She emerged with both hands raised, showing long, dirty nails, and raving curses at us and God. Hers were among the most terrible oaths I have ever heard, and I shall not repeat them in my narrative, lest God should curse me for doing so.

"You dare to order me about, Priest. Return to your town and command the sheep who follow you about like the dull-witted beasts they are! Curse you. Now go!"

The hag's words to Draco reassured me he was not her ally.

"We'll not go until we've had our say," he scolded.

Her hands still raised high and her eyes closed, she turned toward us. "You need not explain to me, Priest. My Master makes me fully aware of what you want. Valon comes boldly to question Hildegard, as does his doltish companion from the Loire."

Those words, spoken in the old hag's raspy voice, gave a new chill up my spine. How could she have known of Valon, and of me? We've only just arrived and we came unannounced. Even Lord Ethelred did not know we were coming.

I had no time to answer my own quandary, however, for at that moment the diabolical hag began to utter her oaths and curses in an unknown tongue, which was contrived to sound like Latin, the language of God, but which was not—it was the evil, mocking tongue of Satan himself.

"*Driasmus in tumultum et cum stantium mosques!*" she roared her gibberish at Valon, moving her hands back and forward at his face as she did so. Turning her palms toward his face and continuing her curses, I saw she had tattooed on her palms diabolical symbols. They were dreadful to me.

"Noquantium nostrus meantiums et caustum malvet, Valon!" she railed, and then seemed to relax her entire body and fall into a trance as if the evil she intended was done.

Valon stepped toward her, entirely undeterred by her evil. "Flail about with your curses and dark wishes as you choose, Hildegard. My business is not with your Master but with you, and it has nothing to do with your devotion to Satan."

The witch stood motionless, her eyes fixed on the ground. I thought for a moment she would not emerge from her trance. Still, Valon was undeterred by the hag's strange behaviour.

"Draco here believes from something you told him that you have testimony to give about the murder of the girl, Monica. I am here, the agent of your King, to learn the truth of this murder."

The word 'truth' seemed to revive the Witch. She jolted herself into a cold, challenging stare at Valon, then fixed upon his eyes, which she could see better than I, in the moonshine and candlelight. She stood quite still for the longest moment and then spoke.

"The King wishes to learn the truth from Hildegard?" The question so amused the hag she broke into cackling laughter, laced with new oaths, directed at Charlemagne himself. Her blasphemies were now more than I could endure.

Still, Valon persisted, unaffected by the wild gyrations before him, nor by the witch's stink, which seemed to increase in her moments of emotion.

"Hildegard, I tell you the King is prepared to hear the testimony you give."

"And why should I help the Great Charles? One reason please and I will give you what you want."

"This, old woman. The Synod of Frankfurt, of which you have not yet heard, perhaps because your Master has not wished you to learn of it. The Great King of the Franks required his Bishops and high churchmen to declare a new law against the burning of witches, under pain of death."

The hag seemed bewildered at Valon's announcement, which clearly, she had not heard. A further moment's reflection caused her to say, in a sly way and with a sidelong glance at him, "What is it you wish to know, Valon, and what good will it do to have the testimony of a witch?"

Almost at the drop of the word 'witch', there arose such a howl of the wolf as I had never heard before. Looking wide-eyed out into the darkness, the old woman said, "There, there, Lacunars. There, there." Then, turning once more to Valon, one eye closed, she whispered, "I saw it all, Valon. I saw the Monster."

CHAPTER 14

What the Witch Saw

"You saw the murder?"

"Aye. I saw it alright. From my hiding place in the wood bin, near the village oven."

"What did you see? If you saw all, as you say, then tell me all. From the start. And first, tell me how you could see anything, in the dark of night and in a narrow street."

Valon's question seemed to challenge the old woman, who sneered and then answered with even greater determination to tell her tale. "I could see as clear as I needed, Mon Sieur, because it was moon bright. If that may answer your first question," said the hag, mockingly. "No one saw me, but I was not more than a stone's throw from the girl. Oh, Hildegard saw it all," she chided. "Even from this cave, old Hildegard sees more than people think."

"In that case, what did Hildegard see?"

"The girl, Monica. She came into the street and walked past me, but not seeing me at all. She strode a few paces further and out from a doorway stepped the Monster."

"Monster?"

"Yes. He laid hands on the little thing, he did and threw her to the ground with one effort. Then, he fell upon her and did his foul work, first strangling while holding one hand over her mouth, then tearing at her clothing until it was gone. Then he had his way with her. Again, and again."

The old hag began to cackle uncontrollably but soon calmed herself. Never was a laugh more misbegotten.

"Yes, again and again. He was at his work with her for most of an hour. But the little thing was dead long before. Long before," she repeated dolefully. "Yes, dead, or as good as, long before." She shook her head.

"This Monster… So, you saw him clearly?"

"Oh, yes! As clear as I see you now."

"Tell us then. What did you see?"

The witch leaned in and looked side-to-side. Then lowered her voice.

"I saw him do it, Valon. Oh yes, old Hildegard saw what she saw, and no one may say she didn't."

"Old woman, I'll not say that I am prepared to believe all you say, but I am prepared to listen."

The witch's eye squinted, and she dropped her hands.

"It was Lord Ethelred who killed young Monica. And a more savage attack I never saw in my life."

"The Lord!" I exclaimed. "You cannot mean it!"

"Oh, but I do, Abbot Theodulfe, whose mother died in the Spanish Marches at the hands of the Muslims."

"How did you know that about me? About my mother?"

"I know much that my Master tells me. And, I know what I saw that night, Theodulfe, whose father died at the same time. The Moors flogged him to death, did they not, priest?"

"Curse you, witch! You have your knowledge from the Devil, and woe to him who trusts in your knowledge, Hildegard, for how can a man trust the word of Satan himself?"

I was about to give the Witch my pilgrim's staff across her foul back, but Valon stepped forward to stay my hand.

"Knowledge is one thing. Witness is another. I care not what your Master tells you, Hildegard. That is between you and him and, eventually, between you and God. What concerns me is your witness to what you saw. And for that, I said I am prepared to listen, and I am."

Valon's intervention angered me and it even crossed my mind that he was far too amiable toward such as Hildegard. *Was he somehow possessed and even able to deceive me?* I wondered.

Now staring into the night, her cold eyes fixed on some unknown distance, the old woman gave out with another of her satanic incantations, and then, turning to Valon, whispered eerily, "There is more to tell the King of the Franks, who you said is now a protector of witches. One more thing. Yes."

"I am still listening, old woman."

"The Monster had a companion. A most interesting companion, too." She smiled her wicked smile. "As I watched I saw emerge from the shadows, from whence the Monster came, a small man who merely watched. A little man, no more than half my size even. The smallest man I ever saw. And when the Monster finished ravishing the girl and even eaten of her flesh, the little man came forward and said, 'You have finished. Now, we must go.' And with that, he took from his sack a thin rope and put it round the wrist of the Monster, Lord Ethelred, and they walked away together, into the darkness."

"Ah, there was one other thing, which may be of no consequence."

"What was that?" I asked.

"As the companion slipped his rope on the Monster's wrist he took something from his *sacullus* and handed it to him."

"Handed what?" Valon asked.

"Don't know. Could not see. But I remember at the time thinking it was almost as if the Monster was being paid for his good work."

This last set the witch to cackling in the most evil manner.

"Can you describe this companion? You say it was moon bright enough to see Ethelred," Valon questioned.

"Never saw him before, but he was clearly a troll, don't you see? Lord Ethelred was acting according to some control over him by the dwarfs and trolls. The forests hereabouts and to the east are full of them, and I can tell you they are troublesome creatures. Wicked!"

The incredible turn in Hildegard's story hardly seemed to affect Valon, who continued to question as if all was quite as he expected.

"You called Lord Ethelred, 'Monster.' Why do you say that?"

The witch again raised her palms to Valon's face and for a moment closed her eyes. Then opening them wide, she said in a low voice, "His face. That's why. His face! His eyes were the eyes of a monster. I could see only the Monster in his eyes."

Valon showed no emotion, but said, "Now I shall ask you a question that you may find odd but I want you to consider well before answering. You have seen Lord Ethelred in the past. When you saw him then did you see the Monster in his face and eyes, or did he have that appearance only on the night of the murder?"

The witch looked quizzically at Valon for a moment, then closed her eyes, mumbled, and considered to herself. "Oh, it was Ethelred alright—his long red hair—but his face had a different look to it, that night. He had the Monster in his face that night."

"But, not before?"

"No. Not before."

CHAPTER 15

The Word of a Witch?

After parting with Hildegard, we retraced our steps, again led by Draco and our candle bearers. I was pleased to leave the evil hag, whose stench continued to offend, but even more relieved to hear nothing of wolves. As we descended the hill, I wondered what Valon made of the witch's testimony, for he remained silent and utterly absorbed in his own thoughts. As we came once more into the precincts of the Abbey, I could no longer forebear to ask.

"I fully understand what the old woman said, Valon, but do you give it any credence at all? Surely not—the word of a Daughter of Satan himself!"

"I do not judge on the one side or the other just now, Father Abbot. At the moment it is merely useful to have her witness. Of course, what she says is interesting, but I agree with you that she could have no credibility before any trial at law. For now, I merely keep her words in my mind, and test them against all else that we hear."

"Seems a dubious approach to me, Valon. I shall never give the Witch's words any credence at all. She speaks with the voice of another, who is evil. If she says it was Ethelred who did these terrible crimes, it is because the Devil has deemed it in his interest to punish the Lord of Châlons. To me, it is a credit to the character of Ethelred that the voice of Satan wishes to condemn him."

"Indeed, Theodulfe, but the Devil works his mischief in strange and contorted ways. Perhaps he wishes us to disbelieve the witch's testimony so as to protect his child, Ethelred?"

Valon's logic befuddled me, momentarily.

"I found it interesting to hear some of the odd details of Hildegard's story. The dwarf, for example," he continued.

"A minor demon, surely. One of Satan's assistants, guiding the Monster in his outrage. This is clearly a tale of Satan's mischief. Consider. He created a being in the form of the good Lord Ethelred—a mindless and profane brute, who requires one of Satan's assistants—a dwarfish troll perhaps—to guide him in his evil. Do you not see, Valon? The Devil has made a Monster in Ethelred's likeness to do his bidding. His evil."

"What you say, Theodulfe must be taken into account. It seems plausible, indeed, and I do not rule out that we must be constantly on guard that what we are investigating is the direct work of Satan. And, that may be what we report to the Great Charles eventually. But, still, we must reserve our judgment, for we have much to learn."

"Agreed. But I tell you. Either the hag is lying in order to compromise an innocent man whom the Devil hates. Or Satan has made a diabolical twin of Ethelred to do his bidding here."

At this last, Valon stopped and turned to me for a moment, a look in his eye that I could only interpret as fright.

Draco, Bodo, and the brother monks listened intently to our exchange but made no intervention themselves. The talk of Satan's machinations was clearly so disturbing to the simple Draco, however, that he, too, was suddenly seized by inexplicable fear and excused himself abruptly. Overcome, he ran from the Abbey court and toward his church.

"Whatever made Father Draco behave thus?" I asked, wondering if any of the others had a better surmise than my own.

"He is mightily disturbed by these events and such talk, Father Abbot. Draco has a peasant's heart, which means he feels deeply the presence of evil in this case and suffers the fear of it to influence his behaviour," Athalfe replied.

"Aye," said Bodo, "as would any man of good sense. The good Father is right to run to his house and take refuge against the evil that lurks in this village."

At that very moment, a strong wind buffeted us, but only briefly and then was gone. Odd, because there had been no breeze that night.

Valon looked after Draco as he scurried-off. "Or, perhaps frightened by something he'd forgotten but just remembered," he mused to himself.

CHAPTER 16

The Day of Saint Walaric

12 December AD 794

Next morning, we found the monastery in great commotion. Word had arrived from the Convent of Saint Agnes that Lady Céleste, eldest daughter of Lord Ethelred, would return to her father's manor and planned a stop at the monastery before proceeding.

Abbot Hugo told us excitedly of her intention. "The Lady Céleste, though a sister of the convent, is nonetheless a formidable woman, Monsieur. She is intelligent and talented and a woman of an outspoken disposition. There's little doubt she will one day succeed as Prioress at St. Agnes."

"But why should she choose to stop so close to her home?"

"Word is, Monsieur de Valon, that she learned of your presence here and your investigation of the murder at the convent, and so she wishes to meet you and speak."

"From what I've learned, I believe it will be useful to speak to her as well," Valon said. To which I added, "And this decision of hers to seek you out may indicate she has

something to tell. One can hope."

Within three hours, the gates of the monastery swung open to greet Lady Céleste, who traveled with two other sisters and several men-at-arms from her father. A young woman with the fairest, flawless complexion, her dark eyes rivaled those of Valon himself. She held her head high in an imperious way, though she seemed to move with a quiet spirituality. Valon, seeing her from the Abbey steps where we were speaking, fell back slightly on his heels, opened wide his eyes, and lost entirely the train of our conversation. It was a reaction I had not seen in him, and I wondered at it, briefly.

Abbot Hugo rushed to welcome the Lady, betraying no hint of the antipathy that was said to exist between the Abbot and her family. *If such feelings exist, they clearly do not extend to the Lady herself.*

Hugo quickly made the introductions, first to me and then to Valon. I observed from the outset that my young colleague and the Lady seemed to have a natural intimacy. Like characters, I thought.

"I will look forward to an early opportunity to speak at length with your ladyship," Valon said and bowed. Sister Céléste smiled an obvious welcome at the invitation.

Shortly after the midday meal, we sought out the nun in the small but well-made garden that connected the pilgrims' hostel to the Abbey's cloisters. Valon expressed his sadness at the murder of Sister Helena, noting that he knew the Lady Céléste and she had shared a special bond. Céléste seemed moved and now less guarded about Valon's interest. I noted also that the hand which Sister offered on greeting remained in Valon's hand long after, and she made no effort to withdraw it.

"During our investigation at the convent, the Abbot Theodulfe and I learned not only of your close friendship with Sister Helena but we also gathered some additional evidence, most of it perplexing. I hope you will assist us to understand some of this," said Valon.

Sister Céléste's eyes saddened at talk of the murder, but she nonetheless responded readily. "I will gladly tell what I can, Monsieur de Valon. Anything. Anything that can help bring justice to my dear Helena. I will do it."

"As you probably know, Sister Helena was found at the foot of the hill, near the junction with the road to Châlons. And she was probably killed there very early that day. Can you think why she might have been there and at that hour? Anything at all?"

Céléste hesitated, too long I thought. "No, Monsieur. I do not know," she said in a stiff way. I was startled to think that she seemed to be lying. I wondered if Valon saw it too.

Valon frowned in disappointment at the response. "Might she have been there to meet someone, for example?" he pressed.

"I have no reason to think so, Monsieur." Again, her response was stiff and cool.

"No reason? You are sure?"

"Yes, Monsieur," she said, now with emphasis, "I am certain."

Valon looked at me as if to say he doubted the Lady's candor.

"My Lady, during our examination of Sister Helena's chamber we found a small metal bowl with ash in it, perhaps a burned piece of vellum or parchment. Can you suggest what that might have been and why Helena might have burned it?"

"Oh no, Monsieur. I do not know. Burned, you say?" She paused. "I cannot think what that might have been."

"To your knowledge, was your friend upset of late? Did she seem changed in her behaviour, or sad perhaps?" Valon asked.

Céleste sighed faintly as she hesitated. "No, Monsieur de Valon. Helena seemed much the same. I saw no change in her."

Producing an object from his *sacullus*, Valon then asked. "This fine gold ring was also in Sister Helena's chamber. It seemed a strange thing to find in a nun's possessions. Do you know its origins? Have you seen it before, Sister Céleste?"

The sight of the ring, which appeared suddenly from inside Valon's cloak, startled Sister Céleste, but only for a moment. She quickly recovered her poise. "No, Monsieur. No, I have never seen it. Perhaps she had it with her from her former life. Nuns sometimes bring things from home," she ventured.

While she spoke, I noticed something odd. She avoided looking at the ring.

"Yes, I suppose that's it. Perhaps her mother's ring. That must be the explanation," Valon agreed. "Well, my lady, I am grateful to you for your assistance. I can wish you had been able to shed more light on your friend's sad death, but then why should you? 'Twas a catastrophe, and who could see it coming. Not the Prioress, nor anyone else. And now, I am left with very little to proceed on."

"I am saddened to hear that, Monsieur," she said, as Valon once more took her hand. She smiled, just a little, and in an undertone added, "Thank you, Monsieur de Valon. Thank you."

"Well, it is not unusual to reach an impasse in such matters. It would seem that Sister Helena has taken to her grave the reasons she was on the path that morning, and that is the end of it.

"Still, if you should remember anything of these questions I have asked, I encourage you to tell me as soon as possible. Time is often a factor in finding a solution in such matters as this."

"Oh, yes, Monsieur. I certainly will."

Valon caressed the Lady's hand as she departed.

When she had entered the hostel, I said, "Valon, I hesitate to say it, but I do not believe she was telling all she knows of this matter. In every answer, she gave I saw hesitation on her face. If she was not lying, at least she held back the truth."

"Of course, you are right, Theodulfe. Sister Céleste is a terrible liar. She was not only lying, but she was also saddened by my questions and what she knew of the truth. She wanted to assist, but for some reason could not. That is what I saw. And that makes me curious. She is hiding something, and we must find it."

"But how? We cannot force her."

"No, but we can remind her as often as possible, that she wishes to help us if only she would. Who knows? She may change her mind, and we must be there to help her when she does.

"And there is another thing."

"What?"

"The ring. This little gold band means something to her. She recognized it. She was surprised to find it in Sister Helena's possession, however. And I believe she knows, or at least suspects, how Sister Helena came by it. We will hope to persuade her to tell us that, in particular. I suspect it is the key to this murder, and perhaps to all the murders we are here to investigate."

"And what of Sister Helena in the meantime?"

"Nothing, I'm afraid. I was being candid when I said we are at an impasse, except for what Sister Céleste may tell us. So, for now, we must divert our attention to the tragedies here in Châlons, which may be linked, somehow, to the murder of the young nun. I cannot see how, but I do not accept the coincidence of so many murders of young girls and a young nun. There is a connection, and we must find it."

"I wonder if something might be gained in that regard by accepting the invitation given us by the Jew, Mathias. Recall his note that Brother Boethius delivered," I said.

"Indeed, I do, and I am thinking your very thoughts, Father Abbot. I've sent Boethius to tell the Jew we will wait upon him this evening, at the seventh hour."

"What do you imagine the Jew will tell us?"

"Why, Theodulfe, I thought you knew. He is going to tell us the name of the murderer."

CHAPTER 17

What Mathias Told

The Jew's house stood midway in a street of merchant houses and their warehouses, all squeezed together. Most were as drab as the warehouses, and the house of Mathias of Tours seemed in especial disrepair. A broken shutter hung precariously by a single nail, while stones fallen from their mortar and street debris littered the entrance. Valon pointed to the *mezuzah* on the doorpost —the sign of a Jew's house.

We knocked and announced ourselves to a servant who seemed reluctant to open the door but finally beckoned us to enter. Once inside, I discovered a far different abode. The exterior of Mathias' house expressed a calculated message of poverty and shabbiness, whereas the interior told a story of wealth and refinement, including fine furniture, tapestries of silk, ornaments of gold and silver, all resting upon carpets from the East of splendid design and manufacture.

Mathias lives outward penury and inward luxury. He undoubtedly has purchased this life at the cost of interest charged to Christians by the sin of usury and by demanding excessive profits for the grains he buys and sells.

"Greetings, My Lord Valon. Father Abbot. Twice and thrice greetings and welcome to my poor house. Won't you be seated?" He motioned us to several finely cushioned chairs in the room nearest the front. "Please. Please."

We turned with a start to see behind us the same wizened little man we'd encountered at the flogging, only now dressed in a robe of finest silk.

Once seated and served an unusual herbal drink, Valon spoke. "We have your note, Mathias, and are eager to hear what you have to tell that may be useful to us, as you have said."

"Yes, well I can offer some information, Monsieur de Valon, only that. It is for you to make of it as you please and as you may, of course."

"And that is?" Valon followed quickly, though with no hint of irritation in his voice.

"Allow me to be candid in advance of what I must say, Monsieur. I have observed the terrible events in Châlons with a mixture of curiosity and fear.

Curious, because I wish to know, as any righteous man would, who could do such terrible things. And fear, because, at the beginning of the murders, more than one townsman whispered that it must have been done by 'the Jews.' I know too well where that sort of loose talk can lead. I barred my doors twice in those days, I can tell you.

"I've taken an interest in these events, as you might imagine. And, I know that almost everyone in the town has come to believe that the murders were done by Lord Ethelred himself, or perhaps by him and his loathsome son, the One-eyed ogre whom you have met."

"Yes. So we understand," Valon agreed, without emotion.

"I do not share that belief, and that is why I have asked you here. I believe you seek justice, Monsieur, and I do as well. Though I have no regard at all for Lord Ethelred and his family, I say he is not the murderer you seek."

"And how do you come by this conviction? Valon asked.

Mathias responded quickly, just a little flustered. "I have evidence that the crimes, or at least one of the crimes—was done by another. That is how I know."

Valon shifted in his chair, as Mathias walked to a small wooden box on the nearby table and took from it an object that at first, I could not identify. He handed it to Valon, and then said, "It's a small wooden cross, My Lord, of the kind worn by all the monks of St. Benoît du Lac, except for the Abbot, whose cross is much larger and more ornate."

"Yes. What of it?" I asked, not liking where he was going.

"It was found in the hand of one of the dead girls. Taken from her frozen hand by her father and given to me. The man who has done some work for me asked my advice what to do with it. I bid him give it to me and keep his silence, and he has."

I was outraged at the suggestion. The Jew was clearly pointing his finger of suspicion at one of the monks of St. Benoît, a heinous accusation. And yet, Valon seemed not the least disturbed.

"Is this father prepared to say the same to me?" Valon asked.

"If you require it, Monsieur, though you can understand his reluctance. He is easily intimidated by what the object implies. And yet he wishes his daughter's murderer to be punished."

"Well, this is an interesting object, but it proves very little. The girl might have found it. She might have been carrying it herself, as a talisman against evil perhaps, when she was attacked. It proves nothing, in itself."

"As you say, My Lord Valon, but I have more to offer."

"More? What, pray?"

"A less dramatic piece of the puzzle, but one that at least coincides with the cross. And in this evidence, I must beg a measure of forbearance on your part, Monsieur."

"You have it if it is useful to our investigation." Valon leaned forward.

Mathias paused a moment, obviously collecting his thoughts, but also perhaps having one last bout of indecision about telling what he was about to relate.

"I have some dealings, Monsieur, with a man of the neighborhood who is thought to be a well-known bandit. In fact, he is a criminal whose enterprises extend well beyond robbery upon the roads."

"I see. No wonder your need of forbearance, then," I said.

Mathias hardly paused and kept his gaze upon Valon. "I have it from this man that he was approached by one of his associates, a colleague in one of his criminal activities, you see, who testified to him that Abbot Hugo hired one of his own band to kill a girl of the village and to make it look as if Ethelred had done the crime, to make it look that Lord Ethelred was the murderer."

Valon's jaw tightened.

"So you believe the Abbot is the villain behind the murders and intends to blame Ethelred. But why? Why would he do such a thing?"

"The disputed lands, of course! It is well known Monsieur, the Abbot, and Lord Ethelred have disputed the late Lord's bequest of land to the Abbey these many years. And it is also known that the Lord is pressing his case, which is believed to be a strong one. The Abbot has good reason to wish to discredit and remove Ethelred, for that would assure his victory in the suit, don't you see."

"That may be so, but your evidence is far from proving that he encouraged brutal murders to accomplish that purpose. What you say is suggestive, but hardly proof. And you offer the evidence of a criminal to support it." I added.

"I know that My Lord, and so I offer it in private and for what value you may find in it. But there is one other thing you may hold in mind."

"Oh?" I said.

"The Abbot Hugo. He is personally engaged, Monsieur. Because of his family."

"I don't understand."

"Abbot Hugo comes of a family to the north. A noble family—he is a younger son and so was fitted for the Church—a family, you see, that finds itself an enemy of Lord Ethelred."

Valon shifted again in his chair but said nothing.

"The animus goes back to events of an earlier generation, even before Ethelred's father, but the bad blood has persisted for decades, and the two families hate each other. In the present generation, there has been a suit at law over the right to control a bridge across the Marne some distance from here. It is a matter of collecting a toll, you see. The matter has dragged on in the courts for some time, and that has only estranged the families the greater. So, you see, the Abbot Hugo is personally interested in the ruin of Lord Ethelred and his family."

Valon and I exchanged glances.

"And then...well, then for what value it may be to you."

"Yes," Valon encouraged.

"It is known that Abbot Hugo has at least one friend in Ethelred's family, and perhaps an ally."

"Oh?" I asked.

"Yes. Lord Humphrey so has long wished to enter the monastery. Hugo has encouraged this vocation. And Ethelred opposes it. They say, in fact, that Ethelred detests that his second son, who might well succeed him because Lord Godfrey is so infirm, should become a monk in Hugo's charge." Having said all this, the Jew leaned back in his chair with a knowing look.

Once in the street and well beyond Mathias's hearing, Valon spoke his mind about all we'd heard.

"I cannot know why Mathias of Tours might want to cast suspicion upon the Abbey, but he certainly has. And, if what he says is true, it is at least cause for us to broaden our own suspicions, it seems to me."

"But, what can one believe of a Jew?" I observed. "One cannot trust a Jew, and we dare not take him seriously when he casts suspicion upon the Church, Valon. Jews are enemies of Christ's Church and will do whatever is possible to injure it. The man should be flogged. Surely, we should give him no credence at all! A Jew!"

Valon made no reply.

CHAPTER 18

The Day of Saint Lucy
13 December AD 794

Next day, while the brother monks and I observed the hours of the Benedictines of Saint Benoît, Valon and the soldiers kept to a different discipline, and we did not see them until breakfast next morning, after Lauds. I was uncertain what we would do next but soon found Valon had charted our course with great precision. That entire day he wandered about the Abbey, looking into every cranny, and more important, asking questions of anyone who would answer. I assumed he was following up on what the Jew told us, but what else?

Just after Compline, I saw him again, but only briefly, and what he conveyed was of the first importance.

"In the past days, Theodulfe, I have become convinced that the solution to this problem lies not here at the monastery, but rather at the manor of Lord Ethelred. That is why I have sent word through one of the brother monks that we seek accommodation there, beginning tomorrow."

Valon's decision without consulting me annoyed me, but I stifled my anger because I approved that he was shifting his gaze away from the Monastery and the Chruch.

"If Ethelred is associated in these crimes, as many suspect, might he not refuse us? Might he not wish to keep us at a distance?"

"Yes. He might be so inclined, but he cannot refuse the Missi Dominici. To refuse us is to refuse the Great Charles himself, and no lord of the manor in Charlemagne's realm would dare do that."

"Yes, of course. I sometimes forget our authority."

"That is because you retain much of the humble priest, dear Theodulfe, though you are now an abbot and a Missi Dominici."

As we spoke thus, one of the brother monks approached, handing Valon a small piece of parchment. He unfolded it and read, his face expressionless as he did so. Refolding the scrap, he placed it inside his tunic.

"I must meet Sister Céleste, who asks me to come alone. Perhaps she wishes to tell what she knows, or a part of it, even sooner than I had hoped."

"I will go with you, Valon. We should both hear her out."

"We should, but that may prevent her from speaking freely. No, best we meet alone as she demands."

I did not like to see Valon meet Sister Céleste alone. The looks exchanged between them earlier made me mindful of Sister Céleste's situation as a *religieuse*, and I thought it quite improper that the two should meet alone and at night. Still, Valon's insistence that more was to be gained from meeting alone seemed valid, so I put aside my concerns and about Valon's immortal soul. As he departed, I decided to spend his absence in prayer for the two, trusting the power of prayer to stand between them and their sinful inclinations. *Deus conservare sine paccato.*

Valon told me later what transpired as my prayers that God preserves them from evil lifted to Heaven. Valon made his way quietly through the cloisters garden to a small rough door in the north wall of the monastery, which opened into an orchard. Sister Céleste's note told him to expect to find her just beyond the gate and among the nearest trees. He lighted his way with a small candle, which in the dark of the night did little good.

"Sister. Sister," he whispered, as he closed the door behind him.

Almost as soon as he uttered her name, there came a rustling in the leaves among the nearby trees.

"My Lady, is that you?" he whispered in the direction of the noise.

At the moment he expected a reply there came a terrible stink, almost as of a rotting corpse, though more terrible, he later told me, than any stench he had known on the battlefield. He recoiled at the putridness of it and immediately sensed danger, but at that moment he was set upon from behind by a fierce attacker. Two muscular arms encircled his neck, both jerking in such a way as to break it. At the same time, whatever the attacker was, he had climbed onto Valon's back and locked his legs around his waist. Valon fell backward to the ground, so as to crush the attacker and dislodge his grip, but without success. The choking grip persisted and even tightened.

Now drawing a small knife from his censure, Valon moved to thrust it into the leg of his attacker, but at that moment a terrible blow landed upon his head, knocking him almost senseless. Lights flashed and flickered across his vision. The blow had come from another attacker, this one at his front, and so Valon struck out from the ground with his feet and felt himself connect with a kick to whoever had stuck him. The kick landed with authority, for the second attacker let out a howl. Still, Valon was dazed, and worse, he dropped his knife.

Meanwhile, the choking attacker who still held Valon on the ground with arms about his neck showed no sign of relaxing his grip. Feeling a rock at his right hand, Valon seized it and imagining the place to strike, brought it back swiftly, hoping to connect with the attacker's head. He did and the effect of the blow was to cause the attacker's arms to relax just a little so that Valon was able to slip away.

As he did, however, the second attacker recovered and delivered another blow, apparently with a cudgel. The strike narrowly missed Valon's neck but landed upon his shoulder with such force that he fell back against the wall door.

Suddenly, the door opened and two hands from inside grabbed him and pulled him backward, while at the same time closing and latching the door against the pursuing attackers. Bleeding from the blow to his head and suffering from the sharp pain in his shoulder, Valon turned and fell into the arms of his savior.

Even in the dark and half-conscious, he could see it was the mute slave girl. One arm around his waist, his arm over her shoulder, she pulled him slowly through the cloisters. Both staggered forward, making their way— Valon in and out of consciousness—to the main steps, where both fell into the arms of one of the brother monks.

"Father Abbot! Father Abbot!" Boethius called excitedly, as he ran toward me in the refectory. *"Father Abbot, Monsieur de Valon is injured! It's Monsieur de Valon!"*

"Injured! Where?"

"At the main steps. Just beyond the doors."

I hurried to the entrance and there found several monks already gathered, some holding candles to light what they were observing on the steps. Valon lay there bleeding from his head, as he drifted in and out of consciousness and uttered senseless phrases about "the stink" and "arms."

Very quickly the Brother Apothecary arrived to treat the bleeding wound, just behind Valon's right ear. Not waiting for Abbot Hugo, I ordered Valon to be taken to the infirmary, where he could be better cared for. Several of the monks lifted and carried him as the Apothecary directed. The slave girl, meanwhile, seemed to have disappeared.

Martin, Boethius, and I began our prayers immediately at Valon's bedside, kneeling and repeating first the Litany of All the Saints. Our vigil commenced at the time of Matins and continued until Lauds. In the meantime, the brother Apothecary administered herbs and maintained a damp cloth upon Valon's forehead. When once I looked up from our prayers, I noticed that the slave girl had somehow slipped into the infirmary and sat on the floor in a dark corner, her eyes closed.

The Apothecary's methods interested me, such that I suspended our prayers for the moment and inquired about his formulae.

"The wound at his head, Father Abbot, must be bathed first in vinegar, from our apples. Then, it is my practice to dress every wound in a poultice of my own concoction."

"A concoction?" I asked, hoping to hear more of it.

"Indeed, Father Abbot. It is one that I have from the ancients, but one also that I have used myself on the battlefields of the Frisian War when I was a soldier. Treat the wound with a combination of myrrh, yarrow, henbane, and hemlock—all crushed and mixed in the poultice."

"And the stones you have placed on Monsieur de Valon? What are they?"

"Yes. I also have it from the ancients that a smooth, warm stone placed upon the thighs, shoulders, and forehead may draw out the evil humors. I have read it in the philosophy of Theodosius of Antioch that such stones were used with great success by the noted Roman physician Publius Livi in the first century before our Lord's birth. The stones themselves came to me from an eastern healer who had traveled much in Persia, Father Abbot, and so they possess special properties, have no doubt of it."

"I see. Publius Livi, you say?"

By mid-morning, Valon regained full consciousness, though he lingered in pain about his head for the remainder of that day and much of the next. While he kept to his cot, the brother monks and I maintained our vigil and the repetition of our prayers for Valon's recovery. And in all this time the slave girl made no sound and did not stir from her corner. Her behavior seemed to me most strange, more like that of a loyal dog than a human. And as I contemplated how she had rushed to Valon's rescue against his attackers, I laughed to myself that she was certainly a wolfhound.

Finally, after several hours, I saw in Valon's eyes full recognition of me and the brother monks.

"You have had a narrow escape, Piers de Valon."

"Yes. Escape. I remember my escape. Saved by the garden door. And Pepin...closed it. Pepin saved me."

I glanced to the corner, where the girl made no gesture of hearing what Valon said.

Then Valon told us the story of his struggle that night, in the orchard. He spoke what he knew of the attackers, one very large and the other small, but very strong. He spoke of the arms around his neck, from which there seemed no escape, and of the blows delivered unexpectedly by the accomplice. And then he told us of the stink—the putrid odor that preceded the attack and seemed to attach to the small attacker.

"It was God's will that you should live, Valon. His will preserved your life."

"I believe it, Theodulfe. I do indeed. And it was He who caused Pepin to follow me and help me. I know that, too."

And with those words—the first he'd spoken clearly in two days—Valon rose slightly on his cot and looked at the girl, who sat motionless and oblivious in her corner. Then his head fell once more upon his pillow and he slipped into a long sleep, from which he did not awaken until next morning.

CHAPTER 19

We Are Unwelcome at the Manor

Within the hour after breakfast next morning we took our leave of the good Benedictines of the Abbey and joined Sister Céleste and her entourage. We proceeded southeast through the town and toward the opposing hills, on the highest of which stood the great Manor of Châlons et Passey. Valon, not quite recovered from his ordeal, said nothing to Céleste about the events in the orchard, nor about the message that had taken him there. In fact, they rode side-by-side in silence, his long black hair now covering the wound that almost killed him. Behind him rode the slave girl on her donkey, still seemingly oblivious to events, and the brother monks, Bodo, and Athalfe, behind her.

In less than an hour, we came in clear view of the Lord Ethelred's Manor. It was not a manor house at all, by the standards of our own day, but rather a fortress, whose forbidding grey mass seemed to rise out of the surrounding forest, almost as a lifting fog. As we drew closer, its eerie grayness seemed to darken. It had no great battlements but featured a tower at one corner that ascended three storeys above the main block. In the mist of a dark winter morning, Ethelred's fortress seemed to show disdain for all that lay beyond it and I thought as we proceeded up the hill that it signaled a sort of calculated arrogance.

The road up to the manor turned off from a path that joined the village high street at a distance of no more than a hundred yards from the town's outermost buildings. The manor itself sat no more than half a league, if that, from Châlons and was situated high enough upon the hillside that it was visible from many parts of the town.

Lord Ethelred's freeman Steward, Dagbert, met us at the gate and escorted us through the inner court to the great steps and doors of the Lord's hall. At the entrance stood Ethelred and his entire family. Preceded by the Lady Céleste, whose return clearly delighted her father, each of the family greeted us in the most formal way. When the formalities had concluded and we were shown to our chambers, I imagined that I had never received a cooler reception in any house I had stayed. Ethelred and his kin were not pleased to accommodate us, but as Valon supposed, felt obliged to do so because they dared not affront the Great Charles.

More important perhaps, much of the time during the greetings Ethelred had a vacant look in his eyes. *Evidence, perhaps, that the Bishop's description of his failing mind is accurate.*

That afternoon, Valon took the soldiers and the brother monks aside to give them special instructions concerning our stay at the manor. I learned later from Brother Martin that they were told to insinuate themselves particularly into the lives of the Manor's staff and servants to learn from them what they could. Bodo and Athalfe, in particular, were to mix with the men-at-arms, a large number of whom seemed to stand constant guard about the house.

In that first afternoon, only Céleste seemed to welcome our stay. The others ignored us, until gathering for dinner made that no longer possible.

I once noticed Valon and Céleste together on a bench in the precincts of the great hall, where Valon's hand touched the Lady's folded hands as they spoke. Another time that afternoon, Brother Martin and I saw the two of them in the great court of the manor, walking slowly and closely in the direction of the garden. I preferred to tell myself that Valon was continuing his effort to glean valuable information of Céleste, for we had agreed that she had withheld from us in our first interview. But I continued to worry that young Valon had developed an unhealthy attraction to the beautiful lady and that she was attracted to him. *No good can come of this.* As I waited for them to return, a presentiment of death came over me.

CHAPTER 20

A Miserable Family

The great hall of Lord Ethelred's fortress manor house served as a dining hall as well. As we entered, I observed a large fire pit at its center where large logs tossed upon an iron grate burned warm and bright. Smoke ascended through a generous hole in the roof and blackened the ceiling.

Valon and I came down the great stairs together and found the lord's family already gathered to greet us. The exchange was correct but reserved. *Were they merely on their guard at strange agents of the Great Charles, or were they concealing something?*

Father Draco was in our company, as was Dagbert, the Steward. There were several near the table whom I could not identify and who had not been introduced upon our arrival —a young man afflicted with the hunchback condition and another, rather handsome, lad dressed all in black. I learned in due course that the elder was Godfrey, the Lord's eldest and heir. The next son was Humphrey, the son who Father Draco said was called Humphrey the Pious, because of his intention to enter the monastery.

The giant, Guillaume, we had already met. According to Draco, he was accounted his father's favorite, even though he was the third son and unlikely ever to succeed. The last was called Mordune the Poet because he was widely noted as a writer of beautiful verses and songs. Dressed all in velvet and furs, Mordune wore about his neck a scarf of the purest white silk, and upon it, there was made all in fine needlework the image of a strange creature—what is called a *monkee*. Mordune held the hand of his twin, Céleste, to whom he was said to be devoted.

As we waited for Lord Ethelred to arrive, Valon and I engaged Father Draco to one side of the great stair.

"I am curious, Brother. Mordune seems a very popular man and the only one of the family, except Céleste, who is the least gay and happy," I said.

"That is so, Father Abbot. He is popular with everyone and is unfailingly in good humor."

"And what of young Humphrey—his desire to become a monk?"

"No one is certain, Father Abbot, but it is said his father will not hear of it. Some of the townsmen say that Humphrey hates his father because of the Lord's opposition, but I do not know that to be true."

"I see. And does Humphrey hold himself apart from marriage in the continued hope of becoming a monk?" Valon asked, now listening more intently to our conversation.

"Oh, yes, Monsieur, but his pious nature makes him greatly reserved. Of the entire family, only the Lady Céleste and young Mordune are popular with the townsmen and tenants. And, as fraternal twins they are, of course, very close to one another. The other—the One-eyed—is regarded as a scourge in the countryside."

"And do Guillaume's crimes extend to rape?" Valon pressed—his dark eyes narrowed and intense—as the question made Draco uncomfortable.

"Yes, sadly," he answered, looking down to avoid Valon's gaze. "And more often than is common elsewhere. Sadly, his father does not restrain him, and I cannot. Believe me, I have tried, but the power of the Church and regard for his own eternal soul does not move him. Humphrey, who is called The Pious because of his love of Our Lord, is unable to influence him to the good, though he has tried also."

"And the Lord's other daughters, the ladies Ann-Marie and Gertrude?" I asked.

Draco demurred. "I'll say little about them, if you please, Father Abbot, except to note that both are known to enjoy the company of men."

"As you wish, Draco, but tell me more about Godfrey the Hunchback. You do not describe him as popular with the people."

"Godfrey is a morose and bitter man, Monsieur. He has been dispirited since his youth and is reclusive in the extreme. Perhaps it is because of his deformity and his misshapen face, which seems distorted by pain into a perpetual scowl. He is seldom seen by the townsmen." Draco leaned in even closer. "He keeps to the manor and here to his chamber," he said, casting an eye to either side and his voice hushed, "where many believe he practices the forbidden arts. Perhaps that's why he wears only black—the color that is loved by The Evil One."

"And what of relations between Lord Ethelred and his successor?"

"Ah, well you should ask that, Monsieur, for it is a topic of near-constant talk in the neighborhood. Lord Ethelred makes no mystery of his disdain for Godfrey. He laments that he will be succeeded by a weakling, who has never trained in the arts of the warrior and who is unlikely to produce an heir. Ethelred jokes openly about Godfrey's hump, and meanwhile, he makes no secret that he favors Guillaume, who is as much like his father as any son could be."

"But, why is Humphrey not his favorite then? After all, he is the second son and next in line."

Draco again looked at pains to answer, clearly wishing to withhold but unable to do so.

"It is a complicated thing, Monsieur de Valon, and I would not know of it except by the confidentiality of the confessional. So, you will understand that I cannot answer candidly. But I will say this, which is no secret to anyone. Ethelred hates his second son, and the feeling is returned on two accounts. Humphrey wishes with all his heart to go into the Monastery of Saint Benoît and to follow the discipline of the monk, and his father has set his face against this, because he detests the monastery and its Abbot on account of their suit at law, and because he has vowed that he will lose no other child to the Church. Then too, Lord Ethelred regards his son's love of the Church a sign of weakness. Ethelred's mind cares only for the affairs of the warrior and preparations for war—things that interest Humphrey very little. And so, Ethelred considers him a disgrace to the line."

"That leaves only the Lord Mordune," I said. "What then of his relations with Ethelred? Is he also at odds with his father?"

The lines in Draco's brow deepened; his eyes narrowed. "All seems well between them on the surface, Father Abbot, no bad blood so you would notice it and no one speaks of a strain, and yet ..." He stopped himself short, hesitating to finish his thought.

"And yet, there is a gulf between them, also," I pressed.

Draco's face grew long, as he considered a moment. "There is something that troubles…at least, I believe there is ..."

"Oh; what then? Be clear with us, Draco," said Valon, in a stern voice.

"I have it from Lady Céleste, who loves her brother dearly and is distressed by it, that Mordune is indeed troubled in his relations with Lord Ethelred for another reason entirely. You see, Mordune shares the suspicion of many in the village that his beloved mother, the Lady Editha, was murdered by his father. According to Céleste, he is tortured by such suspicions. He is of a sensitive disposition, you see, and it pains him to believe such a thing of anyone."

At these terrible words, I crossed myself.

"And does Mordune have cause to believe such a thing? What do you know of it?" Valon asked.

"Not that I know, Monsieur, but then what do I know?" Draco's replied evasively and with a shrug of his shoulders and uplifted eyes. "I only know Mordune's suspicion and that because I have it in confidence from Lady Céleste, who is disturbed by it. Mordune suspects his father killed the Lady Editha, or as good as because Ethelred is besotted with his young cousin and wishes to marry her. He could not have her while his wife lived, and since her death, Lord Ethelred has made a contract of marriage with the young woman—a daughter of the Comte de Meaux. Aside from his warrior skills, it is the only thing he seems to think of, according to Céleste."

"I see," Valon said, considering all he had heard. He might have questioned further, except that we were suddenly called to table by the Steward, who announced the arrival of Lord Ethelred. He and his children wore the same long faces as at our arrival, and though his greeting to us was proper, it was only that—proper. Once seated and served our ample provisions of viande and bread, Ethelred rose to speak.

He was dressed in greater finery than at our first encounter in the square. His robes were of fine linen and silk, embroidered with intricate designs of animals, plants, and mythical beasts. Still, upon his wrists, he wore the brass-studded leathers.

Now, as he stood, I was able to study his features and stature more completely. His head was large and his face round, with pronounced jowls, squinting eyes, and a flat nose with large nostrils. He held himself erect, his broad shoulders square, his feet apart, and his fists upon his hips.

"I cannot say I am surprised at your arrival, Monsieur and Father Abbot," he roared, a scowl across his face, "for the recent tragedies in our territory have sickened everyone. And mark you well that I know what the folk say about me in all this."

"And what is that, my Lord?" Valon asked as if he had not already heard.

"The peasants and freemen say that *I*—I, their Lord, mind you!—that *I* am the murderer! How they have come to this wild speculation is beyond me, but I can tell you it is entirely the invention of some who would poison relations between me and my people." He looked at the Father Draco.

Then, briefly, he seemed to drift, apparently losing entirely the train of what he was saying and stammering to find it.

As Ethelred spoke, I observed how red-faced he became, how boldly the vessels on his forehead and neck stood out, and how the word "murderer" rolled from his tongue.

"It's the damned witch, Hildegard, father," Guillaume said vehemently, now also on his feet. "May Our Lord damn her to the Hell that belongs to her Master!"

"That may be, and I do not discount what we have learned of old Hildegard's ravings. But it is possible that she's put up to such lies by others, who are both saner and eviler," Ethelred offered, a wolfish grin on his face.

"Who might that be?" I asked. "We are here to learn what we can of such things, and I assure you that we prejudge nothing."

Lord Ethelred hesitated to answer, and again began to drift, so Guillaume rushed to respond.

"The Master of lies in this, Monsieur, is the Abbot of Saint Benoît du Lac, and his own Master, Bishop Ambrose. They hate my father and us because we have beaten them off at every turn as they try to rob us of our domains in Passey. What they could not gain at law they have sought to gain by the foulest of ways. By seeding hatred between the people and my father."

I expected Father Draco to rise and depart, but he sat motionless, listening placidly to the terrible accusations and seemingly unconcerned by them. Instead, it was the Lady Céleste who rose, with her companion nuns, and left the hall.

Valon rose to the assertion, as he watched the Lady depart.

"My Lord, do you charge then that Father Abbot and his Bishop are guilty of the murders, all as a pretext to undermine you and win their dispute with you?"

"Or, perhaps to avenge themselves on us, Monsieur," The One-eyed intervened, "for our successes at law. That is what I believe," he growled as he swilled his wine and took another bite of lamb joint he held continuously as he spoke.

Ethelred then answered. "I myself do not charge that, Monsieur, though my sons may speak as they wish. I tell you this, however. In all my fifty-six years on this earth, I have never wavered in my faith nor in my support of the Church. But these local churchmen have come between me and my people and I cannot tolerate that. I cannot forgive them for that! Surely King Charles will see that! I ask you, would he tolerate that?"

"We are not here to decide the issues between you and the Church, my Lord. That is for the King's justice. Father Abbot and I are sent by the Great Charles to inquire into the tragic deaths in the village, and now perhaps the tragic death of a young nun. But we take what you say into account."

In all of our heated dialogue, Godfrey remained silent and inattentive. In fact, he seemed rather not to hear at all, but to be thinking other thoughts entirely. Though Humphrey also remained silent, his eyes focused in a keen interest in what was said, and his face betrayed a pained expression at his father's charges against the monastery and bishop. It seemed to me that he might have disagreed and even joined the departure of his sister, except that he dared not offend his father.

Still, this second son made a strange impression. Dressed in robes and a cowl, like those of a monk, he prefers to affront his father by his clothing rather than by his speech.

As the air cleared and Ethelred sat once more to table, there came into the great hall a little dog, of no particular breed that I could tell. It ran up to Mordune to greet him and the young man took from his plate a piece of meat to give it. But first he demanded the little dog perform, and the creature rose up on its hind legs and began to spin and dance delightfully. Then, the little dog was told to, "Speak," and it barked its plea for the meat. *What a marvelous thing that Mordune should have trained the dog thus.* Draco shouted, "hear, hear!" with the delight that we all felt. Then did we all.

"My Lord Mordune, you have a calling as a teacher of animals," Valon commended—a happy assertion that brought a smile to every face—well, not quite every face, but most. *Neither Ethelred nor his three eldest sons have any taste for laughter and seem even angrier now than they had appeared at the outset.*

"Ah, if only humans were as easily trained," Mordune replied, with a wry smile. Guillaume laughed heartily and added, "Aye, brother. The peasants would be much easier to manage."

I could not help but observe as well how closely the claims of Ethelred concerning the Abbey coincided with those of the Jew, Mathias. My suspicions aroused, I began to consider if Mathias might be somehow in the employ of Lord Ethelred.

As we rose from the table, Bodo came into the great hall and spoke into Valon's ear. The two moved aside, where they whispered some minutes. I did not know what was afoot then, but I learned later that Bodo had learned something interesting from his mixing with the servants and men-at-arms and he reported quickly to Valon.

"What is it?" I asked as Bodo departed.

"Bodo says the Lady Céleste is close to only one of her brothers—her twin, Mordune—and that Mordune and Father Draco are quite close. In fact, the servants say Mordune is estranged from his other brothers. This is a fascinating family, Theodulfe. It will pay us to learn more about their inner workings, I believe."

I agreed though I could not imagine what such knowledge could have to do with the vile murders of young girls. Surely the Lord Ethelred's family seethed with ill-feeling and even hatred, but such emotions are not uncommon, especially in the families of the powerful. And yet, they do not produce a succession of murders that could only be the work of a madman.

As we stood by, the little dog suddenly bolted into the great hall and ran up to Mordune, his master. The young man immediately began to pet the little dog and then to give a series of commands that caused the creature to perform even more of the most amazing tricks. He could sit, roll, stand on his hind legs, and jump on command. In fact, the little creature was capable of doing the most entertaining dance, on command. When the entertainment was finished, the dog jumped into his master's arms, and the two made their bow.

We applauded and shouted our approval, and thanked Mordune and his friend for the performance. The two gave a pleasant end to a dinner that had been generally very unpleasant.

And yet, while everyone smiled their approval, Valon showed no glee at the performance. His face was curiously expressionless, though somehow burdened with thoughts. And after, I heard him utter only one word. "Interesting."

Just as Father Draco finished his evening prayer to bid the Lord and his family a good sleep, the Freeman Dagbert burst into the hall, breathless, his face full of news.

"My Lord!" he erupted, "I'm told there's a body hanging from a tree at the edge of the town!"

CHAPTER 21

The Hanging Corpse

We soon arrived at a large oak standing on the main road to the west, midway between town and the Manor. Leafless now in winter's cold, it served as a landmark to the local folk. As we approached, we saw a number of townsfolk holding torches, brightly illuminating the base of the giant. And there, hanging from a large, low limb—the body of a woman. Only when we arrived beneath the awful tree and stood for the longest moment looking up at the naked, bloodied creature who hung before us like the carcass of a sheep, did I know it was Hildegard!

Father Draco ordered the corpse to be lowered, but Valon intervened.

"No. Do not touch her."

"But, Monsieur, she must be lowered and given Extreme Unction," Draco protested.

"In good time, Father. For now, she is clearly dead and beyond the power of the Last Rites. For now, she must be left where she is, that she may tell me all she can of who murdered her."

Draco's mouth fell, incredulous. "But, as you say, Monsieur; she is dead. She can tell nothing."

Valon merely smiled faintly, then turned the body gently around, revealing a small wooden placard, which hung from about the old woman's neck by a thin cord. As Bodo held high his torch, I read its terrible message:

MELEFISCO NON PATIERIS ViVERE

"My lord Valon, what does it say?" Bodo asked, crossing himself.

"It is the judgment that every witch dreads from the Book of Exodus. *'Thou shall not suffer a witch to live.'*"

Bodo crossed himself again, as did most of the townsfolk who heard Valon's translation.

Valon, meanwhile, kept his gaze upon the hanging corpse, which he now examined closely. "Bodo, hold high your torch," he ordered, and he looked for a long while at everything, including the old woman's hands, the soles of her bare feet, and the wounds on her legs and torso.

The witch had not been hanging long. Her corpse continued to drip blood into a considerable puddle on the ground below. Her body had suffered awful abuse, which made me want alternatively to look and to turn away. Her shift had been torn away, showing that her breasts had been cut and one removed. Her gut had been opened as well, for entrails dangled a bit from their cavity. And, most disturbing, her eyes had been gouged from their sockets, though both remained attached.

Valon commanded Bodo to, "Take her down," even as he continued to examine the cord by which Hildegard was hanged and, for some strange reason, particularly the knot. *A strange man, my companion.*

"It is the hands of a corpse that often tell most about the moment of death, Theodulfe," he explained, noticing my interest in his examination. Taking his dagger from its sheath he used the point to scrape from under the witch's fingernails something, I did not know what. Still, what he found by this strange means seemed to interest him greatly, as he held it on the point of his dagger up to the light of Bodo's torch.

"Yes, this is most interesting, indeed," I heard him say quietly, more to himself than others.

"What is, pray?" I asked, still half-distrusting that anything of value could be found by such means. "Surely the witch has been killed by the local folk, who wish to rid their region of evil."

He said nothing but merely continued his strange examination, to the interest of all who watched. In ten minutes time, he finished, and then said to Draco, "You may perform your ritual."

As the priest knelt beside the body at the roadside, lighted by several torches, the townsmen knelt also and began to pray, as if the witch were a valued member of the town. Draco took from his cloak's pocket the holy water, ointments and other articles required for Extreme Unction, and the rite began.

Valon moved to one side and observed the prayers, or rather he observed the people at prayers. I noticed that in all the commotion, Lord Ethelred and his family stood apart, too, watching from a distance. When Draco finished his ritual, he asked, "Who will take the old woman, prepare her, and see to it that she has a proper burial? She cannot be buried in consecrated ground, of course, so it must be done in the forest."

The question provoked some grumbling, no one came forward, and many stepped back. Finally, there came from the back of the onlookers a man dressed in some finery—a familiar face.

"I will see that she is prepared and buried," he said, with remarkable authority. And with that, he gave orders to some who were clearly his workmen to remove the body to the town.

It was Mathias of Tours, the grain merchant. So it's the Jew who takes mercy on the other outcast, or is it that Hildegard and the Jew serve the same Master?

When Valon and I returned to the manor and were alone in his chamber, I begged his opinions of all we had seen.

"The murder of the Witch was horrid in the same pattern as the others. Seems to me the work of a madman," I offered. "It is one thing to kill a witch, even to burn one but to abuse her in such a way and to hang her out in that fashion…well…that seems beyond sanity. How do you make it out?"

"Whoever killed her hoped that it would seem that some citizens of Châlons took matters into their own hands to kill a witch, and then justified their work by the citation from Exodus. At least, that is what we are supposed to believe. However, I assess that she was tortured and likely with a purpose. Hence the condition of her body."

"Tortured! But, why?"

"Difficult to know, good Theodulfe, but suppose someone wanted to know something from her. Consider this. Perhaps someone knew that Draco took us to question her and that she told us much. Perhaps that same person wanted to know precisely what she had told us. Or, and this is more interesting to me, perhaps that person knew or learned or suspected that she did not tell us all she knew and because of that wished to silence her. That last is a very interesting possibility."

"Interesting? So that is what you meant when you said that word. It certainly is 'interesting.' That would mean that the person who murdered her was frightened that she could implicate him in the murders! That is well beyond 'interesting,' Valon. That is fascinating."

"Yes. And that would mean someone besides or other than, the person Hildegard pointed to is guilty."

"Mother of God!"

"Yes, our thinking must now encompass that Hildegard may have lied to us about Lord Ethelred. Or, perhaps she saw another person that night and withheld that from us. Perhaps that person was paying her to keep her silence. Perhaps paying her to lie about Ethelred. The hellish thing is that the witch's murder now must call into question her testimony.

"And, there is something other."

"What, pray?"

"At first, upon approaching the witch's body, I observed that Lord Ethelred, sitting upon his great horse, watched everything from the road."

"Yes. I did as well."

"I suppose you have noted, Theodulfe, that among the many qualities lacking in Lord Ethelred, *subtlety* is conspicuous in its absence?"

"Yes, but go on."

"Just this. Ethelred's thoughts are always etched in bold relief upon his face, and what I saw there was notable. I saw surprise and distress."

"Good Heavens! Now you say it, that is what I observed as well."

"Let us not make too much of that just now, but we shall retain it in memory, eh?"

"Yes. Agreed."

"I return to our previous conclusion with even more vigor. We are left to suspect Hildegard's evidence."

"Yes, and either way if we do or do not suspect her, it serves the interests of whoever killed her."

"Theodulfe, you have cleverly found the bull point. But the witch's murder, horrible as it was, is nonetheless in our favor because it tells us one important thing."

"Thank you, but I had not realized that I am so clever. What is that one thing, so that I may appreciate my cleverness as much as you?"

"There is an unknown actor here, who is ruthless and very likely involved in the murders, in some way. To know of the presence of such a person is very useful to us. So, we must thank him for making his presence known to us."

"Yes, I see. And now we must find the identity of their murderer. But we are far from doing that."

"True, we are troubled by that, but good cheer, Father Abbot. We have some wonderful questions to conjure with. Such questions are the delight of the investigator."

"Questions?"

"Indeed! I have two before me right now. First, this person who murdered Hildegard. Is he the same person who murdered Sister Helena? And, recall that Hildegard told us she 'saw the face of the Monster.' We assumed she was speaking of Ethelred, whom she had already identified as the brutal murderer. But suppose for a moment she was speaking of two different people and 'the Monster' was the person whom she did not identify to us and who soon killed her."

Valon's thinking stunned me. I had not thought of such things, and once again I stood for a moment in awe of his insight.

"And what of the old Jew who claimed her body? What was the meaning of that? How is the Jew connected in this?" I asked, remembering to Valon how eagerly Mathias of Tours had testified against the Abbot Hugo.

"Aye, those are all questions worth holding in the mind."

"And, now that we are to ourselves," I said, "what did you find upon the witch's hand? It was then, I recall, you said 'interesting.'"

"Only one thing of any interest—a single, short, and peculiar hair."

"A hair? What hair?"

"A red hair."

CHAPTER 22

The Lady Céleste

Rather than speculate about red hair, Valon instead plunged into yet another vexing question. "Putting aside the Jew, how could a young nun of Sister Helena's background be connected to old Hildegard?" he asked, almost to himself.

"That kind of connection seems almost incredible, Valon."

"I grant you that, at least on the surface. But these are deep and treacherous waters, good Theodulfe, and full of currents that may do strange things. There is one other possibility in Hildegard's murder that troubles me more than others."

"Oh," I said, almost afraid to hear it.

"It is possible, I believe, that she was entirely in the employ of the one who murdered her. In that case, her witness may have been purposely distorted, or even calculated to tell us a tale that it suits the murderer we should believe. I suspect we are being manipulated, and that always disturbs me."

This final conundrum disturbed me as well, adding to my confusion as to what I should make of the Witch's murder.

"And what of the Lord and his family?" I asked, wanting to learn if Valon's thinking agreed with my own.

"They are a strange lot, indeed. Lord Ethelred has not been blessed in his progeny, except perhaps for Mordune and the Lady Céleste. One must suspect that the lady sought the life of the Church to escape the life of the Manor."

"Well, we are here, in the midst of Ethelred's family. What must we do?"

"We must learn, and that means exploring all we can of the Manor. I've put Bodo and Athalfe and the Brother Monks to doing so amongst the servants. They will insinuate themselves into the life of the Manor as we may not, and they will be our eyes and ears in the kitchen and wine cellar. Meanwhile, you and I must investigate in our own way. The answers we seek are to be found here, but I beg you, do not press me to explain how I hold this view, for I could not do so."

"I'll not press you, for I believe the same, and do not know precisely why. Was it the testimony of the old Witch, or perhaps the evidence of the Bishop? They have all pointed us in this direction, but that makes me distrust my conviction. Ethelred has many enemies, and they wish us to believe ill of him and his family."

Next morning, as the Lord's family departed breakfast for their various pursuits and duties, Valon took me aside to explain that Father Draco had agreed to distract Godfrey so that we might examine his chamber. Valon had also engaged Draco's knowledge of the Manor, we now had a map of the locations of various rooms and doors, and Draco had told Valon the daily habits of each.

Armed with such knowledge, and assured that Draco would keep Godfrey busy for at least an hour, we climbed to the lonely tower room where the Hunchback lived.

Beyond the third level, we found ourselves upon dark and narrower stairs, which had not been cleaned in some time. Among the debris and cobwebs, I observed the dried carcass of a small cat. We climbed two more levels and found ourselves at a door made of rough oak planks, held together by rusted nails and hung upon large, equally rusted hinges. *A strange place, indeed, to find residing the heir of a powerful family.*

Valon's skill at subverting locks, I learned, was formidable, and we entered the chamber more quickly than I'd expected. Within, all was dark, though I made out many strange objects throughout. I took from my *sacullus* a candle and lit it. The room had not been cleaned in some time and was both dusty and full of grime. Dark draperies, embellished with strange designs and symbols that I sensed to be evil, hung upon the walls. Books and instruments used to study the heavens filled the room, so I concluded that research of some kind filled Godfrey's time.

A large heavy table stood at the center of the room, piled high with papers and books, thrown about in no particular order. At one end stood a mechanical model of the universe, the sort usually found among scholars of the heavens. At the far wall stood a shelf filled with small earthen containers and vials, each labeled in Latin. Upon the same shelf, and in a nearby cabinet that stood open, rested several skulls and assorted bones. Some were large animal bones. One skull, however, was human! My spirit sank to notice that it was the skull of a child.

At the hearth, sat a large iron pot, such as is used in the kitchen to cook, though I could not believe Godfrey was cooking. In it brewed a concoction that smelled of camphor beans.

"This chamber is filled with many strange things, Valon, and much of it seems evil. But, what does it all mean?"

Valon said nothing at first but continued his careful examination of all that was obvious in the room, beginning with the things on the table and moving soon to the shelf, hearth, and great cabinet. He even looked under the bed, and there seemed to find something of interest.

"Well, we have chosen well on our first effort, Theodulfe. Lord Godfrey is clearly engaged very deeply in the Black Arts. To put it directly, he is a sorcerer and one who is quite knowledgeable. From the writings on the table, it appears that he interests himself mainly in two elements of the diabolical sciences—necromancy and alchemy. There is evidence as well that he attempts to divine the future by the stars and dabbles in potions that are designed to control the spirits of others."

I crossed myself and offered a blessing upon the room to free it from any spirits and minor devils that might lurk about.... *defende nos in proelio, contra nequitiam et insidins diabolic esto prasedium.*

"This is the sort of place, Valon, where it is said the demon lackeys employed by Satan live and do their work upon men. Let us quit this place, at once, lest one of them seize upon one of us."

"No, what you say of lurking evil is true. This chamber breathes of it. But we must remain for a bit to do our duty to the King."

By this time, I was convinced that we were likely to encounter a malevolent creature in the chamber, perhaps one that acted as a familiar to Godfrey. For a time almost frozen by fear that such a demon would step out from the darkness and pronounce my name, I forced myself to open boxes and trunks and to look in dark corners as Valon wished. The parchments on the table were rendered in such distorted Latin that I could hardly make out what they said. Others were written in a version of Latin I could not read at all, which disturbed me because I had never yet failed to read such a document. *Was the Latin in the parchments in the demonic form the cackling Hildegard screeched at us when she cursed Valon?*

Much of what I could read pertained to raising the dead to life—necromancy, as Valon said—by means of spoken forms and herbal concoctions known to the ancients, including the Romans of Gaul and Britain. One bound volume—a journal of sorts—represented Godfrey's own researches and thoughts on this and other subjects. *That would be fascinating reading if only I could borrow it for a day or two. A catalogue of the profane and sacrilegious.*

"See here, Theodulfe," Valon whispered, holding in his hand a parchment filled with strange designs and devices. "My grasp of ancient Latin is inadequate in some respects to understand this perfectly, but I can read that it is a formula for a very interesting purpose."

As I read, I, too, was astounded. "Valon, this is a formula for inducing madness in another human. A permanent madness. And, look you here, at the end it clearly says, 'and the substance makes complete the Monster. *Et substantia facit preficere monstorum,*'" he repeated. "Do you see that word? The Monster!"

"Yes. The same as Hildegard. The Monster—*Monstorum.* Not a word that one often sees in Latin."

"But, what could it mean? What Monster, Valon?"

He looked at me in some frustration. "I don't know."

By these secretive means and guided always by Draco's maps, we searched much of the Manor in those first days. Guillaume's chamber and that of Humphrey were unexceptional —Guillaume's full of martial tools, hawking equipage of various sorts, and the stuff of martial games. No books, though there was the expected weaponry and armor, along with a parchment or two on warfare. Guillaume had been to the Frisian War, as had Valon, and so we found many relics of that conflict. The sort of odds and ends a soldier will bring home from war.

Humphrey's chamber was furnished with sacred symbols and several texts. Clearly, he had some talents as a *scriptor*, for he was busy copying a manuscript concerning the punishment of sorcery and witchcraft. There hung from a nail by his small, rough bed a scourge of nine tails, fitted with small brass barbs. It was the tool of a self-flagellating penitent. I was not surprised, for such instruments are common among the faithful, especially in monasteries. I was both surprised and gladdened to know that young Humphrey was of such a spiritual disposition.

On our third day at the Manor, we found Céleste at her prayers in the garden court. A more perfect combination of beauty and spirituality I could not imagine. Waiting a bit until she looked up, we dared approach, and Valon asked leave to speak.

"Yes, Monsieur de Valon. If I may yet assist you. But, how?" she said sweetly, with a slight lilt in her voice to suggest that speaking with Valon was especially welcome.

"I wish to ask further of your friend, Sister Helena, my lady. I ardently wish to do her justice. The Great Charles commissions me and Father Abbot to do justice in this matter."

Céleste seemed troubled at revisiting the subject, but also resigned that Valon and I were compelled to investigate.

"Yes, Monsieur. What is it?"

"I have given some thought to the circumstances of her death, my lady, and I wonder if she might have been at that place that morning to meet someone. A special person perhaps. Did you know or even suspect that the lady Helena might have a lover?"

Sister Céleste shuddered at the question. She rose from her bench and walked a few paces, her back to us. Wringing her hands and even tearing a bit, she turned and said vehemently, "No Monsieur de Valon. No! She would not affront her vows in that manner. Sister Helena was a good and faithful nun, and she would not have done that."

I wondered at the time if Valon considered, as I did, that her protestations were perhaps a little too much, for it also seemed to me that I saw in her face at first blush, quite another answer. As if she suddenly realized that someone other than she now knew the secret. Of course, I told myself immediately that I was inclined to read far too much into a young girl's face.

"So, she never said or even suggested this sort of thing to you? Never asked you about love, for example? The love of a woman for a man?"

Now more composed, Céleste answered directly. "Well, of course, we discussed such things. Women, even nuns, sometimes talk of such things. But not as you suggest, Monsieur. Not as you suggest," she repeated for emphasis.

"You say that Helena would not have dishonored her vows by taking a lover. Very well. But might she have had a suitor, nonetheless a would-be lover whom she refused? A rejected suitor who might have been angry enough to murder her for her refusal?"

Céleste bristled at the suggestion, her eyes flashing, her lips rigid.

Valon continued. "My lady, I found this small piece of parchment in the Lady Helena's hand, as she lay murdered. She clutched it forcefully. Allow me to show it to you and to ask you if you know what it means. I have confirmed from Sister Felicitas that it is not in Sister Helena's hand, and she did not recognize it."

Then, handing the scrap to Céleste, Valon recited what it said:

Sic erunt novissimi primi
et
primi novissimi multi

Though it was the first I had heard of the parchment in Sister Helena's hand, I knew the verse well. "So the last shall be first and the first last," was my rendering from Matthew's gospel.

"My lady, do you know why your friend would have such a verse in her hand when she was murdered? And do you recognize the hand?"

At the sight of the parchment, Céleste lost her composure. She began to weep, all the while protesting that she did not know. "No, Monsieur, I know nothing of it! Nothing of it, do you understand!" she repeated, shaking her head.

Valon relented just a little to give time for the young woman to regather her composure. "There now, Sister, Monsieur de Valon is finished. And you have done well to assist us,"

I consoled, patting both her hands in mine.

Valon, however, was not finished and eagerly pursued what Céleste knew.

He is, I thought, unforgiving in his persistence.

"Can you think why the townsfolk believe your father is responsible for the brutal murders in Châlons, my lady? We have heard little else from the local folk since our arrival."

Now almost again in tears, the young nun looked at her hands and said quietly, "No, Monsieur, I do not. I do not know why."

"Then, My Lady, can you tell me why some believe your father to be implicated in the sad death of your mother? Is there any evidence to support such a notion, for example? Do you share such suspicions?"

Lady Céleste stiffened a little at this last, wiping a tear from her cheek.

"There was one thing, Monsieur, that some thought incriminating, but I dismissed it as a mere coincidence. When mother was found, she held in her hand my father's sash clasp. To some, that was a sign that my father was responsible and so the malicious have wagged their tongues."

Céleste prepared to leave, and as she turned, Valon thought of one last question.

"There is one other matter, Sister."

Turning, she asked, "Yes, Monsieur?"

"Was Sister Helena with child?"

The question fell upon my ears like a clap of thunder in a sudden summer storm.

"Valon, you go too far!" I growled my intervention, now just a little angry at his treatment of the Lady Céleste. "It is ungenerous of you to ask such a question."

He looked at me coldly, as only his dark eyes could sometimes become cold.

"It is not my duty to be generous, good Abbot, but to do justice."

As I prepared an angry retort, the Lady answered. "No, Monsieur," she said sharply, "I did not know any such thing." And then she walked toward the great hall, her head noticeably bowed, her arms at her side, her fists clenched.

"Valon, that was uncalled for. You go too far!" I asserted once more. "You are doing and saying things on your own that we should be doing and saying together. How dare you to ask such a question of that wretched girl, when you have nothing but your wicked suspicion behind it."

"I ask you now. Did you notice as I did that when I showed her the parchment, she recognized the hand?"

"Yes, now you say so. I observed she gave pause," I sniffed.

"More than that. What she saw disturbed her, and she could not conceal it, though she tried."

Valon's gaze softened. "I know you are angry with me, Theodulfe, and I beg your pardon. But I suppose I should tell you that I do have more than mere suspicion behind my questions."

"How could you?" I asked, disdainfully and still angry.

"Because, as you and the others prepared to leave the Convent of Saint Agnes that noon, I returned to the Apothecary's rooms and took my sharp knife to Sister Helena's belly."

"You did what!" I shouted, half disbelieving my own ears.

"And there I found the seed of a child."

CHAPTER 23

Valon the Sinner

As I watched Valon turn and walk toward the Manor, I remained staggered by his admission and almost overcome by my emotions at what he had done. At first, my feelings ran to anger and indignation, so blatantly had he violated our partnership and abused my trust. I felt betrayed and even tricked, and I was then even angrier. But then, it settled upon my brain that this was no ordinary man with whom I was paired, and I was compelled to recognize that his suspicions were not wicked, but true and that by his relentless quest for justice, he had proved himself right.

In the end, I was forced to concede to myself that it meant less that I was affronted than it did that our knowledge of the murder of Sister Helena was now vastly enhanced, and that was a good thing. Though I forgave Valon, I now knew that I could not trust him to abide always by our partnership, for he was too inclined to trust absolutely in his own sense of what justice required. And he was far too inclined to allow nothing—not even his devotion to the King and his loyalty to the *capitulary* under which we worked—to dissuade him. Sadly, I thought, Valon is a rogue, and utterly ruthless.

Later that same day, I have it from Valon himself, the Lady Céleste sent her woman to Valon, begging a private meeting in the Manor's chapel, where she was accustomed to pray in mid-afternoon. Valon met her there, unknown at the time to all but Athalfe.

"My Lady wished to see me?" he asked, hoping that his earlier questioning had prompted Sister Céleste to be more candid, for we agreed that in previous questioning she had lied or withheld.

"Yes, Monsieur de Valon. I have thought a great deal about our last meetings and about the questions you asked, especially about my dear Helena. I confess I have been terribly conflicted and confused in all this, not knowing which way to turn. No, not knowing at all."

Sitting beside her on the bench and taking the lady's hand in his, Valon sympathized. "My Lady, it's only to be expected that these matters would be difficult for you, and I can assure you I have known that from the beginning.

In fact, it has been clear to me that you've been unable to be candid with me, and I make allowance for that."

Now taking Valon's hand in both of hers, Céleste smiled a little at Valon's assurances.

"I beg you Monsieur; be patient with me. I must think these things through in my own mind and above all, to make certain that what I know—or rather, what I think I know—is true. Please, give me time—only a little more time—to sort this through."

Valon softened entirely toward her, now caressing her hand, and then kissing both. "My Lady, I will wait for you as long as it is necessary, in this matter and in all other matters. You must know that, for we have spoken much to each other in our eyes."

Leaning toward him, Céleste touched his shoulder with her cheek, and said, "I know, and you must know, also, that my feelings are the same. But all that must wait until these terrible things are settled. I cannot do otherwise."

"I know, and I understand. And, I will wait."

And, with a gentle embrace, the two parted—the lady Céleste to her chamber and Valon to the garden, where he hoped to think. And, it was there that I found him, seated upon a stone bench and brooding.

Valon did not notice as I approached, so deep was his contemplation. And he did not recognize it when I sat beside him, hesitating to speak lest I disturb important thinking. Finally, after some minutes, I dared interrupt.

"What is it, young Valon, that causes you to brood so deeply and to do it so often? Youth is a time for much greater gaiety than you seem to feel, though you live recklessly, you do not enjoy it."

He glanced my way but remained silent.

"Is it, my friend, your sorrow at the tragic death of your great love? Your lady, Véronique?"

"No, Theodulfe. Not entirely."

After some further hesitation, he unburdened, telling me of the visions that had become the bane of his life. I knew something of this trouble from Alcuin, but now I learned much more from Valon himself.

"It is my troubling visions, Theodulfe. I am cursed with them by God, for my sins I must believe.

"The most powerful vision of my experience came to me when I was at the Frisian War. It was a terrifying thing I saw in that vision, one night, the murder of my dear lady. It was so real. It was so tragic that I became quite ill and, for several days, I lay in a fever and chill." He put his hands to his face as if reliving the fright.

"Yes, these premonitions of yours are perplexing things. I have thought much about them myself since Alcuin first told me of them."

Valon appeared surprised that I knew of his visions and yet had said nothing to him about them.

"Oh," he said, "so you are aware of my visions, then?"

"Yes, and Athalfe told me of the strange vision of the girl you conveyed to him. The girl on the tower."

Valon looked at me, his face filled with anguish. "I've had another of those visions. Last night, in my bed. That is what troubles me now, Father Abbot. It is one thing to think about things past—terrible things that have already come to pass. But now. This specter of the girl that torments me, it has not yet come to pass, and that is what is so frightening. You see, I know that I am seeing what will come—a tragedy that is yet to happen—and I can do nothing to prevent it. Nothing!" At this last, he clenched his fists and raised them slightly.

"Ease your mind, on these matters. They are evil presentiments, sent to you by the Evil One himself. I have given this some thought, and I've concluded that you are possessed, in a manner of speaking, by a demon of some sort. You must be exorcised, young Valon. The demon must be driven from you so that you are freed from such torments."

At that moment—the very moment that I prescribed Exorcism as the solution for Valon's torment—the slave girl ran from the shadows in the garden and threw herself upon Valon.

"No! No! You must not!" she screamed, and covered Valon with her own body as if to protect him from me.

CHAPTER 24

Elise

The girl, who 'til now had been absolutely mute, shouted over and over her protest. "No! No, Monsieur! You must not submit to such a thing! You are not a Devil. You are a good man. The best man! You cannot have a demon in you, Monsieur. You cannot!"

The girl's animated protest so surprised us that the issue of Valon's visions was lost in our amazement at her behavior. Valon took her in hand, holding her by each shoulder.

"Stop! Calm yourself, girl," he commanded, and yet the girl continued to shake herself and to protest. Valon looked at me, as if unsure what to do. But then the girl threw herself more directly at him, hanging about his neck as if never intending to release him. Now, he seemed even more mystified and at a greater loss to know what to do with her.

With no other apparent option, Valon simply embraced the girl so as to sooth her disquiet and allow the tempest to run its course. It did so in a matter of several minutes.

Then, Valon spoke calmly to her. "You needn't worry on that score, girl. I was not going to submit to an Exorcism, because I do not agree with Father Abbot. I once did think as he does, and I do not yet know the cause of my visions, but I no longer believe they are evil. I do not know what they are, but I cannot see that they have caused evil themselves, simply because I have been allowed to foresee evil. It may well be that God has given such visions to me to enable me to prevent evil. I cannot know."

Valon's explanation, rendered in such simple terms, quieted the girl, who now stood and released him from her embrace.

"Thank you for your effort to protect me, however. And, I am aware that you helped me in the orchard. It was brave of you to intervene. But now that I know you are able to speak, what is your name?"

The girl seemed to recoil, in the knowledge that she had exposed herself by her intervention. Valon repeated his question.

"Who are you, girl? We cannot continue to call you 'girl,' now can we?"

Looking down at her hands, she said quietly, "Elise. My name is Elise."

"Elise, eh? Well, Father Abbot and I are pleased to meet you, Elise. Now that we know you can speak the Frankish tongue, I perceive you speak it with a Frisian accent. How is that?"

Elise hesitated at first to tell more of herself, but realizing all was now lost in her effort to remain mute, she relented. "That is because I am Frisian, Monsieur. I was captured by Franks when I was a child. They came to my village early one morning. Killed almost everyone—my family and took me into slavery. I did not know the Frank tongue at that time, so I did not know what was happening to me, but I soon learned."

There was a moment of uneasy silence, as Valon and I both reflected upon the suffering of our former enemies, even the innocent, all in the interest of bringing the pagan and apostate Frisians back to the faith.

"Those who captured me sold me into slavery in the Frankish lands, where I have been sold and resold several times. The last to buy me from my old master was that band of thieves and murderers you met on the road."

Valon did not hesitate. "Well, all that is the past, and we shall not question you further about it. By right of combat and under my authority as Missi Dominici, I claim you as my chattel now, and Father Abbot here will prepare the proper document for me to give you your freedom. Whatever else happens to you in the Frankish lands, I can assure you that henceforth you will be a freeman."

The girl began to cry with such a display of tears as I have seldom seen. Her gratitude to Valon seemed inexpressible and she vented her glee in uncontrollable tears. For some reason, she fell to kissing, over and over, the ring he wore on his Jupiter finger.

"And if you eventually decide to return to your homeland, I will see you are able to do so and that you have money to give you a dowry sufficient to find a husband."

"But that is not what I wish," the girl said decisively.

"Well, what then?" I asked.

"I wish to remain in the Lord Valon's service," came the quick reply. "That is what I wish."

Valon looked at me, clearly amused.

"That is easily done," Valon answered, "because I haven't the time to attend to your future just now anyway. I am preoccupied with other matters."

Elise smiled her approval and walked away in a manner I thought saucy. Valon's only reaction was a shrug, which I did not entirely understand. And yet the subject of exorcising the demons who put visions in his mind was lost in the commotion surrounding Elise.

I saw neither Valon nor Elise the rest of that day but later learned that he spent most of it questioning Bodo, Athalfe, and the brother monks about what they observed in the household. I learned from Brother Boethius that

Valon was unhappy with how little they had found and urged them to find more and to be especially attentive to the goings and comings of servants.

It was then that Brother Boethius confided to me a troubling moral circumstance, which gave me pause about both Bodo and Valon, but which I decided to hold in my mind in order to give Valon the leeway he might need to gather his information. Boethius reported that Bodo had become intimate with one of Lord Ethelred's daughters. Boethius and Martin observed him the night before, in the scullery with Gertrude, the eldest, who was known as both licentious and dull-witted. According to Boethius, the two spent more than an hour wrapped in the sin of lust, which he felt compelled to observe from its outset to its vile completion, so as to be able to report in full to me the depth to which Bodo had been corrupted by his association with Valon. I assured Boethius that God would judge him less harshly for his pleasure in Gertrude's nakedness and her sin of fornication, knowing that it was done in my service and in that of the Great Charles.

Later, when Boethius reported this sin to Valon, he was aghast to learn that Valon already knew of Bodo's wickedness and had even encouraged him to use his power over Gertrude to learn certain things about Lord Ethelred.

"Valon is a ruthless man, Brother, and that is the end to it. Let us pray for him, and offer prayers as well for Bodo's immortal soul."

"But, may we not intervene to chastise both the Lord Valon and Bodo and to stop this perversion, Father Abbot?"

"Leave such concerns to me, Brother. I will remonstrate with Monsieur de Valon and Bodo at the proper moment."

As I assured Boethius thus, I noticed at the other end of the long gallery Brother Martin hurrying as if in search of something, or someone, a look of urgency on his face.

Boethius and I hurried after him, and as we turned from the long gallery and out a door to a small side court of the Manor, we saw that Martin had found both Valon and Bodo. He was clearly telling Valon something he thought important.

"What is it, Brother?" I heard Valon ask, as we approached.

Paying little attention to us, Martin reported. "I have watched the routine of the kitchen, Monsieur, and in the past two days, I observed something unusual. Yesterday, I noticed that at the end of every meal served to the family, both breakfast and evening, Dagbert the Steward takes a large box of the same food to someone. At first, I merely observed the taking, thinking to make sure that I was observing something that happened after every meal. Then, last evening, I took it into my mind to follow Dagbert, who carried his box through the long corridors and rooms found in the level beneath the Manor. Though I risked much to follow and did so as closely as I dared, I lost him."

Valon frowned. Martin paused as if to collect his thoughts.

"Yes, go on. Go on!" Valon urged.

"This morning, Monsieur, I followed again, and this time I was able to learn why I had lost Dagbert the day before. He disappeared behind a cupboard that he pulled from the wall of a mostly empty storeroom in the wine cellar. I did not dare follow beyond the secret door, so I waited for him and, in only a bit, he returned by the same entrance."

Martin again paused. Valon glanced at me, his eyes shining with excitement.

"Please continue, Brother," Valon encouraged further, now with even greater intensity in his voice.

"I hid myself in a cranny of the passageway until Dagbert passed on his way back to the kitchen. Then, I rolled out the cupboard and entered the secret door. It led down a steep wooden ladder to a level of the Manor even below the cellar! As I descended the ladder, I feared there might be someone below—the very person to whom the Steward had delivered his box of food, perhaps—and that I'd be found out."

Martin's face now shone with excitement. He rubbed his hands together nervously. "Happily, I was not observed. Once at the bottom, I could not see well enough to proceed, however, and I had no candle with me, so I did not care to risk it. Instead, I decided to find you, Monsieur de Valon, to tell what I've seen."

Valon's eyes narrowed as he listened to the last of the brother monk's story, and in a moment, they flashed with the excitement of decision. In that same instant, though, Valon's expression changed to horror as a woman's scream shattered the silence of the small outer court.

CHAPTER 25

Paris, 6 rue de Longchamp
21 December 21 1918

That scream caused me to grip the arms of my chair with both hands. Teddy looked up and smiled.

"I hope you will pardon me for pausing Theodulfe's narrative," he said, "but I fear my voice is failing and of course the hour is late. Cousin, may I suggest we continue at the same hour tomorrow evening? I can assure you my voice will be fully recovered by then."

"Of course," Montclaire allowed. "You've given us much to consider, Teddy…er…or rather, you and the Abbot have done so. We will benefit I'm sure from a day to digest all you have read and to reflect."

"And what do you find most worth reflecting upon, dear brother," asked Modestine, not wanting to let go. "We have learned so much that is new, I hardly know where to begin my reflecting. I am utterly confused."

"I am as well," Clarisse sighed. "The murder of the nun is out of character with the other crimes. That's clear,' she said. "So, does it have anything to do with what the Messi are investigating? I cannot see that it does, though Valon is certainly interested in it."

"And that ring. The one Sister Helena had," I said. "That interested Valon too, and when he showed it to Céleste, it seemed to me that Theodulfe thought she recognized it, even though she denied it. What was that about? Why would she do that?"

"Perhaps she was keeping a confidence with her dead friend," I said. "That would be consistent with her character…to be loyal in that way."

"All good questions," Montclaire observed, and we have answers to none of them. "Grist for our mill."

"And there are villains enough to go 'round. Ethelred's family is full of them, not least that One-eyed brute. And Godfrey. There's a suspect if you ask me," Clarisse frowned.

"I hesitate to say this," Modestine interrupted, "but Abbot Hugo seems a sly fellow to me. And we know he has reason to hate Ethelred—that lawsuit over the land, eh?"

"But to kill young girls!" Clarisse protested. "An Abbot? I do not accept that, sister. There is a monster at work in all this. A crazy man! And yet, so far I do not see that any of the men we have encountered is insane. Suspicious, Oui, but insane, Non."

"And what of that Witch?" I asked. "There's a frankly unhinged *woman* if you ask me. Might she be a murderess and making it look like a man had done the killing. Perhaps she hates Ethelred or is in league with someone who does. Maybe she was murdered as revenge."

"And that wolf creature who protects her. There's room for some insanity there, I'd wager," Clarisse said, looking at Modestine.

"One thing seems particularly strange to me," Teddy puzzled, "It's the relationship between the good priest, Father Draco, and Hildegard. A man of God? In association with such an evil woman? How can that be? There must be more to that story. Should we suspect Draco, even, though he seems a good sort?"

"Indeed," I agreed. "I do not trust that pair and I certainly do not trust Hildegard's evidence. A tissue of lies, I suspect, but to what purpose? To shield someone who is the true fiend? Or was she being paid?" I shook my head. "There's so much to speculate."

Montclaire had mostly listened to our observations and complaints. "I for one intend to lose a bit of sleep tonight worrying who was the source of that scream," he smiled.

I too had a restless sleep that night, and as I turned from one side to the other, I imagined the old witch screeching her curses. The wolfish protector made a startling appearance in my nightmare as well.

Next morning, I found Montclaire's sisters at breakfast. They reported that Montclaire had gone out early, 'to enjoy the snow,' according to Clarisse. I complained of my restless night and found that they had suffered the same. "Teddy has much to answer for," said Modestine, mostly with a tired sigh and only half-joking.

At the mention of his name, the professor entered. "Do not blame me, dear cousin," he said from the doorway and then proceeded to the sideboard where he scooped up a slice and toast. "I am merely the reader of the story. If your sleep is troubled, blame Theodulfe, or perhaps that devil Valon."

Later that morning, most of our party went out to shop the boulevards, but I preferred to spend my day about the library and especially the salon, where there were books to read and music to be heard on the new Edison Phonograph.

Montclaire returned at mid-afternoon and joined my reading in the library. By 6 o'clock everyone had gathered for brandy, where the chatter was all about what surprises the good Abbot would soon spring upon us.

Teddy disappeared after dinner but returned just before 7:30, once again holding the ancient manuscript in his hands. As we resumed our circle in the salon and Petrovsky turned down the lamps, the professor stood and began to read. And as before, I closed my eyes and suddenly it was Theodulfe's voice that transported me once again to Ethelred's grim fortress and like Valon and Theodulfe, I heard that startling scream.

PART THREE

Draco's Discovery

CHAPTER 1

The Tragic Day of Saint Digain

21 December AD 794

We dashed toward the frightful sound and, in the time it took me to utter silently the Lord's Prayer, we turned the corner into the great forecourt just in time to see a ghastly sight—the Lady Céleste plummeting to earth. Before my eyes, her small body struck the cobbles with an awful thud. I gasped as the crumpled body of the young nun quivered once and then fell still.

Several men-at-arms, servants, and others gathered round, and then Lord Ethelred came hurriedly into the court, followed closely by Guillaume and Humphrey. For a long moment, the Lord stared at the motionless corpse of his daughter, a pool of blood forming about her head. In death, she retained for a moment all her angelic beauty, but quickly her complexion faded to the icy whiteness that signaled the departure of her immortal soul.

Draco came into the court from the direction of the stables and Godfrey came a moment later limping from the same direction. The priest knelt and began to pray and to anoint Céleste with the last rites of the Church. I whispered a prayer that Our Lord must take her to His side, though the horrible thought had already entered my mind that the lady had taken her own life.

These thoughts were the work of a second, broken as Lord Ethelred released a wail of grief such as I had never heard from a human, and never wish to hear again. It was of an intensity and guttural quality that sounded almost supernatural in its proportions. Immediately, the great warrior fell to his knees, took the broken body of his child in his arms and began to wail and sob in a more human way. It was a pitiful thing, and in that moment, I questioned all my convictions about Ethelred, including my certainty that he was guilty of the murders.

It was then that Lord Mordune and Céleste's sisters came from the Manor. At the foot of the steps, when her twin saw her, he screamed in anguish and began to weep as bitterly as any man I'd ever seen. His sisters did the same.

Knowing what I did, and suspecting much more of the bond between Valon and the Lady Céleste, I glanced at my companion, expecting to find him descending into anguish. Instead, he was much less caught up in the emotions of the moment than he was in observing, by a multitude of flitting glances, all that was happening around the dead girl. Suddenly, the energy of his silent observations, as I could see it in his quickly shifting eyes, changed my thoughts from sympathy for Ethelred to wonderment at Valon's powers of concentration in any situation. *What must he be thinking,* I mused? and to wonder what he was thinking. In the flicker of an eyelash, he ran up the steps and into the great hall, with me and Bodo close on his heel. I had no idea why I was following so determinedly, except that by now I had concluded that the most interesting place on earth at any given moment must be where Monsieur de Valon happened to be.

He stopped only briefly to take in what was to be seen in the hall itself, and then dashed quickly up the stone stairs toward the tower, taking its steps by twos and even threes. We ascended the fifty feet or so to the top floor and battlements of the tower in a matter of a few seconds, during which I had no time to tell myself I was too old to do what I was doing—that I could not climb so quickly. At last, by means of a long, rough-made ladder, we arrived upon the tower roof from which Céleste must have jumped.

"Yes," Valon said, as we came onto the roof, "she fell from here because there are no window openings on the courtside of the tower from which she might have fallen."

I do not know why, but I immediately looked over the battlement, from the point at which she must have jumped, down into the court, where the crowd still stood and where the inconsolable Ethelred continued to kneel and hold the body.

By now, a light snow had begun to fall, and I drew the fur of my cloak's collar about my face, as a wind raked the tower top. Still, we could hear Mordune's weeping, even from the battlements.

I turned back to the roof and saw Valon walking about, studying intently every square inch of the surface, even as the snow began to scurry about in the wind on the tower roof. At a point near me, he dropped to his knees and then on all fours and looked more closely at the stone surface, near where Lady Céleste must have stood before going over the edge. And yet, I saw nothing and could detect nothing of what he was finding if indeed he was finding anything. In the next moment, however, he rose to his feet and looked first at the battlements, and then over into the court, where Lord Ethelred continued to grieve, and where the snow now fell and swirled about vigorously.

"Lord Ethelred must have loved the Lady Céleste very much. His grief is remarkable, even by the standards of a loving father," I said, giving voice to thoughts I had had for some minutes.

"Yes. Remarkable in a man who seems always so devoid of emotion. We are seeing another side of Lord Ethelred, perhaps."

As Valon spoke, I continued to look down into the court. I do not know why, but my gaze fixed on Mordune who stood at his father's side, still weeping beyond control as his father continued to embrace and cradle the lifeless body of his daughter. I was shaken to tears myself at the sight, and when I turned to Valon and saw him emotionless, I was angry.

"You seem unmoved by this tragedy, Monsieur de Valon," I said, in a reproachful voice. He did not seem to react but replied. "You deceive yourself, good Theodulfe. My

sadness rivals that of Lord Ethelred, for I truly believe I am in some large measure responsible for this tragedy. And yet it is my duty to imprison my feelings in an iron box within my soul, to be opened later when I, too, have the luxury of boundless grief."

"How do you reproach yourself for this tragedy? It is none of your doing, surely!"

"Let us consider it as we must, as the King's investigators. Lady Céleste has either jumped to her death, or she was pushed, for icy as it is up here, it is only a remote possibility that this was an accidental fall. The battlements are such that it would be difficult to slip over the edge. If she jumped, then it must be that her emotions were stirred to such intensity that it drove her to madness. It would require that for a *religieuse* to do such a thing. Consider, Theodulfe, who it was in the past twenty-four hours who stirred the poor girl's emotions to such intensity. There is only one answer. It was I, pressing my questions in the garden. It is possible that I pushed her to the edge.

"And then there is the other possibility. If she was pushed, I too am implicated in that."

"What! Good Heavens, man, you are in no way guilty of that!" I protested, taking Valon's arm.

"Yes. Again, it is entirely possible that my questions inspired Sister Céleste to act in such a way that prompted someone to murder her. Let us suppose she was aggrieved by what I suggested. That she thought about it and perhaps even allowed her own submerged suspicions to come to the surface. And, let us suppose further that she confronted someone with those suspicions—someone whose possible guilt was a source of terrible anxiety to her. And let us suppose darkly, Father Abbot, that the person she confronted responded in panic and anger and pushed the Lady Céleste over the battlements."

I crossed myself at the thought of the terrible things Valon supposed, for I knew his surmises were true. Our presence and investigation surely played a part in this tragedy. *May Our Lord forgive us our part*, I lamented silently, taking to heart what Valon had said.

But then the Lord put into my mind the truth that I was compelled to press upon Valon. "Even if what you say of these possibilities is true, my friend, consider this. It was always within the Lady Céleste's powers to trust in God's justice and mercy, by telling you, or me, what she knew or suspected. If what you suggest is true, then Céleste chose to keep her own counsel. And that is not your fault, nor mine. We may wish it otherwise and lament the tragedy of it, but the Lady chose her course and it was her choice to make."

When Valon ended his assessment of Céleste's actions and listened attentively to my rejoinder, he next did something I had expected from the first. He found a corner of the great hall, and there on an oaken bench, he sat for several hours in the silence of his own thoughts, sometimes showing an inexpressible anguish in his eyes. As I sat by him in his silence, it came to me that Valon was now suffering his emotions to have their way, and I now knew what I had suspected in the case of Sister Céleste, his usual detachment had failed. He had come to see her as a man sees a woman, and that was now, undeniably, also a part of our investigation. I wondered what it would mean in the long sweep of our search. There was no way to know.

Later, I ask Athalfe about this strange quality in Valon. "It is the heart of the extreme warrior, Father Abbot," he advised. "I have seen it in war. Those who are the very best at it allow no emotion to enter into their minds until it is safe to do so."

Near midnight, I could keep my vigil no longer. I excused myself to my chamber, leaving Bodo to stand watch by Valon and admonishing the lout not to sleep.

"Yes my Lord Abbot. As you say."

Later, near the hour of Matins, there came a terrible banging at my chamber door. "Father Abbot! Father Abbot!" a voice insisted. "Father Abbot, come at once! It is Monsieur de Valon!"

Valon's name roused me from my deep sleep, and I sprang from my bed into the cold, dark room. Unfamiliar with it, I fumbled and stumbled for a moment to find my way to the door, which I unlatched. There stood Athalfe and behind him the brother monks.

"It's Monsieur de Valon! He's possessed, Father Abbot. The Evil One has taken control of him! Come at once!"

CHAPTER 2

Valon is Possessed by a Demon

I quickly found my sandals and tunic, wrapped my cloak about me, and bid the others lead me to Valon.

Making our way through the darkened corridors by torch, we finally reached Valon's chamber, some distance away. The Lord's family was preoccupied elsewhere with the death of Lady Céleste, and so did not notice the stir caused by Valon's sudden instability.

When I arrived, however, I found Bodo and Elise just inside the room, where our light revealed Valon, collapsed in one corner and raving. The sight of him was terrible. His eyes goggled and glared like a mad man. The linen tunic he wore was soaked in his own sweat. As he sat there, he cursed, babbled incessantly, and threatened death to anyone who approached. Worse still, it was clear that at some point he had lost control of his bodily movements. Athalfe's description of a man 'possessed' seemed apt. There was certainly a demon present, in some form.

I ordered Bodo and Athalfe to rush at Valon, take him in hand, and force him onto his

bed so that we might deal with him, while I sent Brother Martin to the monastery to fetch the Apothecary. Valon's strength was too much for the soldiers, so Brother Boethius and I joined them to subdue him. Using a rope found by Bodo, we managed with great difficulty to tie him to his bed, though he struggled mightily against the bonds.

"Valon is indeed possessed by a demon," I concluded, prepared to recite the Rite of Exorcism over his quivering body.

But when I told Boethius my intentions and bade him assist me in the Litanies and readings of Scripture, the girl Elise flung herself upon Valon as if to protect him from me, and shouted that I must not call down any spells upon him. In near the same state of furious excitement as Valon himself, the girl's violence extended to scratching and biting at Bodo and Athalfe. They were finally able to subdue her as well and tie her to a chair in the corner of the room, where she continued to scream as if we were about to murder poor Valon.

"She believes you are going to call down evil upon him, Father Abbot," Athalfe shouted over the girl's screams and screeches. "She is a pagan, after all."

"Let her scream. Our business is with the demon in Valon."

Soon we were able to commence, first with the invocation of all the Saints, then Scripture, and then the Exorcism proper, to drive out the demon.

"I command you, unclean spirit, whoever you are, along with all your minions now attacking this servant of God, by the mysteries of the incarnation, passion, resurrection, and ascension of our Lord Jesus Christ, by the descent of the Holy Spirit...

"I cast you out, unclean spirit, along with every Satanic power of the enemy, every specter from hell, and all your fell companion, in the name of our Lord Jesus Christ. Be gone and stay far away from the creature of God. For it is He who commands you....

"I adjure you, ancient serpent, by the judge of the living and the dead..."

And so on, until the ritual was finished. Just then, the Apothecary arrived to administer a potion of herbs. The combined effect of Exorcism and the concoction caused the unclean spirit to spring from Valon's body in a violent convulsive movement. Brother Martin told me later that at that moment he saw a dark specter leap from Valon's chest. Then Valon fell into sleep.

"Thank you, Brother Apothecary. Brother monks, Bodo, and Athalfe. I believe we have saved Lord Valon from the Evil One. I am now convinced that Satan himself is at work here, determined to divert us from our mission."

The Apothecary observed further. "Possessed? Perhaps. I have seen this excitement in others, Father Abbot. It is a kind of brain fever that borders on madness. However, it often subsides or seems to, after a rest."

"A fever? Madness?"

"Yes. Similar to them. I have seen it when I was a priest in the service of the Army. And then I did not notice anyone perform the Rite of Exorcism," he said, with an air of skepticism.

"If not demons, what do you believe to be the cause, then, Brother?"

"I have seen it only in one circumstance. Grief."

CHAPTER 3

Valon's Troubled Soul is Saved

By next day, Valon had recovered sufficiently his spiritual composure that he announced to me he was prepared to press our investigation. As Bodo released the rope that had bound Valon to his bed, I watched his face and demeanor carefully for any glimpse into his spirit. I wondered if the demon was still there, lurking in his apparent recovery. And yet, I perceived only that he was now even more determined.

"Theodulfe," he urged, "we must complete our search of the Manor. I am more convinced than ever that we will find the answers to all our questions and also the murderer here, under this roof. And, we must look to the first opportunity to find what it is—or more properly—who it is that the Steward takes food every day."

So, it was that I thought, which came to his mind first when he recovered his senses. The Steward and the food.

During all of that evening, Lord Ethelred and his children busied themselves in returning the body of the Lady Céleste to the Convent of Saint Agnes. It was said among the servants that they would not return until the next day when the body had been prepared and could be returned to Châlons for her funeral. The absence gave us the opportunity we sought to make our final searches of the Manor, so after Compline, we joined forces before the door of Lord Ethelred's chamber.

Again, Valon easily opened the lock and we entered by candlelight. Littered with all manner of weapons and armor, including several long swords, knives of various origins, and much chainmail, the chamber was a mess. I observed also pieces here and there of equestrian fashion—iron bits, Avar stirrups, spurs, and such—and also equipage having to do with falconry. Though a mess, it was the chamber one might expect of a warrior. It included maps of the domains and a large old trunk fitted with iron studs and filled with documents that mostly concerned the history of the family of Châlons and the domains belonging to it. On the Lord's massive table, lay a sheaf of parchments having to do with the long suit at law with the Abbot of Saint Benoît du Lac concerning the disputed lands. I read several and came to understand how complicated the affair was. When I told Valon about the documents, he bid me read all of them and make myself conversant with the issues in the dispute. I did not welcome that assignment, but undertook it, while Valon made his investigation of all else in the chamber.

At the end of almost two hours, I had surveyed all the parchments and Valon was satisfied he had observed all in the chamber worth seeing. As we exited, he told me he found nothing of any interest to our concerns, while I confessed that the suit between Lord Ethelred and Abbot was deadly dull.

"What was the substance of it?" he asked, as we made our way down the passage toward the stairs that led down into the great hall.

"Lord Ethelred's father had detached substantial portion of his domains—more than ten thousand hectares—to the Abbey in fee simple in return for a guarantee that the monks of Saint Benoît would make a Chantry and then undertake daily prayers, including one hundred recitations of Our Lord's Prayer, for the repose of his soul. Moreover, once each year the Bishop of Reims was to come to the Abbey and offer a Requiem Mass for the same purpose. And both were to do so in perpetuity."

"What of that? It is no more or less than many of the Frankish nobles have done toward the Church and especially the local monasteries."

"In this instance, Lord Ethelred charges three things to recover those lands. He claims that his father never made such a gift and the documents supporting it are a fabrication of the Church and Abbot. He charges further that the documents are ambiguous as to what lands particularly are included and he disputes the descriptions in the document. And, he claims to have evidence that the terms of the legacy have not been kept by the monks and Bishop. In all of this, he has been unsuccessful in his suit—until now."

"Oh?"

"Yes. But, he recently obtained a judgment in his favor before the court of Duke Odo. And he is preparing to place the suit before the Great Charles because the Bishop is clearly intending to appeal to the King."

"It would seem, then, that the Church and monastery must worry that Lord Ethelred will prevail."

"Yes, and timing also seems interesting. The final confrontation between the two is at hand."

"I see what you mean. Just as these awful murders have occurred."

"A coincidence? I shouldn't think so."

"Yes. I suppose the Abbey must worry, but what of it?"

"Only this, Father Abbot. It is a strong motive to discredit Lord Ethelred to the King, so as to undermine his suit. And in all of this, I am recalling what Mathias of Tours told us of Abbot Hugo."

"You cannot mean we must suspect the Church! Valon, you go too far in your suspicions! The Bishop and Abbot have been our strongest allies in this and deserve our thanks. And as for the Jew, well, he has the blood of Our Lord upon his hands, as do all his race. He is cursed and cannot be believed."

"Spoken as a worthy Churchman, dear Theodulfe, and none shall begrudge you your love of the Church, nor your attitude toward the Jew, though I do not share it. Nor will any gainsay your claim that I cannot prove what I suspect. Still, I would suspect the King himself if that is where the evidence points and I will do justice for all the dead girls, no matter who is guilty. And I'll hang that Bishop myself is he is behind this!"

Though I continued to chaff at Valon's sinful insinuations, I cared not to affront him, no more than he did me. And so the issue subsided and we talked of it no more that night. Instead, we continued swiftly down the corridor to the chamber occupied by Mordune the Poet.

Again, Valon quickly defeated the lock and we entered another darkened room. Even before our candles lighted our way into the chamber itself, I smelled a stink of animals, such that I gagged. It was not so much the stink of the stable as of the menagerie, for I had smelled the same when once I visited the collection of the Great Charles himself at Aachen. It was that stink that now met my nostrils.

Our candles quickly revealed the source of the odor. Mordune's chamber walls were lined with cages—small and large—all containing animals. Some held ferrets and weasels of local origin. In the smaller were mice and rats, of many colors. And in the largest, an amazing sight—the first ever I saw. A creature known as a *monkee*.

"Good Heavens, Valon! Look you there in that cage…the *monkee*."

"I have already done so. Interesting."

"Tell me. You said that on the night you were attacked in the orchard you smelled an offensive odor. Was it the stink we now smell?"

"No. This is terrible, but the odor that night was worse and different."

As I gazed about the room all else in it seemed both neat and usual. Upon examination, I found nothing the least unusual. Valon discovered a box of small toys, leashes of various sizes, and a collar that obviously belonged to Mordune's small dog, the one that had performed so amazingly at our first dinner. That creature was nowhere about, so I presumed the family took him along to the convent.

Valon continued for the longest while to inspect the small chest of toys and leashes, and while he did so, to consider what he had found. *Odd*, I thought, *that he should linger so over such a box. Why not look more to the cages and to the animals inhabiting them? And particularly the monkee, whose eyes seem a human thing.*

"What have you made of this?" I asked, not expecting to hear more than I already thought.

"The stink is difficult to endure. Mordune has a fascination for animals, which is not troubling in itself. He also clearly has a talent for the training of them, which we saw in the little dog's performance at dinner. It leads me to wonder, however."

"To wonder what?"

"Only this, good Theodulfe. What might these other animals be schooled to do, and to what purpose? Of course, I can only pretend to a certain curiosity at this point, but still…"

I could not imagine what Valon meant by 'still,' but I did not care to ask. I concluded I would know in good time.

As we stepped into the corridor and relocked Mordune's chamber, Brother Boethius came scurrying toward us, his face bright with something to tell.

"Father Abbot. Monsieur de Valon. The Steward has once more taken the box of food toward the stairs that lead to the lower levels. Come, quickly!"

CHAPTER 4

Into the Underground

We hurried after Boethius and found Brother Martin in the great hall, ready to guide us after the Steward. We retraced steps we had followed several nights before until we were past the wall cupboard that was actually a door into the undercellar. Once past that, we heard footsteps coming down the long corridor toward us, so we found a place behind several large wooden boxes to hide and wait. Before the Steward returned around a corner in the corridor we could see the approach of his lighted torch by its shadows on the wall. Then he came, now without the large box in his arms.

When he had passed and closed the cupboard door behind him, we emerged from our corner, lighted two torches, and moved quickly on tiptoes down the stone corridor—a tunnel it seemed to me—in the direction from which Dagbert had come. We turned a corner in the passage and proceeded swiftly down a long stretch until we came once more to the wall and strong door that had previously prevented Valon from continuing. And, even before we had arrived, we once more encountered that peculiar stench that Valon described as like no other. He was, I discovered, correct.

At the end of the corridor, just in front of the door, sat the box of food, waiting to be retrieved. However, it was clear the box would not be taken-in by opening the large door itself, which seemed to be seldom moved, but rather would be pulled through a trap at the door's base, at floor-level. The trap was just large enough to accommodate the flat box, which rested in front of it.

"We must wait," Valon whispered, motioning toward the box. "Whoever or whatever eats that food will come for it," he continued and then motioned us to back away slightly and find a place on the floor.

As we did so, Boethius and Martin smothered their torches, but Valon took from his *sacullus* a small candle, which he lighted to provide us a dim light. And, there we sat, waiting for the person whose food was in the box.

As we sat on the cold, damp floor, I wondered who that person could be. Was he a person who for some reason prefers to live behind the impenetrable door? Or, another, whose duty it was merely to fetch food for others.

And, why would anyone reside behind this heavy, locked door, except a 'prisoner'? If the food was for a prisoner and his keeper, who were they, and why were they imprisoned here?

Minutes stretched to near an hour, as we sat, growing more chilled and looking at the box. The stench, which I thought must come from beyond the door, continued to torment, no matter how long we remained in the corridor. Though such a thing seemed unimportant, among all the issues of our investigation, I nonetheless wondered what could make such a stink.

My thoughts soon turned to Valon—about whom I seemed to learn important things every hour of our association. He was fast becoming the oddest man I'd ever met. I asked myself why does he seem so peculiar? His determination? His strange visions? His singular ability as a warrior? I looked at his face, as it shown in the dim light of the candles, and considered the strength of his gaze, fixed on the box.

Soon, from beyond the door —soft steps.

Valon heard it, too, and held high his candle. We stood well back from the trap at the foot of the door and fixed our gaze on the box.

CHAPTER 5

The Arms of the Troll

The sound of footsteps grew louder, until whoever approached stopped just short. There was a long pause as if the person might have heard us. My heart stopped. Suddenly, the trap opened, and from it came a strange sight—one I had not expected. Two arms and hands reached out to grasp the box. I put my hand over my mouth to gasp silently, as I saw them. The arms, the hands, they were small—the size of a child's, and yet they were covered with hair. Clearly human, they were also those of an animal of some kind.

Valon's gaze grew even more intense, as he, too, watched the hands. When they had disappeared and the trap closed, he looked at me, his eyes and face betraying the same astonishment I felt. We looked at each other for a long moment, no one saying or even whispering anything. We had all seen the thing, and there was no need for comment.

The sound of footsteps retreated down the corridor beyond the door, and we relit our torches and turned to retrace our steps to the cupboard door. When we'd passed the secret entrance and were climbing the stone stairs, I thought to ask Valon his opinion. But somehow, it seemed pointless to do so. How could he, or I, or anyone, make sense of what we'd seen?

The fires in the great hall burned low, and a damp chill hung in the cavernous expanse. I looked up to see snowflakes descending through the opening in the ceiling.

"I know your thoughts, Theodulfe," Valon volunteered, finally. "We saw it. A small creature with human-like arms and hands. But we cannot know that it was indeed human. That must wait until we see the rest of it, and we will surely do so, eventually. For now, it's enough that we have seen what we've seen, and we must add that into our thinking about this investigation."

"But that seems so little to make of the extraordinary thing we've seen."

"That's not all, however."

"Oh? And what other?"

"Recall the testimony of Hildegard. Her witness to what she saw the night of the girl's murder. Remember she told us that she'd seen not only 'the Monster'—who she seemed to identify as Lord Ethelred—but also a demon, who guided the Monster. She called that creature a small man and said he acted as the Monster's companion."

"Yes, I remember now you mention it. That's it then! We've just seen the demon. And the food—it must have been for the monster!"

"I do not know who or what he is, Theodulfe, but I believe we have just seen the arms and hands of the companion. And we now are asking the same question: Was that box of food intended for the Monster? What lies beyond that door? That is what we must now determine."

"But, how? Should we assert our authority? We have the power to demand to go beyond, and with the protection of the Lord of Châlons."

"Yes, we certainly do. But, consider. If we do that now, without sufficient consideration, we may discover something interesting, but at the expense of solving our mystery. How can we know what such a demand might produce?"

"Yes, I see what you mean. But, what then?"

"I cannot be certain, good Abbot. But I believe we must know more about someone who may have been the first victim in this mystery."

"Who?"

"The former Lady of Châlons, who jumped—or fell—from the tower."

CHAPTER 6

A Previous Tragedy

"How might we do that?"

"Not here, though Bodo may yet learn something of interest from the servants. He has a singular talent for persuading one of the Lord's daughters to tell all she knows."

I sighed inwardly and greeted the assertion with the indignant silence it deserved, and then I said a quiet prayer for the sinful Bodo's salvation.

"We must go to the monastery," Valon said. "I believe Abbot Hugo may have something useful to say on that score. At any rate, Lord Ethelred and his family must pass there and through the village today on their way home with the body of Lady Céleste, and I wish to observe that passing."

Within the hour we found ourselves once more entering the great gates of Saint Benoît du Lac, this time greeted by the Abbot himself, along with Brother Otto.

"Welcome, My Lord Valon. Welcome again, Theodulfe."

Greetings accomplished, Hugo led us into the precincts of the Scriptorium, where several of the monks busied themselves copying the great texts of the Church. From there, we followed him through a small door into the *Bibliotheca* of the monastery, past several hundred volumes of bound parchment and vellum that filled shelves. A warm fire crackled in a great hearth and we took comfortable chairs. To one side there was a large window, through which streamed the brightness of a sunny but crisp winter's morning. The old Abbot wrapped himself in a cloak of bearskin as he sat and bid us do the same.

"How may I assist, Missi Dominici? You have but to ask."

Valon hesitated, gathering his thoughts before proceeding. Even as he did, his face seemed troubled by what he wished to ask.

"Father Abbot, I know of the friction that has existed between you and Lord Ethelred. It is common talk, as I have learned. And, I can assure you that my investigations have nothing to do with the merits of this suit, in any way. The Great Charles will sort it out in his own justice, I have no doubt."

"Yes, Monsieur de Valon, we trust he will and we pray he will find that the donation of the former Lord of Châlons was a valid one."

"Nonetheless, I believe you may be able to give evidence of a particular kind concerning Lord Ethelred…or, rather concerning his late wife, Lady Editha."

Abbot Hugo grew noticeably uneasy at the name. He had clearly not expected Valon's line of questioning.

"How do you reckon that, Monsieur?"

"To put it boldly, Father Abbot, I learned that you and Lady Editha were close. That you were her Father confessor and that you advised her in her affairs generally."

The Abbot seemed even more guarded that Valon knew of his relations with Lady Editha. I learned later that Valon had obtained this information from Bodo, who had gleaned it from servants' hall gossip, and from the girl Gertrude, with whom we had already learned that Bodo had contrived a disgusting sexual liaison. May Our Lord have mercy on his soul and take into consideration that he is but a simple and dimwitted oaf whose life as a soldier has left him a slave to his most vile passions!

"It is as you say, My Lord. Lady Editha and I were friends, and I was her confessor. She was the most blessed of women, and I do not doubt that, despite the circumstances of her death, she is even now in the arms of Our Lord."

"So then, you believe the Lady did indeed take her own life. You give no credence to the rumors that she was murdered by her husband, that he might contract a marriage with his cousin?"

Hugo did not flinch at this additional suggestion.

"No, I do not discount such rumors entirely, but I have no proof."

"Do you then have information that caused you to believe the Lady took her own life?"

Now, an anguished look came upon the old monk's face, and he stood and looked out the sunlit window, considering, I thought, what to answer, or perhaps not to answer at all.

"I believe it, Monsieur, because I know how distressed the Lady was at her husband's determination to marry his cousin. She knew he was even searching at canon law a way to put her aside, and she despaired that her own efforts to prevent her husband's plan would fail."

"Ethelred actually took steps to annul his marriage to the Lady?"

"Yes. He entered a petition in the Ecclesiastical Court of the Bishop of Reims to that effect, charging the vilest actions on the part of the Lady, and even offering evidence she had practiced the dark arts."

"He charged that she was a sorceress?"

"Yes, sadly."

"And how did the Lady respond to these charges. Did she offer a counter-petition to the Bishop?"

"She certainly did, and I am pleased to say that I advised her on the matter. It angered and disgusted me that she should be treated thus. That she who I knew to be a blessed woman in God's eyes should be put to such abuse."

"Was that all? She merely rejected the claims?"

"Yes, and more. In her counter-petition, she argued that Lord Ethelred was enamored of his cousin and motivated to put Lady Editha aside in order to marry again. Lady Editha claimed, therefore, at Canon Law that Lord Ethelred should be prevented from marrying the girl, by virtue of kinship."

Valon seemed a bit confused. "You say, 'by virtue of relationship'?"

"Yes, the Lady maintained that in any case, the Bishop must deny Ethelred dispensation to marry his cousin by virtue of being within the proscribed degrees of kinship."

"Oh? And what effect did this have?"

"Very little real effect, because it was eventually denied. The Bishop observed that he could not rule until he had taken time to consider. He clearly intended to dither. Then he denied her petition on grounds that her case was weak. And yet, the Lady's demand sent Lord Ethelred into a rage that lasted for weeks, and I can tell you that during that time the Lady Editha feared for her life. She told me so. It was clear that if Ethelred succeeded in putting her aside and attempted to marry his cousin the Lady intended to block it by renewing her petition."

"Well then," I intervened, "is that not reason enough to suspect that Ethelred killed her, to prevent her renewed petition? He clearly intended to pursue his plan to marry his cousin."

"I suppose so, Theodulfe, but again I must say I have no proof of it. You see, on the day the Lady jumped from the tower, Ethelred was out hunting with several of his neighbors. He returned to find his wife dead. How could he have done it? No, I have thought much about it, and have come to believe that the Lady was driven to despair by the effort to put her aside and by the rejection of her petition. Lord Ethelred's influence and authority were not easily denied, and the Lady knew it. No, she was driven by the brute to kill herself, but jump she must have," Hugo lamented, shaking his head in sorrow.

Valon leaned back in his seat, folded his arms, and considered for a long moment what the Abbot had said. We sat in silence as he did so. Finally, he asked, "To your knowledge, Father Abbot, was any other member of the Lord's family prepared to take up the Lady Editha's petition to prevent Ethelred's marriage to his cousin?"

The question seemed to shake the Abbot just a little, it seemed because he had not thought it himself.

"Why, yes, Monsieur, now that you ask it. I have also been a confidante to Sister Céleste. She asked me not a month ago if I thought she might renew the petition. She had clearly learned of it from her mother, and was inclined to proceed with it if her father seemed to make good his intention to marry his cousin."

"But when the Lady Editha fell from the tower it all became moot," I suggested.

"Yes. Quite."

After some thanks and well-wishes, we took our leave of the old Abbot, who sat in thought before his hearth, as we closed the door of the *Bibliotheca.*

Once we were in the monastery's outer court, I observed to Valon, "Lord Ethelred is a most despicable character. And, he certainly seems to have had motive to kill his wife, even if there is no direct evidence. And, even if he were hunting at the time, might he not have caused her to be murdered? Hired an assassin?"

"Aye," Valon replied, "all that you say is true, or at least plausible. And, it seems at least that Ethelred stands guilty of driving his wife to jump from the tower. But…"

"What? 'But,' what?"

"But we are not here to convict the Lord of Châlons of being a cruel and heartless husband…of being a singularly despicable man…or even of being profane and hostile to Our Lord's Church. All that seems clear, but did he kill innocent girls and brutalize them? That's our issue and, so far, what do we have to connect him to those murders? The ravings of a witch who is now dead and the unfounded charges of villagers who hate their Lord for other reasons?"

"Still," I said, "Ethelred is our most likely villain at the moment, and may we not find the evidence we seek if only we persist?"

Valon listened intently to my assertion and seemed to consider it carefully. But then, Brother Martin approached us excitedly.

"Father Abbot. Monsieur de Valon, Lord Ethelred comes with his family!"

CHAPTER 7

Valon Weeps

As we ran to the monastery's tower and climbed the three levels to the top, we heard the horns of Lord Ethelred's heralds announcing his approach to the town. We peered over the Abbey's wall and out into the town square, where the villagers themselves began to assemble and to await the arrival. Then, from the west, we saw a column of riders. First came the Lord's Steward upon a white horse, followed by a column of men-at-arms riding two-by-two. Next, came a file of twenty wagons and carts, in the first the Prioress of Saint Agnes, followed by more than a score of her nuns. Behind the nuns came a flat-bed wagon pulled by two black horses, and upon the wagon, the small, simple box containing the body of the Lady Céleste, returning to her home and to burial in the crypt of the Manor's chapel. After the wagon, rode the Lord Ethelred of Châlons, his face ashen and laden with grief, his shoulders stooped noticeably, such that he seemed almost to collapse with each step of his great horse. A more dejected man I had seldom seen. Next, came, two-by-two, the sons and daughters of the Lord, first among them in line Guillaume, then Mordune, who rode in the wagon with his sister's coffin. And after these, another train of men-at-arms, again riding in their file of two.

The troop road silently, and as they passed onto the cobbles of the square, we could hear only the clatter of the wagon wheels and the clop-clop of horses' hooves. The villagers stood in silence, all with heads uncovered and bowed, in obvious respect for Lady Céleste. I noted that no man of them looked upon Lord Ethelred, and for his part, he looked only ahead, as if in thrall to his grief.

As the procession neared, a gentle snow began to fall, and the great gates of the Abbey opened. From it, the Lord Bishop and Abbot emerged, assisted by five monks—one to the front with a cross, followed by four acolytes, each swinging a censor that emitted a cloud of incense. When the Bishop approached, he stepped from his monks and circled the wagon carrying the body of Céleste, at each side sprinkling the box with holy water and blessing the corpse. That done, the Bishop and Abbot returned within the gates, followed by the Prioress and her nuns, who were to reside in the Abbey's pilgrim's hostel during their stay in Châlons.

All this accomplished and the Abbey gates once more closed, the solemn procession moved forward in the direction of the Manor. The snow now fell with greater authority. In only a few minutes the procession moved out of our sight and hearing.

In all this, I watched particularly the Lord and his family. Averting my gaze to Valon, I noted to my astonishment, that he was weeping—a look of indescribable grief upon his face.

CHAPTER 8

The Jew Incriminates

We had scarcely descended the steps from the tower when Valon received a summons from the Prioress to meet her after Compline, in her study just off the refectory of the pilgrims' hostel.

"Whatever could she want?" I wondered aloud.

"I do not know, but I suspect it touches upon the death of Sister Helena. Or, perhaps that of Céleste. Let us hope she is able to shed some light on both."

Just then the Brother Warder approached, an expression of urgency on his face.

"Father Abbot. Monsieur de Valon. There is a man at the gate who wishes to speak with you."

"Bring him to me," Valon ordered, a little irritated I thought at the interruption.

"I may not do so, Monsieur," the brother pleaded. "He is a Jew, My Lord, and he may not enter."

We walked quickly to the gate, where we found Mathias of Tours, standing with several horses and servants, and a wagon. He was wrapped against the cold and falling snow in a great cloak of furs.

"A bit late for travel, is it not?" Valon observed. "Hardly the sort of weather for travel."

I thought Mathias looked frightened as he answered. "My Lord Valon, it is late and I dread the snow, but I have decided to risk it. Châlons is no place for me just now. Before I leave, however, I wish to tell you why. I have been threatened, I believe on account of things I have said concerning the Abbot."

"Threatened?"

"Yes. I received a message early this morning. It says I and my household will be burned alive if we do not quit the town immediately."

Valon's eyes flashed anger. "If you choose to stay, Mathias, I will give you the King's protection."

"Thank you, My Lord, but I know these people well, especially the powerful among them. The King is far away, and they are here. I believe it is best for me to go, at least for a while."

"As you wish. But what must you tell me before leaving? You said you wished to say something."

"Indeed. It concerns old Hildegard. Something I have held back from you and everyone, though I believe some suspect it."

"The Witch? What about her?"

"She has a son. He lives still in the forest, near his mother's cave."

"A son?" I repeated.

"Yes, and a strange one he is. You see, old Hildegard kept him out of sight because of his appearance."

The Jew paused as if to reconsider what more he had to tell.

"You see, the boy is...he is misshapen. The folk hereabouts...well, those who know of him and have seen him, believe that he is a *loup-garou*, Monsieur. A werewolf."

"Utter nonsense!" Valon replied, now even angrier.

"Yes, I know. I do not believe such things. However, there is something peculiar about the boy, and you will see it when you find him. And, Monsieur, you must find him, because he knows much of his mother's dealings, including who she had business with. That boy can tell you much, and that is what I've come to say before I leave. You must find him and discover what he knows."

"How do you know all this?" I pressed him.

"Last night, when I had my servants clean the corpse of the witch and prepare her for burial, the boy came knocking about my door. He wished to see his mother a last time, and so I let him in. As he entered, I noted he had his face covered, but I could see his hairy hands and forearms. 'Twas him, alright.

"He told me he was grateful to me for seeing to his mother. I assured him it was the least I could do for a sister outcast. I took the opportunity to ask him if he knew who had killed his mother, and in such a brutal way. Who hated her so."

"And?" Valon pressed.

"And he told me that he would tell you. He wishes to see you, Monsieur. Of course, I promised to pass the word to you, and so I am here as I leave Châlons."

Mathias moved to leave, and Valon inquired after him, as he disappeared into the darkness.

"But where will I find this boy?"

"If you go to Hildegard's cave, he will find you, Monsieur. The boy sees everyone who travels in the forest. He will find you."

The seventh hour found us at the Sister Prioress' door and entering a chamber that seemed especially bare of the usual necessities, even by the standards of a monastery. The elderly nun, her posture erect and gaze direct, motioned us to sit by her fire, which blazed in the hearth. As we each accepted a cup of mulled wine, she explained.

"I have asked you here, Messieurs, to convey some of what transpired at the Convent of Saint Agnes during Lord Ethelred sojourn, and to tell something I have learned of Sister Helena's death. It may be important to your work."

"I am grateful to you, Sister, for your help."

"Well, now, as to Ethelred. While he was at St. Agnes, I had ample opportunity to speak with him and to observe him. I believe he is genuinely grief-stricken by his daughter's death and his emotions are something I never expected to see of him, quite frankly. While at dinner one evening in my study, just the two of us, he found himself a little in his cups and let slip something that may be important. He became quite emotional and asked me for the prayers of the Sisters of my convent. It was then he told me he believes one of his own family wishes to kill him, and that one of his own is even responsible for the terrible murders of girls in Châlons."

Valon and I leaned forward in our chairs at the same time.

"I was surprised, of course, and asked who he believed guilty. Of that, he would not speak, but he said further, almost as if to himself, that a family's secrets are the stuff of mischief and murder. Yes, Monsieur, that's exactly what he said. Mischief and murder, and family secrets. Odd, is it not?"

"Yes, Sister, very odd indeed, though the more I see of Lord Ethelred's family, the less odd it might seem," said Valon. "They are a peculiar lot. Of course, Ethelred would deny it all if I approached him with what you say, and so it is doubly useful to me that you have told me. And you said you have additional information regarding Sister Helena?"

"Yes, Monsieur de Valon, I do. It has struck at the heart of our community—our convent—that two of our beloved sisters have died. These are sad times, and to think that the two who were the best of friends and are now both dead."

"Yes, an odd double-tragedy, but I must suspect they are linked and that both may have some connection to the horrible deaths of girls in Châlons."

"I cannot speak to those suspicions, Monsieur, but I can provide one additional piece of information. When news of Sister Céleste's death reached the convent, one of the Sisters asked to speak with me about Sister Helena. It was Sister Brenda, who was closer to Sister Helena than most and who worked with her in cleaning the public areas of our refectory and stairs."

"I see."

"Sister Brenda told me she had known something about Sister Helena that she had been bound to keep in confidence when she should not have. She begged my forgiveness, and of course, I forgave her readily. It was then she told me something that shook me."

"Oh?"

"According to Brenda, Sister Helena was preparing to run away from the Convent and to

marry. She'd been enticed by a man—Brenda did not know who—to come with him on his promise of marriage."

"Did Sister Brenda know *anything* of this man?"

"Only one thing, Monsieur. Sister Helena told her he was a man of some substance."

"A man of substance, you say. No more than that?"

"I regret, Monsieur, but that is all Brenda was told, not a village youth as one might suspect, but rather a man of substance."

As we left the Prioress, the Sister Warder approached and asked to speak with Valon. I excused myself, and the two were able to speak privately to one side of the corridor. Then, in a moment, the Sister Warder departed and I returned from the discreet distance where I had lingered.

"What was that about, if you may tell?" I asked.

"Nothing. A bit of tittle-tattle that I must keep to myself, if you please. But it was nothing," he assured.

I learned later that the Sister Warder had given Valon a message from a man. A Jew. The Jew—clearly Mathias—wished Valon to see him in the garden of the convent, near the door that led down the hill. He reportedly wished to meet Valon alone, because he had more to tell, which he did not wish me to hear. He believed, he said, that I was hostile to him because of his evidence against the Abbot.

Fearing Valon might once again fall into a trap, I quickly dispatched the oaf Bodo to follow him and watch him from a distance. He later reported that he did so.

That seemed reasonable to Valon, who went to the garden as soon as we parted. He waited there in the dim light of the torches across the cloister, for "the Jew," whom he assumed to be Mathias of Tours. Bodo, who watched at a distance from the cover of hedges, heard a sound behind him. As he turned, he felt the dull thud of something striking his head.

Valon meanwhile sat on a stone bench thinking of all the Sister Prioress had related. Not far into his musing he too was struck from behind and fell to the ground, unconscious.

CHAPTER 9

The Pit

When he awakened, his head throbbed with pain, and he found himself in a place both cold and wet. Worse, the place stank of rotting corpses. Valon's confusion in the dark persisted for some time, as he felt his way around the strange place where he lay. He could sense that he lay in mud or muck of some kind. Soon, his mind cleared sufficiently that he could tell he was in a deep pit, and when he looked up, he could see in the distance the mouth of the pit and beyond it, stars in the sky.

The thought of shouting for help somehow seemed at odds with his throbbing head, so Valon contented himself to search of his *sacullus*, in which he knew to find a flint, dry straw, and the stump of a candle. Though the *sacullus* itself was wet, the straw and flint remained dry. After a half-hour's effort Valon was able to light his candle and see more clearly his surroundings.

The pit was perhaps ten feet across, with rock walls too steep and smooth to climb. With him in the muddy floor of the pit lay the rotting carcass of a small deer—the unfortunate creature had fallen in the pit. *My fate*, Valon thought, *if I do not find a way out of this*.

A few minutes of clear consideration told Valon that whoever had put him in the pit knew that shouting for help would gain nothing. The place, he concluded, must be far from people. Still, he decided it was worth the effort to should occasionally, especially if he heard a sound. So, he decided that he must listen carefully for any sound.

Several hours later, Valon saw the first light of dawn above him and soon the floor itself was lighted. The pit appeared perhaps thirty feet deep, and now able to examine the surface of its walls, he was more optimistic. It appeared the irregularities and crevasses in the wall made it just possible to climb, and so he began to think how to do so. Soon, he was climbing, feeling his way up the steep surface, finding any small recess to place a foot and any protruding rock for a handhold. By tedious climbing over the first hour, he found himself ten feet above the pit's floor and even more encouraged that it would be possible to escape. Plotting every move carefully, he reached out to seize a rock that extended invitingly from the wall and pulled himself still higher. But then, the rock gave way. He crashed to the floor, a cascade of rubble falling after him.

Luckily, his fall was broken by the deer's corpse, but still, pain wracked his body. Eyes closed, he uttered a prayer to All the Saints and lay for a long while, thinking about his life and his endless misfortunes. He thought also of the Great Charles, who had foolishly entrusted a great mission to someone stupid enough to be lured to the convent garden a second time. *And consider where it has got you,* he reproached himself. *In this pit, which you must share unto death with a stinking deer.*

Hours passed in such consternation, and those passed into a day. As darkness settled upon the pit's opening for yet another night, it somehow signaled to Valon that there was no escape and he would pass a long succession of such days. From the Frisian War, he knew how long he could persist without food and water—he had gone that distance before. *How long,* he asked himself, *before I eat that rotting carcass, and whatever is in this water?* Dreadful thoughts. *First, I will drink my piss, as I once did in the War.*

Soon, he could see the moon through the mouth of the pit, and as he looked at it, he thought he could hear a noise—a muffled scuffling from above. *An animal, of some sort,* he concluded. *No reason to arouse your expectations. Yes, an animal. Perhaps he will fall in, like brother deer, and give me a meal.* And then, only the silence of the forest night, and a familiar, wet cold settling into the bottom of the pit.

Valon passed yet another night thinking of all manner of things—the Great Charles and the Mission he'd given to him, Lady Céleste, friends and companions he'd known in the War. He even decided to review the evidence of the murders, the great mass of conflicting evidence he had collected so far. *So much evidence and no clarity.* He sighed. *No clarity at all.*

Hours later he began to drift in and out of sleep, despite the cold of the water and the hardness of the rock at his back. And in that half-wakefulness, he felt and heard many things, none of them quite real. Singing of angelic voices, the deep tones of Charlemagne's voice, the dreadful wailing of Lord Ethelred as he cradled the broken body of his daughter in his arms. And then, amongst the other unreal sounds, a strange voice saying in Latin, *"Occupo is. Occupo terminus funis quod escendo is. Escendo is.* Take it. Take the end of the rope and climb it. Climb it."

Rousing himself, Valon shouted, "Who sings to me so beautifully? Who speaks to me in Latin?" Though he knew that it was merely his wild imaginings. *Or, it must be God, inviting me finally to Heaven.*

"It is I," came the reply once more in Latin. "It is I who speaks to you. Now, take the rope and climb it."

More convinced than ever that his mind was tricking him, Valon took up a handful of the cold, putrid water and splashed it in his face. He then looked to the pit's opening and could see nothing except stars. "Who? Is someone there?" he asked, this time hoping for a reply, but knowing none would come.

"It is I," came the quick response. "Take the rope and climb." And again, it was said in the most perfect Latin.

Valon could see no rope but began to feel about the slimy walls of the pit in the darkness. Finally, his hand touched a rope. It was real! A rope! Putting aside his disbelief, he scrambled up the rope, using his legs and toes against the wall to boost every move of his ascent, but sometimes missing on the slippery rocks.

Twenty minutes of effort brought him near the mouth of the pit. Dirt loosened by the rope and by his movements began to come down on his head, and yet he continued to pull himself up, hand over hand. When he'd reached the rim of the pit, he followed the rope over the edge and continued pulling until he was able to scramble over the edge and, at last, to rest on the surface.

There he lay, exhausted, hearing nothing, and seeing nothing of who bade him take the rope and climb. The speaker of beautiful Latin. Where he lay, he found beside him a burning torch, stuck in the soft ground. He took it up and held it high.

"Where are you?" he demanded. "Who are you? Come out!"

"I am here," came the hesitant reply, from behind a nearby tree.

Still on the ground and recovering his wind, Valon was unprepared for what he saw. He gasped, as from behind the tree stepped the *werewolf*.

CHAPTER 10

The Creature

The sight of the creature so frightened Valon that he recoiled, and began to scramble about for something—anything—to use as a weapon. He brandished the torch. In only a few seconds, however, it occurred to him that there would be no need of weapons. Whatever the creature before him was, it was to him that he owned his life.

"I apologize, friend. It's just that your appearance is so unusual you at first startled me. Please, forgive me."

"Do not concern yourself of that," the creature said, still speaking Latin.

"Do you speak only Latin? I ask because I notice that you have only spoken Latin to me. Do you not know the Frankish language?"

"I speak only one language—the only language that my mother gave me. Only Latin."

"Well, aside from your appearance, that may also mark you as unique. I have never before in my life met anyone who could speak only Latin. And your Latin is as perfect as I have ever heard it spoken."

The creature laughed. "No one has ever found me remarkable for my Latin!"

"What is your name?" Valon asked.

"Name?" the creature asked. "I have no name. No need, as you might understand."

"Yes, I see." And then changing the subject, "The Jew, Mathias of Tours, told me of you. You came to see him...to see your mother."

"The witch was not my mother. Not my real mother. But she was the only mother I ever knew. She found me in the forest. Abandoned from the town. Left to die, because of what I am, I suppose. She fed me and taught me to speak and to care for myself."

"How do you live? What do you eat? Animals?"

"No." He laughed again. "I sometimes find dead animals to eat, but mainly I live from what I find. What I find on bushes—the berries—and the roots I dig. The witch taught me to dig roots that are to eat. I also eat what I find under rocks."

"And your clothing?"

"From Father Draco. I never allow him to see me, but we have spoken, in the darkness. He has good Latin, like yours. He told me of God, and of Jesus Christ. He told me also of baptism and wished me to have it, but I did not think so. I did not think I wanted to have the baptism," he said vehemently.

"Well, that is your choice, as far as I know. Why did you rescue me? How did you know to find me here?"

"I saw you thrown in there. At first, I went away and decided to mind my own business. You are no friend of mine. But after thinking I decided that the witch might want me to help you. Father Draco would want it, too."

"You saw who put me in the pit?" Valon pressed.

The boy recoiled sheepishly. "Yes. They came into the forest in the evening. I could smell them. One—the big one—carried you on his shoulders, like a sack of grain. The other—the dark one who led him—carried nothing. They lowered you into the pit. They wanted you to live and to starve down there. Otherwise, they would have crushed your head before throwing you in there."

"Yes. You are right. That was one of the things I thought about, as I sat down there. Why did my attackers put me there, alive? Why not dead?"

"I don't know. But I saw them lower you, so I knew you were alive."

"You say you saw them put me in the pit. Who did you see? Who put me in the pit?" Valon encouraged. "Who did you see?"

"Couldn't see their faces, but there were two of them. The big one who carried you was very large, like Lord Ethelred and The One-eyed. As big as them. The other was a slight man, smaller than the usual. He wore black and told the other what to do. 'Go here. Put him there,' he would say. That kind of ordering about. They didn't speak in Latin, but I know what he was saying."

"Was the smaller man so small that he is a dwarf? That small?" Valon asked.

"Ha. So you know about the troll, do you? No, I have seen the dwarf. It wasn't him, said the werewolf. "The man in black was merely a small man."

"You've seen the dwarf?" Valon exclaimed.

"Yes. In the forest. I've seen him sometimes."

"Did you know that Hildegard saw him also—saw both the dwarf and the giant who murdered a girl in the town? Did she tell you of that?"

"No. I did not know that."

"Do you know who killed her? Who killed the witch?"

"I did not see it, but I know she spoke to one other from the town, besides Father Draco. They met from time to time and talked of the secret knowledge that Hildegard had from the Evil One. Sometimes, they argued.

She did not like him, but he paid her for potions and so she spoke with him. She laughed one time that he was even more evil than the Evil One himself!"

"Who was the visitor?"

"I don't know," Simon answered. "I don't know his name and did not see his face. I could only see that he dressed in a black robe, like Father Draco."

"A monk, then?" Valon pressed

"I don't know," Simon answered.

"You say the visitor bought potions. Potions for what purpose? Do you know?"

"Yes. The Witch told me. Potions to make others do as you wish."

As the boy-creature spoke Godfrey's name, they heard a rustling among the leaves behind them and they turned. Elise stepped out from the brush, startled to see them. Taking in the sight of the two and a look at the boy convinced her to draw a knife, apparently to defend Valon.

"No! No need of that!" Valon shouted. "He's our friend!"

As Elise relented, she nonetheless staggered forward in amazement at the sight of the boy-creature.

"He's not a werewolf. Only malformed, by God, like those who are born lame or blind. Think of him that way," Valon reassured.

"Yes, My Lord," she said in a quiet voice, but still casting a suspicious eye on the boy.

"I am amazed. How do you come here?" Valon asked.

Elise hesitated. "Looking for you. I saw them take you from the garden and down the hill, but I could not follow in the darkness. I have continued to search in the forest in the direction they took you. Now I am lost myself. So, it's not I who have found you, but we who have found each other. Where are we?"

The boy answered. "You are north of the town. Half the distance from the convent to the Manor. This pit belongs to Lord Ethelred. It is said that in the time of his father, they dug silver here, but it has not been found here in many years."

Notice the elevation of the sun," said Valon, as he came to his feet.

"We must return to the convent. Theodulfe will be worried and exorcising demons from everyone in sight to find me. I'm sure he has sent out the soldiers and brother monks to find me, and they have likely gotten lost, as you did."

"That is true," Elise declared. "I heard them shouting in the forest."

"Will you guide us as quickly as possible to the convent or to the road?" Valon asked the boy.

Motioning for them to come, the boy headed swiftly into the trackless forest, as if he knew his way by some secret path. Within the hour they came to the road.

"Go that way up the road and in only a little while you will come to a path to the convent."

As Valon and Elise moved onto the road, the boy said, "One thing. Simon."

"What do you mean?"

"I told you I have no name, but that is not so. I call myself Simon. Father Draco told me that I may have a name like other people if I am baptized, so I have given myself that name."

Valon stepped forward, took his hand, and said, "Simon, I owe you my life and I thank you for that. Even more, I tell you that the Great Charles smiles upon those who save the lives of his Missi Dominici. We shall meet again, my friend."

CHAPTER 11

We Return to the Manor

Valon's sudden disappearance left me agonizing almost to illness at the possibilities. I dispatched the brother monks and the two soldiers to search for him, both in the precincts of the convent and beyond. I did not wish to cause a commotion at the absence, because it occurred to me that Valon might have disappeared of his own will and for reasons he believed would advance our investigation. Also, I did not want to alert those who might oppose us, now that Valon had disappeared.

When Valon and Elise suddenly appeared in the refectory, therefore, it was cause for quiet celebration among those of us who looked to him as the leader of our mission. In the quiet of the convent's chapel, he told us the story of his abduction, his time in the pit, and rescue by Simon. It seemed a frightening revelation, but at the end of it, one question loomed more obvious than others.

"We might wonder who abducted you, Valon, but my quandary is why they did not kill you outright. Why take the trouble of placing you in the pit, alive?"

"Aye. That vexes me as well. Why that? There are several possible answers, but one stands out in my mind because it is somehow more disturbing."

"What is that, pray?"

"Hatred. That the villain we seek has now, for some reason, come to hate me. That is a possibility that must give us pause to consider."

Valon slept much of that day, and as we departed the convent next morning, intending to return to the Manor, he told me of his conviction that it was now time, by any means possible, to investigate the subterranean corridor beyond the strong door. The early morning chill of December seemed to pierce my cloak and fur, as we made our way from the town to the Manor. The grass and shrubs at the side of our path glistened with frost and the white clouds gathering in the west promised snow. It was in the air.

When we neared the Manor gates, Valon began to explain. "I now know how to defeat the inner door of the passage."

"How is that? The door was not only locked but bolted from the inside. And it is strongly made. Would take a ram to batter it down. And if we did that our adversaries would know we'd been there."

"You are correct, but I have found the perfect solution. I am going to use the best means at my disposal to trip that bolt."

"And that is?"

"Elise!"

CHAPTER 12

Beyond the Strange Door

"Valon, you cannot take a child—a mere girl—into such danger! It's unconscionable!"

"I have already considered that. And, you forget one thing, Theodulfe," he cautioned, as we entered the great hall, a wry smile on his face.

"And that is, my son?"

"You forget that no mere girl who is with Valon is in any danger at all. Ergo, good Theodulfe, the scheme is entirely conscionable. Besides, Elise has more grit than any warrior in Charlemagne's army. I've already seen that."

Somehow the logic of Valon's assertion, based on all evidence I could summon, was convincing, so I was forced to the only objection remaining to me. "And have you told Elise what you wish? What is her opinion?"

"I have already *acquired* her agreement, good Theodulfe. I have put Bodo to tell Elise of the difficulty and what she must do, and I have a message from Bodo that both will await us in my chamber as we return."

We climbed the stone stairs to the second level, where both Valon and I were well-situated. Entering his chamber, we found Bodo, whose history of vile fornications had been the object of my constant prayers since coming to know his wicked character, and Elise, who seemed to me as scruffy as usual. She was just a slip of a thing, and I wondered just how Valon proposed to use her to defeat the door.

"We have important work to do this night, Elise, and you are to lead us in that. Are you prepared to be a good soldier of the Great Charles, and to do as you are told?"

"Oh, yes, Sir, I am!" she said enthusiastically, as she came to her full height.

"Good! Now I want you to come over to that bench with me and I will instruct you exactly what we are to do this night, and what your part will be. When we arrive at our destination, you must then do exactly as I have instructed, and with very few words. Do you understand?"

"Yes, Monsieur," the girl repeated, smiling proudly.

For the next five minutes or so, the two sat in a corner of Valon's chamber and the Missi Dominici instructed his new soldier in the part he wished her to play that evening.

When all was finished and we were joined by the brother monks, we left the chamber and made our way down the stone stairs to the first level. As we arrived, we could hear chanting coming from the great hall where the Lord and his family, led by Father Draco and attended by the entire household, were at prayers over the body of the Lady Céleste. It was the preface to her funeral, which was to be held next day in the Manor's chapel.

Shielded by a wall, we slipped past the sad ceremony and found our way once more to the stairs that led to the subterranean portions of the manor. Once past the secret entrance behind the cupboard, we moved silently by candlelight down the dark passage, around the corner, and toward the inner door. In only a few minutes, we stood once more before the ironclad door, which seemed as formidable as it had previously. We also found the same unusual stink as before. Brother Boethius vomited at the first sniff of it.

Lighted by a candle in Bodo's hand, Valon first defeated the great lock. Hearing the inner tumbler fall, he declared it open. Then, turning his attention to the trap at the bottom of the door, through which those frightening hands had taken the box of food, he inspected it carefully, again lighted by Bodo.

"I believe it is unlocked," he said in the faintest whisper.

Then, turning to Elise, he said, "Alright, soldier. It is now your turn, and remember the Great Charles is counting on you."

Nodding, but without a word, the girl lay on her back, her head pointed toward the trap. Valon pulled at the trap, opened it, and the girl moved to slide through, headfirst and still on her back, but she was prevented from passing by the thickness of her chest.

"Curse the luck!" Valon growled. "I thought she was flat enough to fit!"

Valon pulled her up. Taking his own scarf, he wrapped it tightly around the girl's chest, so as to pull her breasts even flatter than God had made them. "Now, try again. You'll fit," he reassured.

"Good Heavens!" said Boethius. "I had no idea you could do that!"

Bodo cast his eyes heavenward but said nothing.

This time, she passed easily. Once she disappeared behind the door, Valon passed through the trap a short ladder that Brother Martin had carried. The ladder allowed Elise to reach the bolt near the top of the door.

In a moment, we heard both the lower and upper bolts move very quietly so as not to reverberate down the passage. Elise was clearly well-instructed on how to move the bolts and did as she was told. Then, there came only silence from the other side, as Elise and her little ladder waited quietly in the darkness for Valon to push the door open.

Still lighted by Bodo's candle, Valon took from his *sacullus* a small pouch. With a finger, he scooped out what was in it and took it into his mouth. Then stooping, he spat a bit of the contents on each hinge.

"What is that?" I asked.

"Butter."

Then, his hand on the great door's handle, Valon pushed with a jolt. The thing moved with hardly a sound. On the other side stood Elise, smiling her glee and relief at being reunited with us.

"Well done, girl," Valon said, and rubbed the mop atop her head and untied the scarf around her chest. Then, taking the girl's hand and giving it to Brother Martin, he said to her, "Wait here with the brother monks. Understand?" The girl nodded.

Leaving the monks and Elise to guard the opened door and to warn of any approach, we three ventured in, lighted only by Bodo's candle. Once inside, the stink was far worse than when the door was closed. Our going was difficult, such was our caution to make no sound and such was the darkness of the passage, despite our light.

As we approached and peered round another turn in the passage, we could see at a distance a faint light emitted from one wall.

"A door," Valon whispered.

Inching slowly down the passage, our hands on one wall and without the light of our candle, we came within a few feet of the door. We could now see that a dim light was coming from a small window in the door—a peephole and no more. Bodo and I hung back, while Valon moved forward, crouching to avoid the window. Then, slowly rising up to gain a glimpse through the hole, he gasped to behold a horrible sight.

CHAPTER 13

Into the Darkness

There in the dimly-lighted cell, stood a large filthy man, mostly naked and chained by both arms to the far wall. His head was covered entirely by a black cloth masque. He stood, muttering and groaning to himself as if a tethered animal. It was a pitiful sight. Then, as if for no reason at all, the prisoner erupted in growls and shouts of incredible pain, which resounded down the passageway.

"A mad man," Valon later concluded, "and kept a prisoner."

When Valon had finished his inspection of the prisoner, he motioned me and then Bodo forward to sneak a look. When we had, he signaled us to follow him still farther down the corridor into the darkness.

When we had progressed perhaps ten yards into what seemed complete darkness, Valon again whispered, "Let us see where this goes."

The sight of the creature in the cell had sapped my taste for more exploration, but nonetheless, Bodo and I followed Valon into the shadows, still feeling our way slowly along the wall. When it seemed safe to do so, Valon took from his *sacullus* a flint and dry twig of fatwood and lit his candle. The light gave us leave to proceed more quickly down the stone tunnel, which seemed to grow smaller by all dimensions from this point forward.

Now, as we stooped slightly to advance, we soon came to a wall, which appeared to be the end of the thing. At that wall, however, we found a ladder, rising through a small hole in the roof of the tunnel. We climbed until we were able to step off the ladder onto a stone floor. Once there, Valon held high his candle.

"Where are we?" I whispered but got only silence in return.

The light from the candle revealed a bare, windowless room of no more than ten feet square. In one wall, there was a small door. Valon motioned us to remain still, as he ventured quietly toward the door. Listening for any noise beyond, and looking under to see if any light could be observed, he lifted the latch slowly and quietly and opened the door a crack. Closing the door, he reported.

"We are in the crypt of the Manor, perhaps fifty yards from the house itself. The crypt is lighted by a small window in one wall."

As we entered the strange room, lined with the sarcophagi of the family of Châlons, and with additional burial places in the walls, covered by carved tablets, I felt a sudden, compelling urge to flee, as if from some unseen but palpable danger. And yet, Valon crept on, toward the entrance to the crypt. Bodo and I followed.

At the door, Valon paused and peered through a small window. Seeing all that he needed, he motioned us to retreat by the same way we had come.

We made our way down the ladder and once more into the dark tunnel. Now, fearing no intrusion from whoever cared for the prisoner, we proceeded with three candles and more quickly past the prisoner, who still groaned and moaned in the agony of his chains, and even quicker toward the door where Boethius, Martin, and Elise waited. Once past the door, Valon wrapped Elise's breasts again, and we left her on the other side with her ladder, closed the door, and listened for her to shift the bolt. She then pushed her ladder through the trap and followed it, again sliding on her back.

"Excellent, girl," Valon encouraged, and taking Elise's hand, led us in retracing our steps toward the cupboard and the great hall.

CHAPTER 14

Who is the Prisoner

We'd been gone for no more than an hour, and upon returning found that the ritual of mourning for the dead Céleste continued. While the brother monks and Elise returned to the servants' hall and kitchen, Valon and I watched and listened from a distance, still unseen by the mourners.

The recitation of prayers was soon finished, followed by the chanted litany of all the saints, led by Draco and answered by the mourners.

"Santa Lucia."

"Ora pro nobis."

"Santa Barbara."

"Ora pro nobis."

"Santa Viviana."

"Ora pro nobis."

And so on, for more than half an hour, intoning the prayer that asks each of the saints to *pray for us*.

Long before the litany ended, however, Valon motioned me to follow him to his chamber.

"We have learned much about the prisoner in the subterranean tunnel, but mainly we know he is very likely there at Lord Ethelred's order. But why? And, who is he? Those are the questions we must answer. And neither will be easy."

"Yes, but does it seem to you that this prisoner has any relation to our investigation? Unusual as his imprisonment is, I cannot think of a single piece of evidence we have uncovered that links this prisoner with the murder of young girls. And, Ethelred may imprison as he pleases. He is Lord here and has the right. Many of the Frankish lords keep a dungeon."

"Theodulfe, you are perfectly reasonable in what you say. There is no evidence, and yet, I sense a connection, if only we could discover it. I come back to two problems, the murder of Sister Helena and the prisoner, and I am utterly convinced that both, somehow, are part of our mystery, and perhaps the most part."

"If that is so, Valon—and I confess I feel the same as you—then we must put our minds to these issues. And, all that we do must answer them."

As I spoke this, Bodo knocked at the door, to tell us Lord Ethelred had ordered that the Lady Céleste would be laid to rest the following morning, after a *Requiem* mass in the Village Church. The Lord Bishop agreed to offer the mass, with Father Draco and the Abbot Hugo assisting. It promised, I thought, to be an especially solemn occasion, and I wondered about my companion's emotions. *They were clearly strong for the Lady Céleste—much stronger than I had at first suspected. Even now I could sense he was fighting through his own grief at her death. But, could he withstand the sadness that her funeral was likely to arouse? Could he struggle past that to do what we must do?* I worried. I did not know.

CHAPTER 15

Requieum aeternan dona ei

I slept poorly on thoughts of how far we seemed to be from a solution. It pleased Our Lord to give me no rest, despite a night of prayers. In that darkness, I concluded that Valon had proved himself a strong and relentless man, and so I had no cause to doubt that his resolve would carry him past the grim events of the coming day. And yet, as I arose that morning there seemed in the chill air of the Manor a palpable sadness that somehow reached beyond the fact of Lady Céleste's death and gathered up into one great heap all the grief that had recently accumulated round the murder of the village girls and the horrible death of Sister Helena. Yes, somehow, it all seemed to concentrate on this day, as if a river of sadness, pouring into the event of the coming funeral.

We gathered with the family for a grim breakfast of cold meats and mulled wine. There was no talk, beyond the briefest words of greeting from Mordune. Ethelred was not yet down from his chamber, and the Lord's children stood as silent as their sister's corpse.

Valon, too, had little to say. His eyes betrayed a night as sleepless as my own. And more, his face seemed drawn with grief; such that I worried anew that he was overcome with his emotions for the Lady Céleste.

Not waiting for Ethelred to arrive and for the funeral cortege to gather, Valon ordered the brother monks and soldiers to accompany us to the church, straightaway. As we descended the hill into the village, we saw the townsfolk gathering in the square to observe the family of Châlons as they processed. We could see, as well, the nuns of Saint Agnes, led by their Sister Prioress, emerging from the Abbey and walking single file to the church. Behind them came the monks of Saint Benoît du Lac, two-by-two, their heads shrouded by their black cowls, and numbering near a hundred. It was a remarkable sight, and, throughout, it was silent. *The silence*, I thought, *of the crypt*.

The cortege bearing with it Céleste's body moved slowly down the path to the town, taking nearly an hour to arrive, and all the while, the Church bells tolled—endlessly it seemed their melancholy tidings. After the simple box was carried into the church by Céleste's brothers and placed on its bier, Valon and I took up our view, standing at the back of the mourners. The Bishop and his acolytes followed the box—*such a small box*, I thought—and after blessing the corpse, commenced the *Requiem*.

"*Requiem aeternam dona ei, Domine, et lux perptua luciat ei. Requiescat in pace. Amen*," the Bishop began his chant.

The funeral mass that followed took most of the morning and after, all those attending and a large number of the townsfolk followed the box solemnly up the hill to the manor, where the Lady Céleste was placed in the family's crypt. And in all this, Valon said nothing, his face ashen. The weight of his emotions, for the first time since I had known him, showed clearly in his entire being. Most remarkably, the bright light was gone entirely from his eyes.

By evening all visitors to the Manor had departed. The Bishop and Father Draco lingered longer than most, as did several of Ethelred's neighbors, also vassals of the Comte de Meaux. The Comte attended as well but did not remain long after the funeral mass. Neither Valon nor I approached him to introduce ourselves. The occasion somehow did not give an opportunity, but he acknowledged our presence by a nod of his head.

While Father Draco remained at the Manor, Valon questioned him further about the Lord's family, and particularly those with whom the priest enjoyed a special relationship.

"Can you tell me, Father, if any of the Lord's children blame him for the death of his wife, Lady Editha? I understand of course that there is an unfounded belief in the town that he was responsible; that the death was not a suicide."

I was startled by the question that seemed to come from nowhere.

Draco's face grew even more distressed. "Yes, Monsieur. I would say that both Godfrey and Mordune are inclined to believe that, and that is certainly part of their hatred of their father. Lady Céleste did not accept it, and it was a source of divergence between Mordune and the Lady because he is utterly convinced that it is true. Though, in her deepest fear, I believe even Céleste may have had her suspicions. But who can know such things?" He shrugged.

"And the reasons the brothers believe this?"

"Only one reason, Monsieur. They believe Lord Ethelred murdered his wife in order to marry his cousin."

"But surely both of them are aware that Ethelred could have found sufficient pretext to put his wife aside if it came to that. The Frankish nobles do it often. Even the Great Charles has done so. Why do they not take that into account?"

Draco hesitated, his expression increasingly distressed. "There is something known that accounts for their conviction. I have not said it, because I consider it no more than a falsehood, but there it is."

"There what is?"

"Both Godfrey and Mordune believe their father was unable to put his wife away because she refused and because she held some leverage over the Lord that prevented it."

"Oh? What leverage?"

Draco's expression changed from uncomfortable to painful. "It is believed, Monsieur, that Lady Editha shared a terrible secret with Lord Ethelred and that she held it over his head that she would reveal it if he dared put her aside."

Valon remained silent for a long moment, obviously considering this last more carefully than anything he had yet heard of the priest. I, meanwhile, was startled at the revelation.

"And, why do you consider this assertion a 'falsehood,' Father? Or, is it merely unproved?"

Draco seemed a little confused by the question but responded directly. "Simply this, Monsieur, that it is unfounded upon any evidence at all. I suppose one might say it is 'unproven,' but that would seem generous to me. An unfounded rumor is an unfounded rumor. I am a simple man, Monsieur, and I do not torture words of their meaning."

"Yes, I see that. Now, you say there was a disagreement between the Lady Celeste and Mordune. Would you say that disagreement has turned to bad blood? And, for any other reasons that you know?"

"Oh, no, Monsieur. I know of no other reason. It seemed to me, in fact, that they remained as close as in the past. They were twins you know—a bond that is lifelong, they say."

"Twins…yes, so I've heard. Connected by that bond."

And then a light suddenly came into Valon's eyes. I noticed it. So did Draco.

"This mystery seems to have many pairs in it, many twins you might say. Céleste and Helena were a pair in the convent, were they not? Guillaume and Humphrey are inseparable, they say another pair. The Steward took food to the tunnel for two—yet another pair. And you and I, Theodulfe, are another pair, are we not? The Missi Dominici always go in pairs."

I found nothing to make of this observation. Curious perhaps, but not germane. And yet, as soon as Valon pronounced it, Draco seemed to find it both interesting and, I thought, frightening. His eyes opened wide, he became more thoughtful, and afterward, he excused himself and left the Manor.

"What was that about?" I wondered aloud.

"Who can know? Draco was seized with some thought that made him fearful and even caused him to run away. Did it seem to you he was frightened?"

"Yes, frightened."

"But, of what?"

"Or, of whom?"

CHAPTER 16

Valon Suspects the Church

It was Father Draco's fright, rather than any of the other events of the previous day, that weighed upon my mind and gave me another fitful sleep that night. As I considered the many possible explanations for Draco's behaviour, I could think of nothing that would suffice.

At mid-morning next day, I sought out Valon but was told he and Bodo had gone hunting with Lord Ethelred and a large company of his family and neighbors. I wondered at this unusual intimacy with the Lord of Châlons. Boethius speculated that Valon may have wished to observe more of the relations between Ethelred and his sons, all of whom were in the party.

Despite the light snow that began to fall at mid-day, leaving a modest covering upon the ground, the hunting party did not return until mid-afternoon. When I saw Valon, he seemed more confident of his conclusions about Ethelred, but I had no notion of what those were.

"Have you considered, Father Abbot, that there is an explanation for these murders that has little to do with this Manor, but signals that we should have remained in the Abbey?"

"And what is that?" I asked, half fearing that Valon had somehow adopted the wild speculation of the Jew, Mathias of Tours.

"I mean simply that Lord Ethelred may be entirely peripheral to this mystery and that the solution may lay with the church—with the Abbey and Bishop."

My heart sank. The Jew had led Valon astray. Then I was angry. "But what evidence do we have of that?" I huffed.

"I have been privy to some information from Ethelred's closest neighbors, who seem to me to have no personal interest in the case at all. To a man, they believe that the Abbot Hugo and Bishop are capable of the meanest actions to undermine Ethelred, who they fear will win the suit before the King for the return of the lands that were alienated by his father."

"Is that true, then?"

"It is. I was able to question three in strictest confidence, and their testimony is that Abbot Hugo especially is a sly and vengeful man who would stop at nothing to win that suit and to protect the Abbey's lands."

"But, Valon, you are suggesting murder! In fact, you are suggesting the most horrible crimes against innocent girls! That goes well beyond devious behaviour or even dishonest dealings. The evidence surely suggests that there is a peculiarly evil and demonic mind at work in all this. Or, is this a matter of Satan himself having his way?"

"That is the appearance, Theodulfe, but consider, that is precisely what one would contrive to make a case against Lord Ethelred, to paint him as a Monster. And, in truth, Ethelred assists such a perception by his own usual demeanor. He is an unpleasant man, and perhaps even an evil man. But still, we must ask, 'Is he the evil man who is killing girls?' All I am suggesting now is that there is a danger we will fall to spending our time trying to prove Ethelred is guilty when perhaps we should be sifting evidence and allow it to guide us where it will.

"And consider another thing."

"Oh?"

"It is said that Guillaume is even now the very image of his father as a young man. In the dark of night might he not appear to be his father?"

* * * *

Early afternoon found us in the market square of Châlons, accompanied by Bodo, and bound, as Valon told me, for the shop of the miller, Osbern, whose daughter was a victim of the Monster. Osbern reportedly also was an enemy of Lord Ethelred. I imagined to myself as we walked that Valon wished to learn what Osbern knew, as opposed to what he merely believed, in his grief and hatred of Ethelred.

Osbern and his wife were at work in their mill, which operated by a large wheel driven by the ample flow of the River Marne. The mill itself was fed by a jetty on the river, which since ancient times had sent a more vigorous flow through the millrace.

Osbern," Valon said authoritatively, "we wish a moment with you if you are able to spare it."

The miller said something to a boy who was helping and then turned full face to us.

"Yes, Monsieur. If I may assist, I will. I know the Great Charles has sent you to investigate our troubles, and for that, we are all thankful."

The miller's greeting seemed heartfelt, and his wife, who continued at the mill, turned to nod her approval.

"The Great Charles and the Archbishop are concerned for your troubles, Osbern, and wish to help. But, in that, I need you to help me, by answering my questions honestly, despite your feelings in the matter. Justice is a dispassionate thing when it is done well, and so we must try to put our feelings aside when doing Justice."

"Yes, Monsieur, I understand."

"It is said that you saw something strange on the night that your…on the night you lost your daughter. Tell me what you saw, without exaggerating and without leaving anything out. I leave you to tell your story as you please."

The miller hesitated as if to gather his wits, or perhaps, his courage. Then he said it.

"I saw the Evil One."

CHAPTER 17

Osbern's Witness

"It was the night of All-Hallows Eve, My Lord. There was some commotion in the town and in the neighborhood—as you might expect—as the folk lighted bonfires and made merry to ward off the forces of evil. And yet those very forces prepared to descend upon my family and especially upon my...upon my sweet Marie." He shook his head.

"In early evening, my dear daughter wished to go out with other children of the town. They were bound for the hillside above the village, where the large fires were to be lit, you see. They told me later that Marie remained there 'til quite late. Her friends remembered seeing her dancing and making merry.

"When it came time to return home, I believe sometime after midnight, Marie and several of her friends came down the hill to the road that leads up to the Manor. There they took the path down to the town's high street. When they arrived at the outskirts of town, several of the girls separated to go to their houses. Finally, Marie was left alone to walk the short distance remaining to our house, you see."

"What distance did she walk alone?" Valon asked intently, a look of the hunter on his face.

"No more than a hundred yards, Monsieur."

"Go on, please."

"Well, at about that time I heard a commotion in the street—a side street that's little-used—a short way down from our house and mill. At first, I didn't know what it was, and then I thought perhaps it was merrymakers who were being too loud."

"But then?" Valon prompted.

"But then, it sounded like a struggle of some sort, and I thought immediately that the merrymaking had gotten out of hand and maybe two of the lads were going at it with their fists. Still, I told myself that someone else could break it up, and I decided to mind my own business."

"So you delayed going to see what was the matter?"

"Yes, Monsieur. I regret to say it."

The burley miller's voice broke at this last admission, then he continued. "I have told myself a thousand times that if only I had responded when first I heard the noise, I might have saved my dear Marie."

"That is not likely," Valon said, I thought too dispassionately. "More likely, you would have been killed along with your daughter. And then your good wife would have become a destitute widow. But, please continue."

The miller seemed buoyed by Valon's candid appraisal. "After a few minutes, it seemed to me no one was prepared to intervene, so I determined to do so. I dressed hurriedly and descended to the street, where I proceeded in the direction of the noise."

Osbern now paused the heels of his hands to his forehead, covering his eyes. "As I approached, I saw a body in the middle of the narrow street, but it was dark and only when I turned over the body did I know it was my Marie."

Osbern paused again, now tearing a bit, his eyes downcast. Brother Martin embraced him and whispered something in his ear—a prayer perhaps, which the burley miller clearly found reassuring.

He continued. "As I could see that it was my Marie, I took her up in my arms. I think I could tell she was dead, but I still intended to seek the help of the monks to care for her just on the chance that she lived still."

"That was a normal impulse. I would have done the same myself," Valon reassured.

"I drew Marie close to my chest and hugged her, and I was almost out of my head in my grief. And, then, as I looked up and down the narrow road, I could see something odd in the shadows. I did not know what it was at first, but then it emerged from the shadows and made its way down the street."

Osbern paused again and took in a long breath as if inflating his resolve. For a moment he seemed lost in a thought that he dared not express. "And then, Monsieur, I could make it out. Well, I could almost make it out. What I saw still puzzles me, and for a long while I dared not admit to myself what I had seen."

Valon was growing a little impatient. "Well, man, what had you seen, then?"

"A demon, Monsieur. Perhaps even the Devil himself—the Evil One. But surely a demon."

At this assertion, Valon's eyes opened wider, both eyebrows raised. "Describe the Evil One to me, so that I may know what he looks like."

"What stepped out of the shadows, Monsieur, was a demon, perhaps only four feet tall or even less. He was heavy-built, with no neck. His arms were long and muscular, and his thick legs were bowed."

"Did you see his tail?" I asked, knowing that is one well-known mark of the Evil One.

"No, Father Abbot, I did not see that."

"Oh."

"As he made his way down the street he seemed to waddle," Osbern continued. "And, quite soon he turned a corner and disappeared. I saw him only a few seconds, but I saw what I saw, Monsieur, and I won't be told that I did not see it," he insisted.

"You needn't worry on that score, Osbern. I won't tell you that you did not see what you saw. But, what else then did you see?"

"Well, then Monsieur, I saw something just as frightening. From the same shadows as the Evil One there came the figure of the Monster, but a figure I knew at once. It was a moon-bright night, you see, so I could see him quite well, only a matter of twenty feet or so from me. I was crouched in the street still, with my dear Marie, but as I looked up again I saw looking at me a monstrous face, but one I knew. It was the face of Lord Ethelred. He snarled at me as if an animal, Monsieur, and then he turned and followed after his master, the Evil One."

"Osbern, you have told me very clearly something that's quite startling. But consider, man. You have said to the Missi Dominici that your Lord Ethelred was roaming the streets of Châlons on All-Hallows Eve and that you saw him in the street where you found Marie, dead."

"Yes, Monsieur, that is what I saw," Osbern said, his chin raised defiantly, "and I know I saw it. He looked at me as close as from here to the mill over there," he said, gesturing toward the great mill wheel.

There was an earnestness in Osbern's face and demeanor that left me certain of his account, fantastic as it seemed. Valon agreed, and when we found ourselves alone, he acknowledged it. "Whatever Osbern saw that night, I believe he has reported it to us accurately, just as he saw it."

"Then why should we not believe him? There seems to be a diabolical intervention in all this that is clear. Whatever is at play here, it is at the Devil's instigation. It is Satan himself who is our adversary here. That is clear. I believe that Lucifer has assumed the form of Ethelred, perhaps to sow discord and hatred in the town. Or, more likely, Satan has possessed Ethelred—taken control of his body to do his mischief in Châlons," I concluded.

"And therefore, what do you make of Osbern's witness, dear Theodulfe?"

"Just this. It is very similar to what the witch Hildegard told. The two leave little doubt of what we face here. The very atmosphere of this place is alive with evil. His presence—Satan's presence—is in the night air. It's in the very mist that rolls in from the River. One can smell it in the air of this place. The stink that has sometimes tormented our noses is the odor of the Evil One. We must perform an exorcism upon the town of Châlons. We must enlist the monks of Saint Benoît and the Bishop, of course, and we must bring down the power of Heaven against the diabolical forces that are running riot in this place!"

"That may well be, Theodulfe. Like you, I sense there is a great evil here. But I am not certain it is Satan who we face, so much as it is a human evil."

"That may be, Valon, but I intend to discuss with the Abbot and the Bishop the possibility of a general exorcism. I fear we must act quickly."

"As you please, Father Abbot, but meanwhile, I will look more to the human side of things. Osbern's witness may have a human explanation."

"But mark this, Valon. Neither Osbern nor the Witch identifies the Monster as Guillaume."

We moved toward the Monastery gate, and as we entered, we found Abbot Hugo in the great courtyard. He greeted us warmly and spoke first.

"Welcome, Missi. I pray that you have made progress in your inquiries and that you can tell me so."

"We have made some progress, Father Abbot, but we are not yet close to a conclusion," said Valon, a tone of disappointment in his voice. "I have but one question to ask you, and then I will leave you with Theodulfe, who has his own proposal for you."

"You have but to ask, Monsieur."

"I know you have lived many years in Châlons and know the region well. I am told that you are a native of Châlons, in fact."

"I have lived here seventy-three years, Monsieur. Châlons is the only home I have known."

"In all your years and in your experience have you ever known—and I say, ever known—this region to be the home of a dwarf?"

CHAPTER 18

Ergard's Sins

The question seemed to startle, just a little. Abbot Hugo's face grew as serious as mortal sin. He paused, not to think, it seemed to me, but to consider if he should answer.

"Yes, Monsieur. But that was many years ago. There was a dwarf born to the town in the early years of Lord Ethelred's father. And it must be more than fifty years now, at the least."

"How so?"

"That is a vexed question, though you could not have known it. You see, this dwarf was no ordinary child. No, he was a bastard son of Lord Ergard, the old Lord of Châlons, born of a village girl whom he had violated. It was a judgment from God Himself, and the old lord saw it as such. He took the dwarf to raise himself because the poor girl killed herself from shame and fright."

"A despicable man and a tragic story," I lamented.

"As you say, Theodulfe, but at least the old lord tried to make amends. He did many years of penance. He took the baby to rear, but it died after only a few months. And, this is important. Old Ergard gave all those lands to the Abbey's Chantry, as payment for the prayers we say daily for the repose of his tormented soul. Yes, he was a profane man, but he was not godless, and he at least did his penance for his sins."

"Abbot Hugo, are you certain that this dwarf died?"

"Oh, yes. There was a funeral. He was put in the crypt. I remember it as a young monk. Oh, yes, dead and entombed."

Valon seemed puzzled and a little disconcerted.

"What was this child's name? Can you remember it?"

"Yes, because it was an odd name. The dwarf child was called Marcon, and I do not know why."

Once more Valon fell silent and seemed not to notice either Hugo or me until the Abbot spoke once more.

"One other thing, Monsieur, since you have asked about the old lord. There was another great sin that plagued his soul."

"How do you know that?

"He told me so. I was not his confessor, the old Abbot Albrecht was that. But I was asked to act as Ergard's scribe in making his will and in conceding the lands to the Abbey. He said much to me in those times, and one confidence he shared was that he found himself guilty of much more than was known. And, he felt himself punished by God for that other thing, though he never told me what it was."

"Another great sin and another punishment, eh?"

"Exactly. I have always wondered about that thing, but I have not known what to think. It is something the old lord took to his own grave, and we shall never know, I suppose."

"Perhaps," Valon agreed. "But only perhaps."

At this last, Valon lapsed into a long minute of thought, as his face became utterly expressionless. His eyes seemed more languid and looking more to the great distance. Then he repeated, "Perhaps," but now as if to himself.

CHAPTER 19

Marcon

Though I remained determined to raise the need of a general exorcism with Abbot Hugo, Valon took his leave and returned to the Manor. As the evening was then falling, I arranged to spend the night at the Abbey, and my brother monks as well.

I learned only later that Valon encountered Father Draco as he crossed the square toward the Church. Draco seemed in a hurry but stopped to pay his respects.

"Good evening, Monsieur de Valon," Draco spoke first.

"Good evening, Father. Might I beg a moment of you?"

"Yes, Monsieur, though I have a duty to perform in only a few minutes," he said.

"I'll be brief. When you left us yesterday, you seemed preoccupied with some thought. Theodulfe and I were a little concerned by your apparent distress. Is all well with you, then?"

"Oh yes. 'Twas nothing, after all," Draco said, a little uncomfortably.

"Good then. I will bid you goodnight, Father."

Draco hurried off, with hardly a good-bye, and in the direction of the Church. Valon watched him disappear into the Church and then continued his own return to the Manor.

It was not until late next day that I returned to the Manor, and there I found Valon at one side of the great hall, with the sinful wastrel, Bodo.

"What luck have you had in arranging an exorcism, Father Abbot? Is Châlons to be made safe?"

"No, it is not. Neither Hugo nor the Bishop favored my idea, and in fact, both seemed rather annoyed that I should think Châlons possessed, simply because some village girls had been murdered. And, of course, the Bishop's permission is required for an exorcism, and so it is now impossible, at least for the moment. It is quite narrow-minded of them, I believe, but there it is. Nothing to be done."

"Yes, I see your point. Narrow-minded indeed."

"And what of your investigation?"

"Bodo and I were just discussing that. Do you recall the crypt? Where the tunnel led?

"Yes, of course. What of it?"

"We're going there again tonight, only this time by the more direct route. And we're going to find a grave."

"Tonight?"

"Yes, I particularly do not wish to be seen."

"A grave? Whose grave?"

"I'll answer that when we have found it."

In the few short hours before full dark, I managed to find food for the first time that day. Invigorated by nourishment, I espied the reprobate soldier Bodo alone in the precincts of the great hall and took the opportunity to remonstrate with him about his sinfulness.

"I know of your disgusting, lustful relations with the Lord's daughter, Bodo," I scolded, as the startled sinner backed to the wall. "I must warn you that your very soul is endangered by such vile things," I continued with a stern face and a furrowed brow.

The malefactor seemed caught off guard and thoroughly abashed. "But, Father Abbot, I am doing no more than Monsieur de Valon has ordered me to do," he whined.

"What! You lay your outrages at Monsieur de Valon's door! You blackguard!"

"But, Father Abbot. Monsieur de Valon has instructed me to learn all I can from the Lord's family and especially the dull-witted girl, Gertrude, who is full of gossip. And…"

"And what?"

"And she will only give up what she knows if she is free to use me as harshly and as often as she wishes. She is insatiable, Father Abbot! She wishes to use me constantly! I go to my bed each night an exhausted and diminished man, but it is all for the good of Monsieur de Valon's investigation."

"You dastardly lout! You use the poor girl to serve your brutish passions, and then attempt to blame not only Monsieur de Valon but now the girl herself. Your innocent victim!"

The disgusting sinner said no more but merely bowed his head in shame. I was so incensed with his outrageous excuses and attempt to blame the poor, stupid girl for his iniquity that I turned and walked away, leaving God to deal with Bodo's faltering soul.

Only a little later, I found Valon with the soldiers. We made certain no one in the Manor observed us and then made out the door at about the Tenth Hour. We moved in shadows toward the entrance to the Crypt, some one hundred yards from the house, just beyond the stables. We had no light as yet, and so were guided only by the brightness of the moon.

"Here it is, Monsieur," Bodo announced a hint of anxiety in his voice.

"Yes, good. Now it's time to light your candle and give me the iron bar to pry the door."

Valon wedged his iron bar in the sill and broke the door open. When we entered the crypt a rush of stale air greeted us, and then, oddly I thought, the aroma of the jonquil at the outset of winter. Yes, very odd. The crypt was festooned with cobwebs, which Athalfe cleared away with his long knife.

At the center of the long room lay several sarcophagi, all in a single file, in ordinary stone, and each bearing upon the top the name of the person inside. Meanwhile, each long wall on either side held compartments, in which others of the Lord's family were entombed and each compartment faced with a stone tablet bearing the name of the person inside. At the far end of the room, near the door through which we had entered last time, there were two sarcophagi, both small and obviously containing the remains of children.

Valon spied the small sarcophagi at the same time and made for them as quickly as he noticed them. And there, to the left of the door, rested one small stone box. On its top was inscribed in small letters.

M·A·R·C·O·N

"Valon, it's the dwarf's tomb!" I whispered.

"Yes, but that was to be expected."

"What! Expected?"

Before I could understand his meaning, Valon had taken from his *sacullus* a small iron bar with which he began to pry open the top of the stone box.

"What are you doing! You cannot desecrate the tomb, Valon! It's a violation of the laws of the Church and an offense against God! Stop! I say. Stop!"

I reached out to restrain his arm, which caused him to look at me as if in a quandary.

"Father Abbot, if my surmise is correct, you will have no cause to condemn me for desecrating a tomb."

At that moment, the top of the box came loose and Valon pushed it aside. Bodo held high his candle, as we peered into the box.

"Empty! It's empty!" I repeated, disbelieving.

"Yes. No dwarf. No Marcon. No desecration, eh."

"But what's this? Why remove the dwarf's body?" And where is it then?"

"Those are all good questions, Theodulfe, but unfortunately they are also all the wrong questions."

"What?" I said, feeling a little the sting of rebuke in Valon's assertion.

"The proper questions are these— where is the dwarf now and why was the dwarf given a funeral? You know…the funeral Abbot Hugo remembers."

"Valon, you've confused me again."

"The answer is that the dwarf is not in the box because he did not die. The other answer is that he was given a funeral because his father could not bear the shame of allowing him in public. And, both answers suggest that the old Lord made his dwarf son a captive, probably in that subterranean tunnel where we found the man in the masque."

"May the Lord protect us!"

CHAPTER 20

Wigord

I remained dumbstruck at Valon's assertions for some minutes, as did Bodo, who continued to hold high the stump of his candle. Valon, meanwhile, carefully replaced the lid to the dwarf's sarcophagus and blew the dust upon it to conceal the fact that it had been disturbed.

"Valon, what you say has startled me. I confess I was hasty in accusing you of sacrilege, and I beg your forgiveness. But if what you say of the dwarf is true, and of Ergard too, then what has come of the dwarf? We found no prisoner dwarf when we searched the tunnel. There was only the prisoner and he was certainly no dwarf!"

"That's true. If my surmise is correct, the dwarf is the goaler, but we shall only know that by further investigation. In the meantime, I am now more puzzled by Father Draco."

"But I have seen no difficulty with Draco. What do you mean?"

"Oh, I'll agree that what I've seen is subtle, but do you remember that day Draco left us abruptly? From that day, I have sensed a difficulty with him. I cannot identify it, and he has not broached it with us, but something is disturbing him. I know it. We must go see Draco and put it to him that he is disturbed. If we prompt him to confide in us, it will be worth the effort. And there's another thing."

"What, pray?"

"Somehow, Draco is at the center of these strange events. He led us to Hildegard. He is intimate with Lord Ethelred and his family. He is a part of the abbey and is a confidant of Abbot Hugo and must also have known of the dwarf, Marcon. He is everywhere in this thing. That leads me to believe that, in some strange and unexpected way, he may be the key to it."

"Yes, I see what you mean. Draco seems always to be there, wherever we turn."

Within the hour, we found ourselves upon the high street, walking briskly toward the church. The afternoon light was beginning to fade and we felt a biting chill in the air. The smells of food cooking in hearths filled the atmosphere, as did those of wood fires being stoked for nighttime warmth.

A slight mist was descending upon the town—a promise, I thought, of a cold river fog in the evening.

As we came to the church, a door at the side of the main entrance suddenly burst open with a great startling bang and Father Draco staggered into the street. Seeing us, he made directly for us, and when he reached Valon, fell into his arms.

"Father! What is it?" Valon asked, as he lowered Draco to the ground and supported his head with one arm. Suddenly, blood came from Draco's mouth, an indication I thought that his lung had ruptured. Then I saw the blood trickling from his chest.

A frantic look came into Draco's eyes as he lay quivering in Valon's arms, his mouth open as if to speak, but only managing a groan. Straining all the energy left to him, he forced into Valon's chest something he'd clutched in his left hand.

"Must tell you…something. Must tell…" he muttered, but then his eyes glazed in an icy stare, and his body fell limp.

Valon looked up at me, his own eyes full of confusion. "Dead!" he lamented, angrily. "We're too late. If only I'd started an hour earlier, poor Draco would be alive, and we would know what he wished to tell us."

"But what is that in his hand?"

Valon opened the dead priest's fist, revealing a torn piece of parchment.

"What is it?" I asked again, as Valon examined it.

By this time, several townsmen had gathered round us, one or two mumbling their consternation at Draco's death—a woman sobbing noticeably at the loss of her priest.

"It's the fragment of a page, torn from a bound volume. See here on the left, the stitching of the binder. There's nothing written upon it, but it appears to be the bottom-most part of a page."

A look of urgency came upon Valon's face. Laying down the dead priest's head and jumping to his feet, he said, "Quick, Theodulfe. Into the Church. We must find where this fragment is torn from. Quick!" he repeated. "Draco's murderer may yet be in there and he too may be seeking the same document!"

We ran into the Church, which was bathed in shadows. A strong smell of incense greeted us as we entered—that and burning candles. A single candle burned upon the high altar, signaling the presence of our Lord Jesus Christ in the form of a host in the Tabernacle, and many small candles burned upon a shelf of votive candles to one wall. The rest was darkness and silence.

Valon ran down the chancel toward the nave, where on the right a door led to the vestry. We reached the door and easily opened it, then stopped briefly to listen for any sound of someone else in the church. Silence.

Valon rushed into the vestry, then lighted a candle drawn from his *sacullus*, which he held high to light our way in the darkened interior. We saw nothing at first, but then a small door.

"There, probably Draco's chamber and study."

"Let us hope."

The door opened easily, though its hinges creaked as we peered into the darkened room. It was indeed a monk's cell, with a small study to one side. A rough cot with a straw-filled mattress stood at one wall, a table in the center of the room, a single primitive chair, a candle on the table. The embers of a fire flickered in the hearth, where there hung a *pot-au-feu*, its contents issuing a putrid stink. In one corner sat another pot.

Valon made directly for the study—a simple affair, where resided a small shelf of bound books. A bare table in the center of the room held a candle in its center, which he lighted. There was a chair at one wall.

As soon as I entered and looked about, Valon handed me his candle. "Here, hold it high." He then took a great tome from a shelf and began to page through it.

"What is it?"

Valon made no answer at first, but then, "It's the *Etat Civil*—the village registry of birth, deaths, and marriages. It seems to have been kept by the serving priest of the Church of St. Agnes de Châlons since the year 712 and… He stopped in mid-sentence as he continued to page through the volume. "Yes, and see here."

"Where?" I asked, now more curious and still holding high our candle.

"Here's our torn page, Theodulfe," he said triumphantly, as he fitted the fragment into the page. It fit perfectly.

"What page is it? What does it say?"

"See here. It's a page from the year 738, the month of October. And it records a birth."

"A birth? What…?"

"A birth in the family of the Lord Ergard, holder of the Manors of Châlons and Passey. It records baptisms in that family. Here see how it reads:

This 12th Day of October In the Year of Our Lord 738

A Solemn Baptism
Ergard, Lord of the Manors of Châlons and Passey
His wife, Clotilde de St. Denis de Paris
A son, Ethelred and A son, Wigord, twins
Born this 4th Day of October In the Year of Our Lord 738

"Twins? By all the Saints!"

"Aye, Theodulfe. Twins. Lord Ethelred was born twin to a brother, Wigord."

Valon continued to page forward in the volume, skimming carefully but quickly as he went. In five minutes, he had moved through the entire volume and then whispered, "And here we come to Father Draco's era and to this year, and we have now found something even more interesting."

"What have you found, then?" I asked, my curiosity now almost insatiable.

"I have found something that is *not* here. There is no record of the death of Wigord!"

"He's alive, then? Ethelred has a living twin? But…how could that be?"

By my candle's flickering light, I saw Valon's face come aglow. Then, with no word to me, he ran from the room.

PART FOUR

Bridgette's Nightmare

CHAPTER 1

We See the Monster

I dashed after him and caught up as we ran down the chancel toward the great doors. When we reached the street, I was at his heels, but still had no notion of where we were rushing. But now my only thought was that I must remain with Valon, to see what he was so determined to reach so quickly. He said nothing as we made our way across the town square, toward the high street.

Now breathless to keep up, Valon moved to the double-quick in his march. We were headed out of the town and to the west, so I surmised we were returning to the Manor. But why?

As we walked, evening's shadows gave way to darkness and an icy fog rolled up from the river, hanging in the glens and low places, but clearly rising. The moon loomed large and full on the horizon, lighting our way as we turned into the path that climbed to the manor.

Valon's pace did not ease as we climbed and if my excitement had not been so keen, I'm sure I would have fallen behind. In a matter of minutes, we reached the Manor gates and found the keeper slouched lazily at his post.

Not stopping to rouse Bodo, Athalfe, and the brother monks, and unnoticed by any in the Manor, Valon made directly for the crypt, and once there, for the stone steps that led to the tunnel. Inside, I relit my candle to guide our way, as we made for the cell and the masqued prisoner.

Breathless, we reached the door. I held high my candle and then gasped to see the room entirely empty. That discovery lighted Valon's face as if by a flash of lightning.

"What is it?"

"Quick, Theodulfe! We have no time to lose. In fact, we may be too late even now."

"Too late for what?" I demanded as I ran after the retreating Valon. "Late for what, and where are we going now?"

"Too late to prevent yet another murder, and we are returning to the town. And even faster than we came!"

Tired to the point of dropping, I nonetheless followed as well as I could. I surprised myself that I was able to keep up. Emerging into the court, we met Bodo and Athalfe and bid them join us as we ran through the gate and down the path to Châlons. A glance at their faces told me the soldiers were as curious as I about our destination, but they said nothing. Once in the path, Valon broke into a full run. The soldiers and I followed. Now, however, my side hurt and I began to fall behind. I stopped briefly to recover my wind. Still, I resumed my march and at least remained in sight of Valon and the soldiers as they made for the town.

Just as we reached the main road and turned toward Châlons, I heard noises coming from the opposite direction, up the main road. They were barely audible but sounded to me like the screams of a woman. Too far ahead of me to hear them himself, I shouted at Valon.

"Stop! Valon, stop! Come here and listen to what I hear."

At first, Valon did not seem to hear me, but then he and soldiers turned, listened, and then hurried toward me. I did not wait for them. I made down the road toward the muffled sounds. But as soon as I did so, I was distressed to realize that I now could hear no sounds at all. Had my ears fooled me? I feared that Valon would doubt me and turn back to the town, but he pursued me and caught me not one hundred yards upon the road. Then we stopped and listened together.

Nothing.

"I'm certain I heard screams. Not loud, but I know what I heard," I insisted even before Valon challenged me.

Still nothing. And, then more sounds, from further up the road. We ran to the sounds, Valon now in the lead.

In only a minute or two we came upon the terrible source of the sounds. To the side of the road, the large shape of a man lay upon a girl—a girl whose clothing had been torn away and who was clearly about to be raped. The hulk of the man moved violently upon the girl. He was biting and scratching at her as if an animal.

Valon did not stop to consider, but ran directly at the attacker, and dived at him. The force of his charged knocked the attacker off his victim. The two rolled into the grass at the roadside and there Valon began to pummel the hulk with his fists, beating the brute's face more rapidly than I have ever seen.

Still, the big man regained his composure and struck Valon at the side of his face with a rock he'd picked up from the road. Valon reeled back, which gave the hulk a chance to regain his feet.

As he stood there came a small figure as if from nowhere, flying through the air at the giant. It was Elise! She jumped upon his back, her arms around his neck, scratching and biting, like a small animal defending its young. In one moment, the hulking figure swung Elise around and tossed her aside with a growl.

Now he dived upon Valon, who was more agile and managed to roll aside from the attack. The brute fell upon empty ground, which gave Valon a chance to take up a rock of his own and bash his attacker on the back of his head. Elise, meanwhile, snatched up a rock of her own and threw it at the beast, delivering another blow to his head.

The Monster let fly an agonized scream, as he rose, holding his head. It was then, when the moonlight struck him full in his face, that we could see.

"Valon, it's Ethelred! God forgive him, it is he!"

CHAPTER 2

Dead by His Own Hand

As I said his name, the giant let fly another loud growl. His face contorted and twisted into a frightening snarl, almost as if he'd become a beast. It was then I knew the truth of old Hildegard's description of him as a 'Monster,' for he had that look about him. He had truly become a Monster.

I expected Ethelred to resume his attack, perhaps on me, but instead, he turned and ran up the road toward Châlons, still screaming his pain at the crushing blow to the back of his head. At some distance down the road he was joined in his flight by the shadow of a small figure, less than half his height. The two continued toward the village, but I thought they might intend to climb to the Manor.

Valon staggered to his feet, aided by Elise, clearly the worse for his scuffle with the brute. Bodo meanwhile ministered to the girl, who had revived a little. "Who are you, girl?' Bodo asked. "What is your name?"

At first, the girl only groaned, and I doubted she could respond at all, but then she uttered softly, "Bridgette... Bridgette Salis." And then she began to cry.

Valon stood, still dazed and unsteady from his struggle with Ethelred and bleeding from the side of his head. I took from my waist a sash of good linen and used it to bandage his head. Athalfe, meanwhile, offered his small skin of wine. Valon opened wide and squirted it liberally into his mouth and then used it to wash his head.

Now more conscious, Valon shouted, "Take the girl to the town, Bodo. You'll find help for her at the abbey. Abbot Hugo will know what to do. When you've seen to the girl, come immediately to the Manor, where the others and I will go. We must be quick. Events are afoot there, which we may not be able to stop."

As we hurried up the hill, Valon explained our haste. "Pardon me, Theodulfe, for rushing you about the town and countryside, but it's been necessary. The events I spoke of concern Ethelred and his twin. I believe that both are in danger just now, and from the same person."

"What do you mean? What person? Ethelred just tried to rape the girl and kill you, man!"

"No, you are mistaken," he replied. "I cannot be certain just now, but I have deduced his existence, you see. There is another person who has been orchestrating these strange events and for his own purpose. I believe that purpose is extremely rational, though the events themselves are intentionally made to look the work of a madman, or worse—the Devil."

"What is this person doing now, that we are rushing about to discover or prevent? Assuming that you are right, that is."

"I cannot be certain of that, either. But he will know that we disrupted what he intended for tonight. And that will frighten him. He will know from the wound I inflicted on the brute that we had a close look at the fellow, and the dwarf will tell the rest—what he surely saw from his vantage point down the road. Oh, yes, the person behind this is even now learning all that has happened, and it must frighten him terribly."

By this time, we'd reached the precincts of the Manor, and Valon quickened our pace even more as we entered the great hall and made for the stairs that led to Lord Ethelred's chamber. It was now near midnight and most of the servants were asleep, and yet as we ascended, we heard noises—shouts, perhaps—coming from somewhere. As we turned into the corridor that led to the Lord's chamber, the shouting grew louder still.

"Quick, we may already be too late," Valon said, and we sprinted toward the shouting. In only a few seconds we turned another corner in the corridor and saw candles at the other end and heard clearly what was being said, or shouted, rather.

"My Lord! My Lord! Open the door!" a voice said.

"Father, open your door! Open I say! Father! Father!" came another shout.

Drawing closer, we saw several of the servants, together with Guillaume, Godfrey, and Humphrey.

"What is it?" Valon demanded. "Why shout at Ethelred's door?"

"We cannot rouse him," Godfrey replied, anxiously. "Incredible as it sounds, one of the servants reported he saw father running through the great hall bleeding and distressed. Suddenly, he ran up the stairs we supposed to his chamber and now he does not answer. We found blood on the floor in the hall and in the corridor, so it seems he's been injured. And yet he does not answer our knock."

"Quickly, we must break the door. Get a ram!"

On Valon's orders, Humphrey and Guillaume took up an oak bench in the corridor to use at the door's lock. It took several jolts to break it loose, but the door eventually flew open, and Valon dashed into the opening.

The chamber was lighted by a single candle, but as we peered in the opening, we saw Ethelred on the floor, in a pool of his own blood. That pool was not about his head, which was clearly injured, but rather at his wrist, which was cut. His eyes were frozen open in death, his face contorted in anguish.

Godfrey rushed forward as if to enter, but Valon blocked him.

"No! Do not enter quite yet. I must see the room as it is."

Valon peered about the room, surveying with a keen eye the entirety of the dimly-lit chamber. I looked over his shoulder, so as to see what he was regarding. There seemed nothing unusual about the room, except that a few things had fallen from the table as Ethelred collapsed onto the floor. In his right hand, there was a knife. His left wrist was sliced, and blood covered the floor around it. His head, meanwhile, bled from the blow that Elise had given him. Beside his head lay a large key, presumably the key to the door, which he clearly locked before committing suicide.

Valon soon stepped fully into the room, it seemed to me on tiptoe. A little way in he looked to either side, I thought at those parts he could not see well from the door. Next, he stood over the body, looking down at it for a long time. He circled the body and table, continuing to look down at the floor. Then, he fell to his knees on all fours and again examined the region around the body, looking particularly at the key.

After a few minutes on the floor, he arose and began to look to the exterior of the room, walking the wall and examining it as thoroughly as he had the floor. There was no window in the room, but rather a series of narrow slits in the wall, from which archers could fire their arrows if the Manor were under attack. Each slot was perhaps four inches wide. There were ten of them.

Just then, Mordune and the Lord's daughters arrived at the door, having been awakened by servants from their sleep.

"What is the matter here? How dare…" Mordune demanded, but then saw the body of his father on the floor and stopped in mid-sentence. "What has happened? My God, what has happened to Father?"

"It pains me to tell you, Monsieur, but your father killed himself. At least, that is what seems the case," I explained, placing a comforting hand on the young man's shoulder.

"Suicide?" Impossible! That is not the case! Ethelred of Châlons would do no such a thing," he repeated convincingly.

Mordune's insistence on that point caused Valon to look at him strangely, with what I saw as a slightly perplexed expression. His eyes fixed for a moment, and then returned to the room.

Then Valon walked to the wall with the narrow slits and examined each carefully. As he did so, at one slit he took something up in his hand—something I could not see myself—examined it closely, and then let it fall to the floor.

"What is it?" I asked eagerly, hoping he had found something useful.

"Oh, nothing. Nothing useful, I think. In fact, I've exhausted all that's to be learned in here. The others of you may come in and attend to Lord Ethelred. At the very least, he must be covered."

As Godfrey prepared to place his own cloak over Ethelred's head, Valon stayed his hand. "Wait!" Valon looked a long moment at Ethelred's face and then said, "Alright. Pardon. Cover him."

When Valon came out of the chamber I took him aside.

"It is suicide then! Ethelred ran from his attempt to murder the girl and you, and faced with your knowledge of his guilt and the certainty that he would be arrested for his crimes, he chose to end his life. At least, that is my interpretation."

There was no reply. And then…

"That is a sound judgment, Theodulfe. It would seem so. And yet I believe there is another explanation that we must investigate. It would seem a frail possibility to you, I admit, but I am now convinced of it."

"But what is this other explanation, Valon?"

Valon looked a little uneasy.

CHAPTER 3

Requiem for a Fiend

Godfrey stepped forward, directing the servants and men-at-arms to wrap Ethelred's body in linen and carry it to the kitchen where it would be prepared for burial. There was no discussion of funeral arrangements, but Draco's death, the events of the night, and the Lord's poor relations with the Abbot and Bishop all seemed destined to complicate the preparations.

Valon and I took advantage of the commotion to slip away and into the outer precincts of the great hall.

"Valon, how can you make anything of the death chamber except that Ethelred killed himself? It seems clear he was cornered, having been seen by all of us in the commission of a horrible crime, and decided to escape his certain punishment by the King by taking his own life. It seems to me that he was likely insane in some way that we cannot understand. Perhaps even possessed in some strange way, eh?"

"Before we can know anything with certainty, Theodulfe, let us look in one place where we might discover something telling. And something that might run contrary to your notion of things."

"And where is that?"

"In the tunnels. I wish to know if the cell is still empty."

"What! I cannot see what Ethelred's prisoner has to do with this, whether he is there or not. Of course, we have already seen once that the cell was empty. For all we know, he may have been moved to another keep for his imprisonment. But Lord Ethelred is able to imprison within his domains and we are bound not to interfere with it. It is beyond our charter."

"That is strictly so, Theodulfe, and I assure you that we will not interfere with the imprisonment. I merely wish to know one thing. Is the prisoner there or not? That is all."

I considered for a moment, and it seemed to me that what Valon wished to do fell within our powers. So I consented to go with him to the crypt, and from there to descend into the tunnel where we had once seen the prisoner. It took but a few minutes to find our way to the now-familiar tunnel and once there we encountered no one. We hurried down the tunnel toward the cell and once at the door, opened again the small peep door. By the light of our candle, we could see that the masqued man was again shackled to the wall and when he saw our light, once more he began to growl and moan and hiss as he had done previously. Clearly, the prisoner was once more imprisoned there, and I wondered what that could mean to Valon. But I could not know, and I believed that Valon could not as well.

Once satisfied with what we'd come to see, we backtracked to the crypt and from there into the Manor's courtyard.

"What does it mean, Valon? That the prisoner is once more in his cell? Where was he before? Surely there's not another cell down there, or we would have found it. So where was he?"

"You have fallen upon the important question, my friend. But I cannot answer that to a certainty, only tell you my suspicions. And yet, I am not sure it is time to share those, for they are *un peu fantastique*. I will say this, it means as much that he is back in his cell as it did that he was previously missing. Both are significant to us. I can assure you of that."

"I apologize, Valon, but that makes no sense to me at all. I am utterly confused."

Not waiting for me to question him further, Valon pressed into the Manor and there, as I later learned, hoped to find Godfrey. We were not disappointed, for the heir was in the great hall, giving orders to this servant and that concerning the care of his father's corpse and preparations for his funeral.

Though he appeared to be a suicide and therefore could not be buried within the church, Godfrey was already insisting to the Steward, Dagbert, that the Bishop and Abbot were to put all consideration of such things aside and agree to have the *Requiem* for Lord Ethelred, as befitted his stature in the region.

"There is a pretty problem," I whispered to Valon. "The Bishop will not be easily moved on that score, and will probably ask our opinion since we have examined the chamber."

"And what shall we tell him?"

"We shall advise him to bury the bastard, for he was not a suicide. He was murdered."

"What!"

CHAPTER 4

Paris, Rue de Longchamp
22 December 1918

A peculiar look suddenly came upon Teddy's face. I thought for a moment he must be ill. Others noticed it too. Clarisse spoke first.

"What is it, Cousin?" she asked sympathetically. "Are you ill?"

The young Professor reflected for a moment and then delivered his greatest surprise. "Sadly, my friends and family that is where the Abbot Theodulfe's manuscript ends."

"What!" someone shouted.

This revelation startled everyone. We had all assumed from the start that Teddy had brought with him a *complete* manuscript—not a mere fragment.

"Teddy, surely this is not all there is," I insisted. "There must be a finish to the thing. Have you searched the old professor's personal documents? Perhaps his solicitors could guide you? His family, I would guess."

"Yes, Sir Francis. I have approached his executors, his family, and solicitor. I've searched all known archives and collections. I have even advertised for fragments that could possibly be the ending of it. And there are none. I have exhausted all hope, and that is what has brought me to you, Gérard."

Montclaire sat expressionless in his deep chair, the only one in the circle who looked as though he'd expected the surprise.

"Yes, I rather thought you had something like this up your sleeve. Hence our wager. You did not intend to withhold the ending. You are missing the ending of your manuscript and wish me to supply it. Is that it?"

The Professor's expression grew quite serious at the question, and his brow raised noticeably. "That is quite the thing, Gérard. I am not toying with you, nor was my wager a *jeu d'ésprit*. I am in dead earnest because I believe the only way to know the end of this thing is for you to use your great powers of insight and analysis to solve the murders."

Montclaire paused for a long moment and drew thoughtfully on his cheroot.

"There seem two issues here that want more thinking out than I have been able to give them, with any confidence. First, was Valon on the right path and was he making the right conclusions in his investigation? And second, what happened that Theodulfe's surviving narrative does not tell us?" asked the Professor.

"Yes, you have posed the bull questions, Teddy. But I am not prepared to pronounce myself—not as yet. However, I will do so in good time, and I will resolve the problem for you and to your satisfaction."

EPILOGUE

Montclaire's Solution

CHAPTER 1

Rue de Longchamp

23 December 1918

When we returned next evening to our circle of investigation, Montclaire quickly challenged Teddy, but the professor surprised us once again with yet another revelation.

"Your manuscript has said all it can," Montclaire observed, "but surely you have done additional research on the family of Châlons. How could any historian resist doing so?"

"Oh, yes," said Teddy. "Although I have now finished reading what apparently exists of Theodulfe's manuscript of the investigation of the Missi Dominici, and I have told you that it is a mere fragment, there is more to be heard."

This information caused a stir in the room.

"Having discovered the manuscript and read it carefully," he continued, "I decided to research what I could of the family of the Lords of Châlons et Passey in the years after 794. At first, I did so thinking I might somehow discover a lead to the lost fragment, but when that was not possible, I became interested to know their history, after the events Theodulfe described."

"Were you able to find anything of importance?" Montclaire asked.

"Indeed, I was. There was much to learn."

"Well, please tell us," Modestine pressed, with a huff.

Teddy cleared his voice, placed his pince-nez squarely upon his nose, and began to lecture, as he would I imagined at the front of his lecture hall at Oxford.

"There is a good deal to be learned about the family of Châlons et Passey, mainly because they soon became immersed in Charlemagne's war against the Avars. In fact, the Duke of Champagne summoned all his retainers into the King's service and outstanding among them, a large contingent from Châlons, which was led to considerable glory by Lord Guillaume."

"Guillaume! Good Heavens! How in the world did he emerge as Lord of the Manor? Whatever happened to Godfrey? And Humphrey?" I demanded.

"Exactly, Sir Francis. I asked myself that very question, and for the longest time, I despaired of discovering the answer. However, I was able to persuade a colleague to do a spot of research for me in the local archives of the Marne regions, where he found a single reference to answer that question. It seems that within only a few months, Godfrey was found by the Bishop of Reims to be practicing sorcery and the worship of the Evil One. It seems that someone denounced him, anonymously. Despite the sanctions against it from the Frankfurt Synod, he was condemned locally to the stake and was burned in the year 795. The testimony against him was from a young woman whom he apparently seduced to be his assistant, but who was rescued by Humphrey the Pious, Godfrey's younger brother, who led the call for his trial by fire."

"But that does not explain entirely how the third son, Guillaume, should end up as Lord."

"Yes, and there is more. It seems that upon his brother's trial and death, Humphrey the Pious was so shaken by the thought of what he had done that he forswore his inheritance and entered into the Monastery of Saint Benoît du Lac, where he ultimately became Abbot and lived a long life."

"Well I'm dashed!" I couldn't help but blurting. "And you say Guillaume the One-eyed distinguished himself in the War, eh?"

"Indeed, Sir Francis, but to no profit to himself. He was killed in combat, and so never enjoyed the lordship of his vast domains. A pity was it not?"

"What then, Professor?" Clarisse asked. "The title passed to Mordune, eh?"

"No. I cannot know why, but next the family of Châlons et Passey achieved something that was rare in Charlemagne's era. The title passed to the female of the line. It was Ann-Marie —the eldest daughter, who became Lord and lived a long and prosperous life in that title. By all accounts, she was a good steward of the inheritance and passed it whole and improved to her son."

"But, what of Mordune then? He was in line to succeed Guillaume. What happened to him?"

"Well, that is a complete mystery, Your Grace. He is not heard of again, beyond the manuscript I have read to you. We can only know that whatever became of him must have happened between Christmas 794 and the time that Guillaume died in 796. It was then that the title passed to Ann-Marie.

"And yet it is clear that tranquility returned to Châlons very soon, for there were no more murders, and Ann-Marie and her husband seem to have been popular among the people.

"The troubles with the Abbot appear to have been resolved, somehow, for I could find no evidence that the Lord Ethelred's lawsuit proceeded."

"Then it is a happy outcome to an unhappy beginning?" Modestine de Montclaire asked.

Modestinewas flustered to hear it, however. "Happy, indeed. And the daughter Gertrude fornicated every night of the Christmas season with the wicked soldier, Bodo? Doubtless, she kept him on as her man-at-arms. The baggage!"

"Er…yes, Teddy sighed, but at least the line continued, Uncle. Surely that is something?"

"A happy ending? Well, so to speak, cousin, but there is still the sad and mysterious events of 794. Will we never know what to make of them?"

"That is the challenge you have hurled at me, is it not Teddy?" Montclaire spoke-up. Not waiting for a response, he quickly added, "And I can promise you my answer. It will be the stuff of our final *séance* tomorrow evening, and my solution will be my Christmas gift to all of you."

Immediately, we dissolved into our chambers and other activities, but I noticed that Montclaire lingered in the library. There, he took up his chair in the far end by the hearth. In the dim light, he took up his pipe and lapsed into a long brooding silence. The others may not have known it, but I was precisely aware of what he was doing. By this time in our long association, I knew his methods, and I knew right away what I saw.

Montclaire had descended deeply into the techniques of contemplation he'd learned from his great mentor—C. Augustine Dupin, the renowned detective of the Rue Morgue fame—in whose course in detection at the Sorbonne Montclaire had commenced his life of investigation decades earlier. It was a peculiar psychological method introduced by Dupin, in which the detective attempted through contemplation to enter into the mind of his adversary or another for that matter, in an effort to learn his motives, his insights, his rationale—to read his very thoughts, and therefore to anticipate his behaviour.

In this instance, I was certain that Montclaire was spending his solitude in the mind of his distant kinsman, Piers de Valon. Yes, the mind of his kindred spirit. I imagined also that he was entering and wandering about the minds of others as well: Ethelred, certainly, Godfrey, Humphrey, Guillaume, and Mordune almost certainly. Father Draco must also have been a mind to conjure with, and Abbot Hugo, too. And then, there was the mind of the Monster, whom we all by now knew to be Ethelred.

I could not, however, imagine how interesting it must be to be Montclaire and to engage in all those strange journeys of the mind, across a thousand years. Only Montclaire, and perhaps the great Dupin, could imagine that, and so I waited with the others for those strange machinations to end and for the detective to speak.

CHAPTER 2

Montclaire Solves Teddy's Puzzle

All next day, we lolled about the *apartement*, visited friends in the neighborhood, and walked about the shops in the Trocadero. But wherever we went, the others and I confessed to a sense of extraordinary anticipation of Montclaire's promised discourse of the coming evening. My patience had worn thin as a cigarette paper by evening. I was but a bundle of loose nerves, as we assembled after dinner in our circle. It was extraordinary. We sat in absolute silence, awaiting Montclaire.

Such was our anticipation that when he appeared in the doorway of the dining room, it seemed dramatic, and I am certain I heard Clarisse gasp. No one spoke, and no one moved to lift a fork until Montclaire sat and spoke.

"This evening, I can now assure you, we will have a resolution to this thing, and there will be no doubt of the Monster in this case. I now know him. His face is even now in my mind, and I will unmasque him so that history will know him for the villain he was."

The tension at the table broke with those words, as Montclaire bid us all commence.

There was no more word of the mystery at table. Conversation turned on the coming Peace Conference, President Wilson and his Fourteen Points for world peace, and the policies of the French government toward defeated Germany. It was, I imagined, a conversation that could be had at a hundred thousand dinner tables in France that Christmas Eve, for it turned mainly upon the great hope of peace. It was that which made that Christmas of 1918 so special and so memorable in my mind—the great shared hope of lasting peace.

Soon after dinner, we all gathered once again in the library, each taking a seat in the accustomed circle. Only now, instead of listening to Teddy read, we looked to Montclaire who stood in the middle, turning as he spoke.

"We are all grateful to Teddy for bringing us this puzzle and so I must begin by telling you, dear cousin, how delightful it has been to share this Season with you."

The Professor acknowledged our "Hear, hear," with a slight bow of the head.

Montclaire paused a moment, as if to collect his thoughts, then spoke. "First, I must tell you there is no true solution that we may know because we are not there. We can only look over the investigator's shoulder from the distance of a thousand years and suppose what he would have deduced if he had deduced properly. That is not the same as knowing."

"Agreed," said Modestine, "but what can we suppose, eh?"

Montclaire smiled. "A great deal, dear Sister. For one, we can suppose from Theodulfe's testimony that Valon rightly doubted Céleste's suicide, but assumed she had been murdered. Pushed from the tower. She was a devoted sister of the Church and nothing she said to him suggested she would kill herself."

"But who then?" I asked. "Who pushed her?"

"It was the person Céleste arranged to meet on the tower. The person with whom she planned to have an anguished conversation because Valon had forced here to finally to confront her suspicions of that person. Much as she hated to do so."

"You are confusing me, Gérard." Teddy sighed.

"Céleste's suspicions were doubtless rooted in her relations with Sister Helena, who had probably said things to her in the past. Disturbing things. Perhaps there were things also that Céleste observed, but chose to dismiss as too fantastical. But now, Sister Helena's murder forced her to begin to think horrible thoughts. About why her friend was murdered and by whom.

"She would say nothing to Valon, however, until she had confronted another person. A person she cared for deeply, but now was compelled to suspect."

"Who then?" I demanded.

Montclaire smiled patiently. "The person who gave Helena that ring. The ring Céleste recognized as having belonged to her mother and which she knew to have been given to one person. The person who wrote that strange passage from Scripture found in the dead nun's hand. Let me ask you, Fitz. Who did Céleste love best? Who would she have resisted suspecting with all her heart? Who would she have confronted before saying anything to anyone? And who is described by the biblical admonition that, 'the last shall be first.' Who was last?"

"Good Heavens!" It came to me. "Her twin! Mordune!"

"Yes. The brother she loved. The brother who murdered her friend because he'd impregnated Helena and could not marry her."

"But the Lady's suspicions do not prove Mordune guilty of such a terrible crime," I protested.

Montclaire looked sympathetically at me. "No. Fitz, they do not. But we know he is guilty because we can prove the next murder he committed."

"And who was that?" Clarisse asked.

"The Lady Céleste," said Montclaire. "She met him on the tower, confronted him with her suspicions, and he pushed her to her death."

There was loud murmuring in the room.

"Oh yes. I can prove that by two pieces of evidence that Theodulfe provided. First, he tells us that he, Valon, and the others heard a scream and ran toward it—to the great court. Theodulfe tells us further they arrived in the time it took to say the Lord's Prayer. Theodulfe would have said his prayer in Latin, of course, which I took the trouble to time last evening."

"And?" I asked.

"Seventeen seconds, in Latin. Only two seconds longer than in English."

"And so?" asked Teddy.

"They arrived in time to see the Lady hit the cobbles, according to Theodulfe, and so we may conclude that she screamed well before she fell. While she was yet upon the tower. Though she might have screamed at her own decision to commit suicide, she probably did not. Our own experience with suicides tells us that they do not scream. Suicide is, after all, a pretty calm decision and most people do it with quiet resignation. No, the lady screamed almost certainly during a struggle with Mordune, when she realized he intended to kill her."

"You said there were two pieces of conclusive evidence," Teddy observed. "The other?"

"Aye. It satisfies me that all of the brothers and Ethelred arrived from outside. Only Mordune emerged from the Manor and later, after the time it took him to descend from the tower where he'd just murdered his sister."

We all fell to silence, as Montclaire's logic convicted Mordune.

He continued. "Mordune had to murder Sister Helena because her pregnancy would have spoiled all his other plans—more important plans."

"What was that?" Clarisse asked.

"Mordune was engaged in an elaborate scheme to be rid of his hated father and after that to dispense with his despised brothers, one-by-one. You see, Mordune was determined to make himself—that last son—the first. Lord of Châlons. Hence that strange verse we found in Sister Helena's cell, 'and the last shall be first.'"

"What plan?" the old Duke asked.

"Mordune somehow discovered that his father was keeping his brothers, the twin and the dwarf, as prisoners in his tunnels. Of course, that did him no good at first, but when Ethelred's mind began to fail and Mordune saw he was becoming demented, he made his move. Mordune, who had a fascination with training animals, decided to train those two unfortunate creatures to do his bidding. They became the instruments of his vengeance upon his father, who he hated for murdering his mother. Have no doubt, he would soon have unleashed them on his brothers.

"It is likely Mordune also made use of Hildegard to supply him with potions to use with Wigord. Remember, Theodulfe described Mordune as dressed all in black and Simon described Hildegard's visitor as dressed in black.

"I believe Mordune also subverted the Steward, Dagbert, and then persuaded the dwarf, Marcon, to use his power over the twin, Wigord, to do what Mordune wished."

"And what was that?" I asked.

"To go on a murdering rampage in Châlons that would turn the town against his father and cause his father to be removed, somehow. After all, Ethelred was going insane and that figured to make it easy to blame the murders on him.

"Draco suspected, perhaps because of something he knew from the confessional, and that was why he was killed. Valon discovered who the Monster and his guide were, thanks to Draco."

"But how would Valon have identified Mordune as their master? That would seem to be a leap. He would have thought it was Ethelred, eh?" I observed.

"He probably did not, until the Lady Céleste was murdered and he knew who killed her. It was then he began to piece all of the collected parts together and to understand Mordune's complete scheme. Although he knew early on that Mordune had killed his sister, he did not want to move against him until he could put the entire picture together.

"I believe he did so by observing Mordune's movements, by noticing when Mordune was absent, for example."

"So Ethelred's suicide forced his hand, eh?" Modestine asked.

"Not exactly. What forced his hand was that Valon disrupted the Monster's attack upon Bridgette Salis. When that happened, and the dwarf reported it, Mordune had to act. He had to kill his father and make it appear he had been the attacker. That would have ended the Messi Dominici investigation, and dead men tell no tales."

"Kill him! Ethelred!" Teddy exclaimed. "But he was found in his locked chamber…the key on the floor mat."

"Oh, I'm sure that did not fool Valon. Mordune had a second key to his father's chamber, as he probably did the chambers of his brothers. He was a clever and conniving man."

"But," I asked, "what happened to Mordune? To the Monster locked in the tunnel cell, and to the dwarf, Marcon? What?"

Montclaire smiled his evil smile. "There you have touched upon the strongest evidence of what Valon ultimately concluded. Isn't it clear?"

"What clear?"

"Valon killed them. He killed all of them."

"What!" Clarisse exclaimed.

There was a long silence.

"You must not think of this the way you would a modern prosecution. The Missi Dominici was not merely an investigator. He was charged by the King's *capitulary* to 'do justice.' Oh yes. Valon was expected at the end of the day to do Charlemagne's justice. And, he did. Quickly and with deadly efficiency, I'll wager. And I would wager further that as he sent Mordune to his death, he had in his mind the sad image of the dead Céleste."

'Killed them? The three? Surely not," said Teddy.

"Oh yes. Murdered the three of them and without a moment's pause."

"And did what with them?" Modestine challenged.

"That is the last supposition I can give you, Sister. He might well have stuffed their bodies in the sarcophagi in the crypt, and if you go to Châlons and open those tombs you might find the bones of two giants in Ethelred's tomb and the bones of a dwarf and another in Marcon's. And yet, I rather suspect that Valon put them elsewhere—in another place where you might find their bones."

"Why do you say that?" Teddy asked.

"Oh, merely because it is what I would have done in his place."

"Where?" Teddy followed.

"In the pit in the forest, where Mordune and the dwarf had left Valon to die. I suspect he threw them—the three of them—into that pit and in the same way they had left him there to die. Alive. And, I suspect further that Valon charged the wolf-boy, Simon, to keep guard over them until they were dead."

"Good Heavens!"

CHAPTER 3

Teddy's Final Challenge

"Compelling as your logic is, Gérard, I'll not accept it. No, not while one other avenue of research is open to us. After all, I am a scholar. We must test your solution."

Montclaire's eyes opened wide, as surprised I to hear Teddy's refusal.

"And what avenue is that, dear cousin? What test?"

"Yes. How?" I demanded.

"We must go to Châlons and find those bones. That's how!" said Teddy, raising his chin.

Modestine grumbled. Clarisse gasped. Montclaire smiled.

"Game on, Teddy!" Montclaire shouted, with apparent glee. "We leave for Châlons on Boxing Day!"

Montclaire's eager acceptance of Teddy's challenge and the short time he set for our departure left me scrambling to make the necessary arrangements for travel. Meanwhile, Montclaire telegraphed ahead to all those whose help or permission would be required for us to conduct our investigation. His name was enough to gain all that was needed.

Travel arrangements were more difficult. In those days, so soon after the Armistice, the Marne region and its rail line were a mess, mostly from the extraordinary destruction of the War. The few undamaged lines were clogged with rail traffic between Paris and the former battlefields. Still, we were able to gain permission to travel to Châlons-sur-Marne, one of those towns that had changed hands many times in the course of the fighting.

We left the Gare de Lyon at sunrise on Boxing Day and by slow progress over dubious rails and a change of trains at Dijon, we reached Châlons on the 27th. Much of the Marne was still in American hands at that time, and Châlons was, as it turned out, headquarters for the American commander.

It was not difficult to find accommodations and then to find the old fortress Manor, but to look at it caused my spirits to sink just a little. Teddy and Montclaire sighed in unison.

The old pile was mostly destroyed by the bombardments. We learned from General Thaddeus Billings, the American Commander of the sector, that the old Manor had been headquarters to both the Germans and the Americans and changed hands several times in the back-and-forth of the War. Lately, it—or rather the part of it still usable—had become a hospital for Allied wounded and mostly housed American and English soldiers.

Our business in the crypt posed no danger to the efficient operations of the hospital, though Billings' mouth dropped a little when we explained our mission. I could tell that in his matter of fact military way, he regarded the entire venture as a bit ridiculous. Still, Montclaire and Teddy explained that the information to be obtained was a matter of some consequence to their family, so the General accompanied us to the old crypt. He brought several of his soldiers, in case heavy lifting was required. As it turned out, opening the great iron door of the thing was a project, mainly because its hinges had not moved for at least several centuries.

A bit of modern mechanics and some grease worked wonders and as the great door's hinges squealed in pain at being forced to work after centuries of rest, the blackness of the crypt's interior stood before us. We lit our chemical torches and walked in, and there before us stood the tombs of the family, including one marked Ethelred. Elsewhere along the wall, were sarcophagi marked Marcon, Ergard, and Guillaume. Others of the Lord's children were buried in the walls, their places marked by stone placards. My heart sank to read the one marked, "Céleste."

Montclaire ordered all of the tops removed from the four sarcophagi and while there were large skeletons in the tombs of Ethelred, Ergard, and Guillaume, the other—Marcon's—was empty and there was only one set of bones in each of the first three.

While the General and his soldiers betrayed their surprise that the one was empty, Montclaire only smiled in his enigmatic way.

"Thus far, you are justified, cousin Gérard," said Teddy, also smiling.

We explained to the Americans that we had half expected the tomb of Marcon to be empty because it was Montclaire's theory that he'd been "disposed of" and buried, so to speak, in another place entirely. And no bones of Mordune either.

By this time, Billings was allowing himself to be drawn into our mystery, but he confessed he had no authority to assist in what Montclaire proposed to do next. That, he said, would need to come from the French military authorities in the city, who were overburdened at the moment with caring for the needs of the population.

Once again, Montclaire's name was sufficient to get approval, and it mattered even more that he and Teddy were willing to pay good wages to ten able-bodied men to assist. By the next day, we were organized and prepared to begin searching the wooded mountainside below the old Manor, first for a cave and then for the pit.

By mid-morning, searchers were systematically scouring the dense forest and brush of the mountainside for any opening that might be a cave. By mid-afternoon, all but two had returned to report that their efforts had been futile, though they made a thorough reconnaissance of the entire hillside.

Then, the other two came running down to the road, breathless and eager to report that they'd found the opening to a cave of sorts, though one blocked by dense brush.

As we approached, it did not seem to me to be a proper cave, but rather a hole in the side of the mountain, now obscured by brush. When the shrubs were cleared away, however, the opening appeared large enough for us to enter, and so we did, armed with proper torches.

Some twenty yards into the cave, I sensed it was remarkably dry and the air fresh. It was then however that Teddy gasped.

On the floor in front of us, we could see the bones—the skull and skeleton of someone who had somehow curled up in a corner of the cave to die.

"Don't touch it," Montclaire cautioned. Teddy agreed.

"We must find someone who knows more than we do about such remains before we disturb them, lest we ruin our own investigation."

CHAPTER 4

The Physician

"What do you propose?" I asked.

"We need an expert. A physician perhaps, to tell us what we must know of these bones," said Teddy. "Perhaps the American General can help?"

Montclaire dismissed the lads until next day, with pay, and we left the cave and mountain to find General Billings at the American Hospital. Montclaire put his problem to the helpful American, and we smiled to hear what he suggested.

"You're in luck, Montclaire. We have here a French doctor. Claude Morin's his name. He's an absolute whiz at what you want. He helps in the hospital, but mainly he's been out trying to identify the remains of soldiers—French, American, German, and English—found on the nearby battlefields. He does remarkable work."

As it turned out, Doctor Morin took a bit of an attitude about diverting himself from his War work to search for bones from the 9th century. And who could blame him?

But Montclaire could be persuasive and in pleading his case he played upon the Doctor's extreme curiosity about found remains. As it turned out, Morin agreed to examine any bones we found but was unwilling to help us look.

"For that," Morin said, "allow me to suggest an alternative."

"Oh?" Montclaire asked, a suspicious tone in his voice.

"My student. I teach at the University of Nancy, you see."

"Yes. And?"

"I had a student before the War. Her name is Juliette Bourdain. She's a marvel at the sort of anatomy and anthropology you have in mind."

We three smiled and looked at each other. "Then let us invite Mademoiselle Bourdain to join us, Monsieur. Can you bring her to Châlons?"

Thanks to Doctor Morin's help, three days later a dowdy young woman wearing thick spectacles and sensible shoes descended from the train from Nancy. In her stiff and abrupt way, she asked, "Which of you is Montclaire?"

Morin had explained all that was needed to her in his telegram and Mlle Bourdain was eager to join our investigation. We arranged her room in the same hotel where we stayed, and the next morning we climbed the hillside and escorted our expert to the cave and its bones.

We each held our torches while Mlle Bourdain knelt over the bones, examining each with her lens, at the elevation of about four inches.

"A boy," she said in her matter-of-fact way. "About twenty years, I would say…no more."

"Yes," said Teddy.

She looked at Teddy with a dismissive eye and then continued her inspection, now focused on the skull.

"There is some malformation about the jaw. I'm not quite… Ah…interesting!" we heard her say.

"What is?" I asked.

She gave me that look to suggest my question was an unwanted interruption. "It is not unknown, Colonel, but this boy had larger than usual canine teeth. It could well be a manifestation of *clinical lycanthropy*—a condition that is rare but well known."

I saw Montclaire smile in the light of our torches.

"Anything else?" Teddy asked.

She shook her head. "Only this. He probably died of natural causes, but who can say for certain after so many years. I can say he died of nothing that would have damaged his bones."

As Mlle Bourdain began to move the skull, she moved the dust from a stone slab on which the head rested, and as she did so, we saw what seemed to be a rough etching on the tablet. Montclaire fell to his knees and began to whisk and blow the dust from the tablet, and then, in the light of our torches, there emerged an inscription. In Latin.

"Can't make much of it myself," I confessed. "My schoolboy Latin fails me."

"I'll spare you the trouble, Fitz," said Montclaire as he began to read. *Mirabilis est vita habemus, utcumque vivunt, eo mondo quo debet.* 'The life we have is wonderful, no matter the way we must live it.'"

"I agree, said Teddy, "and the Latin is pristine."

'Yes. Beautiful."

CHAPTER 5

The Pit, Again

Later that same day Mlle Bourdain carefully removed the bones to Doctor Morin's laboratory at the Hospital. At first, I attempted to assist, but Mlle gave me a stern look to suggest that the task should be left to someone more experienced in removing bones.

Montclaire, meanwhile, assembled the local lads. He ordered them to distance themselves twenty paces from each other and instructed that we would walk up the mountainside, as we had previously, only this time in search of a more difficult thing—a depression. Any depression that might long ago have been a pit. I worried that that description left plenty of room for all sorts of false discoveries. We could spend days digging in the wrong places.

Teddy, Montclaire, and I took our places in the middle of the file, and we marched up the mountainside in relative pace with the others—six of the lads to either side of us. The climb was slow because we were all inclined to take our time and examine every yard of ground for a depression. No leaf was to remain unturned.

An hour into our search, we heard a shout on the left flank. We ran to the noise and there found several of the lads gathered around an undeniable depression in the earth. Not a pit, but certainly a depression, measuring about ten feet across.

The boy who had found the depression smiled, knowing that Montclaire had offered a handsome reward to the lad who should discover the pit. As Montclaire tossed him a gold Napoleon, the others looked a little downcast. Until that is, Montclaire announced yet another reward. "A gold piece to you all if we find a single bone and 100 francs to the man who finds the first."

The lads erupted into shouts and cheers. Someone shouted "Vive Montclaire! Vive La France," and for some strange reason, everyone began to sing a rousing rendition of *La Marseillaise*.

By this time the hour was late. We agreed to meet early next morning with picks and shovels. At that time, word of the discovery had spread, and we were joined by General Billings, Doctor Morin, and the always-serious Mlle Bourdain.

The work was slow going, but by mid-day, the diggers were below five feet. Every additional hour saw more roots and soil tossed from the pit, which now showed its stone walls as clearly as they were described in Theodulfe's story. I had no notion if we would find what Montclaire predicted, but I was now convinced—as I had not been before—that we had indeed found the pit.

By mid-afternoon, it was clear the lads were digging at about eight or nine feet. We watched from the rim as each bucket of earth was hauled up and emptied for close inspection by Mlle Bourdain. Nothing. Then, one of the diggers let out a yell that I am sure was heard in Châlons.

"I've found something, Monsieur," the lad shouted up, holding high in his hand was appeared to be a bone. A large bone.

The object was hauled up to Professor Morin, who washed it in a bucket of water and then took out his lens for a careful inspection. I knew it was an animal fragment of some sort—a deer, perhaps—and so I was unprepared somehow as he looked up in astonishment and said, "A femur. A human femur." Then he smiled.

At that point, we might have celebrated, except that more shouting erupted at the bottom of the pit. A wild yelp announced yet another discovery and then it came into full sight. A skull.

In the next hours, as the lads cleared the bottom of the pit, they fetched up an assortment of bones. Small, large. Some were clearly ribs. Another skull. Bones of a foot. A jawbone. As our light began to fail, we had assembled quite an assortment of bones, all of them carefully examined by Doctor Morin and Mlle Bourdain and each declared human.

When the pit had been cleared of its bones, we all stood speechless for the longest while, and in the stillness of that forested mountainside, I looked down in the pit and thought I could hear the anguished cries of the three who'd been left there to die.

Smiles were the extent of our celebration that evening. Montclaire rewarded each of the lads with an extra day's pay and gave each a gold Napoleon. Like the bones from the cave, our large collection of bones from the pit went with Morin to his laboratory at the American Hospital. We agreed to meet there next morning at nine to hear his opinion of what we'd found.

When we met next morning, it was clear that Dr. Morin and Mlle Bourdain had been so excited about the find they spent most of the night examining the remains. Doctor Morin was ready to render a final report. We listened as if in his classroom at the University.

Pointing to the bones that lay on a laboratory table in three groups, the Doctor began. "We have here the remains of three individuals, all males and one much younger than the other two. Allow me to tell what I am able about each of these individuals, though I caution that the bone fragments are in terrible condition and none of the skeletons is even nearly complete."

"By all means," said Montclaire.

"This first individual, whose remains are most complete, was an exceptional specimen. He was quite tall—perhaps 200 centimeters (6 feet 6 inches). A giant in his day. We have a part of his pelvis and from it, I would say that he was also large. A broad man."

"Montclaire," I gasped. "It's Wigord!"

He said nothing, and Doctor Morin continued, standing over the second assortment of bones, which were arranged on the table generally as they would have been in the body itself.

"Here we have an even more exceptional specimen, gentlemen. This person was a victim of dwarfism syndrome. He was very likely about the same age as the other fellow—perhaps 50 years—and he was no more than 120 centimeters (less than 4 feet)."

"And the other bones?" Montclaire asked eagerly. "What do they tell?"

"Ah," said the Professor. "A person very different from the other two. This fellow was rather young—probably no older than 30 years—and he was from all appearances a perfect specimen of a young man. He was about 180 centimeters (5 feet 10 inches), slight of build, and apparently in good health. What he was doing with the other two is beyond me."

Then, picking up the skull that we all suspected to be that of Mordune, he frowned.

"What is it?" Teddy asked.

"This fellow very likely died by having his skull crushed, just here, where you can see an injury to the area near the left ear. The other two—the dwarf and the big man—have no such injuries."

"Mordune was murdered, then?" I asked. "By the other two?"

The Professor parsed his lips, not liking to be pinned down to an opinion.

"Oui. It would seem so," he said, grudgingly.

I looked at Montclaire.

"But, why would they kill Mordune?" Teddy asked.

I agreed. "Why on earth would they do that?"

"To preserve their own lives," said Montclaire.

"Preserve their own lives? But how?" I asked.

Montclaire dropped me a disappointing but sympathetic glance.

"Quite simple, Fitz. They ate him."

CHAPTER 4

Montclaire's Last Word

I am sure my mouth fell agog, as I rocked back a little on my heels.

Teddy recovered quicker than I. He took up Montclaire's hand, shook it vigorously, and exclaimed. "Gérard, you have been proved right. Amazing. You have told us precisely what Valon did and you have taken us to the proof of it. We have here, clearly, the remains of Wigord, Marcon, and Mordune, from the pit where Valon condemned them to remain and die."

He smiled and continued to shake Montclaire's hand.

Montclaire persuaded the authorities in Châlons that we had indeed found remains of the manorial family and they were placed in the crypt where, I suppose, they belonged.

* * * *

We returned to Pairs in mid-January. Teddy remained with us at Montclaire's *apartement* for several days. Clarisse and Modestine returned also, curious to have a full report on all we had discovered in Châlons. One evening, as we all gathered before the crackling fire in the library hearth, Montclaire revealed to me one last part of the story that I could not have known.

"Yes. There is one other thing, Fitz. Something Cousin Teddy neglected to note in his story. One can forgive him for that because until now it has been a minor fact in our family's history—a thing of no apparent importance."

"And, what is that? This thing of no importance? Does it now assume greater significance?" I asked.

"Indeed, it does. You see we have long known the name of the woman Piers de Valon eventually married, and to whom he remained devoted until his death, many years later. She gave him numerous children, and she is the mother of our entire line, which as you know is among the greatest families of France."

"Yes, I know. A great lineage, indeed," I agreed.

"But now we know the very strange origins from which this great family sprang," said Montclaire, smiling.

"What do you mean, 'strange?' Who was this woman?"

"Until now we have only known her by her name. Elise."